"He's a thug… a really nasty piece of work."

When young Clayton Kerry, member of a notorious Worcester family, is found dead on an abandoned factory site, it looks like an accident. Some even say it was what he deserved. But headteacher Alun Blake's refusal to sugarcoat the truth about the pupil he excluded causes outrage in the local community and sparks a vendetta against him that rapidly spirals out of control threatening both his life and that of his daughter.

When Detective Inspector Summerskill and Detective Sergeant Lyon investigate, they find Clayton's death was by no means as clear cut as it had seemed and that they are at the start of a trail that will take them into the heart of a school and far beyond the boundaries of their city, to crime on a national scale.

As they uncover what really happened, Summerskill and Lyon are brought face-to-face with uncomfortable truths about their own lives and relationships. Personal loyalties are tested, and before the case is through, at least one more person will die.

Sticks and Stones is the third in the Summerskill and Lyon series of police procedural novels.

GW00401033

STICKS AND STONES

Summerskill and Lyon, Book Three

Steve Burford

A NineStar Press Publication

Published by NineStar Press
P.O. Box 91792,
Albuquerque, New Mexico, 87199 USA.
www.ninestarpress.com

Sticks and Stones

Printed in the USA
First Edition
February, 2021

Print ISBN: 978-1-64890-209-3

Also available in eBook, ISBN: 978-1-64890-207-9

Warning: This book contains sexual content, which may only be suitable for mature readers. Depictions of violence, self-harm, homophobia, homophobic slurs, alcohol/drug use, past physical abuse of a child by a parent, bullying, death, and murder.

For Huw, A.A., T.T. And, of course, L.L.L.

Chapter One

"And some sad news just in. A tragic accident today on the site of one of the county's oldest landmarks has resulted in the death of a Worcestershire schoolboy. Fifteen-year-old Clayton Kerry was killed when one of the walls of a building on the site of the old William Fitzmaurice brewery collapsed.

"The Fitzmaurice brewery, once the producer of some of the county's most prestigious beers and ciders, has been a familiar site on the banks of the River Severn for as long as anyone in the county can remember. For decades, however, it has been closed and deserted, its buildings neglected and crumbling. All attempts over the years to procure the site for redevelopment have been blocked by legal wranglings within the Fitzmaurice family.

"James Fitzmaurice, oldest surviving member of the brewing family, today said that he and his family were deeply saddened by the death but that they could take no responsibility.

"We'll have more on that story in our local news bulletin later this evening. And now, over to Duncan Lewis with today's weather..."

The picture on the screen changed to an earnest young weather forecaster in glasses, smiling in front of a map of the country even as a mass of CGI storm clouds crept in from the west.

"Tragic accident." The man in the bed yawned, muted the television, and carelessly tossed the remote control to one side. "It was hardly going to be an *amusing* accident or a *laughable misadventure,* was it?"

Sitting on the other side of the bed, Dave Lyon paused in the act of pulling on his trousers. "And is that all you've got to say about it?"

The man he'd addressed gave one of his typical crooked smiles, laced his hands behind his head, and lay back against the large pillows. The sheets were pulled down low over his stomach, and Dave didn't doubt that their position and the pose had both been deliberately chosen to afford him a good view of the body he was getting ready to leave. It was a great body. "What do you want me to say?" Sean Cullen asked. "That

I'm heartbroken over the death of some kid I've never even met? Touch hypocritical don't you think?"

"You're an MP. I thought that was part of the job description."

Cullen smiled again. Dave's barb hadn't pierced his thick politician's skin at all. But then Dave hadn't thought for a second it would. "And you're a detective sergeant. Didn't you *detect* anything about that report?"

"What do you mean? It was an accident. The report didn't say anything about suspicious circumstances."

Cullen tutted slowly, clearly enjoying himself. "You heard them say the old Fitzmaurice brewery has been closed for years, and I mean years. Even I used to slip through its fences and hide in the buildings when I was a kid."

"Bunking off from your posh public school for a crafty fag with the lads?"

"I was never one of the lads, David, and even if I had been, I wouldn't have wanted them with me while I was enjoying my cigarette and a copy of *Zipper* or *Vulcan* or whatever I'd managed to get my hands on. Anyway, these days the old Fitzmaurice brewery has got more barbed wire around it than the nearest HMP but it's still notorious as a hangout for kids drinking and taking God knows what. Which means, the victim of our *tragic accident* would have had to walk through several very obstructive fences and have failed to notice several very prominent warning signs before he made it to the buildings where he was no doubt in the act of doing something very naughty before a ton of bricks fell on his trespassing little head." Cullen assumed an expression of mock surprise. "I know my constituency, sergeant. Don't you know your beat?"

Annoyed with himself and with Cullen, Dave was damned if he'd show it. Now he thought about it, he did remember some talk back at the Foregate Street station about the brewery, but he was still comparatively new to the area, and neither the name nor the reputation of the place had struck a chord when he'd heard that television report.

Cullen, of course, made no allowances. The product of an Oxford education, where he had been on a winning Boat Race team, and of an adversarial parliamentary system where he had been, when elected to the House of Commons over a decade previously, one of the youngest MPs in the house, Sean Cullen was an extremely competitive man. And that competitiveness, Dave was discovering, extended all the way into his personal life.

Dave took some comfort from the image of the young public school boy Cullen had been, sneaking off to abandoned warehouses to smoke and enjoy gay wank mags. It was good to remember he hadn't always been the high-profile, smug arse he was now. "Well, whatever he was doing, I doubt it was going through his collection of gay porn."

"You think kids have changed so much?"

"No. But they do have the internet. Any young lad these days can pleasure himself blind in the comfort of his own home. Straight or gay."

Cullen reluctantly conceded the point. "Mind you, it wasn't all just about the fags and mags." He yawned lazily, like a self-satisfied cat recalling an empty carton of cream.

Dave buttoned up his shirt, began the search for his shoes, and refused to give Cullen the satisfaction of asking what he meant by that. How was it you could only ever find one shoe when you were trying to leave a guy's bedroom? "Why'd you even want the television on anyway?" he asked as he searched. "You trying to impress me with the size of your screen?"

"I thought I already had impressed you. And I was hoping," Cullen went on, before Dave could reply, "to catch something about my Fitness First initiative. I did an interview about it yesterday for the local news. They said it might be on today. We've probably missed it. Or it's been dropped in favour of the tragic accident. I'll check again later."

"Want to see how good your profile looks on the television?"

Cullen smiled, the sheet over his body slipping down another inch, almost accidentally. "I know how good it looks on television."

Yeah, I'll bet you do. Like the body, Sean's was a great profile. With those cheekbones, there had to be aristocracy somewhere in his family bloodline. "I'm only surprised you haven't got a mirror over the bed."

Cullen yawned. "Too seventies. And it would get in the way of the cameras."

Missing shoe found, Dave stood, reached for his jacket, and forced himself not to look up at the ceiling over the bed. *A joke. Just a joke. Don't give him the reaction he wants.* "I'll see myself out, shall I?"

"I think you know the way by now."

At the bedroom door Dave stopped, hand on the handle, and looked back. Cullen's eyes were closed as if he was already drifting into sleep. "You never ask me to stay." It was a simple fact, calmly stated.

Cullen didn't open his eyes. "Would you?"

Dave considered. "No. See you later."

"I look forward to it."

Neither man suggested when or where that might be.

This had been their third hookup at Cullen's house since that night they had walked out of Gallery 48 together, and this was pretty much the way it had ended the previous two times. Dave couldn't see that changing any time soon.

*

Claire Summerskill looked up from the pile of staff review forms on her dining table. Across the room from her, the television was showing a picture of a teenager and the newsreader was giving the as yet sketchy details of his death. The picture was a school photograph, a head and shoulders shot with all the charm and warmth of the mugshots she was used to down at Foregate Street. But the familiarity of this one had caught her attention. It wasn't just the sulky *I'm only doing this because I have to* expression. It was the uniform, specifically the red, green, and white tie that was still visible even though the boy in the picture was wearing it rebelliously loose, the knot so far below the undone top button of his shirt as to almost be cropped out of the picture. "He's from your school."

Tony, her oldest son, lounging on the nearby sofa, rolled his eyes. "Can see why they made you detective inspector."

"They made me DI for doing over snarky young perps so don't backchat your mam."

"Yes, *Mam*." Tony returned to the lurid graphic novel he was reading.

Claire went back to her paperwork. It was nice, this moment, just the two of them. Okay, she was finishing off soul-crushingly dull admin, and he was deep into some four-colour nightmare with levels of violence and sexual suggestion she knew she probably wouldn't approve of if she examined it too closely, but still, it was nice and all too rare. And she secretly loved it when he called her *mam,* even if it was semi-sarcastically, and had the rural drawl of a Worcestershire accent behind it rather than the south Wales music of her own voice. Yes, it was *nice.* Just her and Tony. Sam, her youngest, fast asleep upstairs.

Of course, it would have been nicer still if Ian, her husband, had been there with them, even if things between him and Tony had become difficult lately. "He's growing up," Ian had said. "Turning into a young man. Bound to be a bit of horn-butting as the young colt challenges the old ram, especially when he's a step-ram." Ian was shit when it came to metaphors, but he could be really kind and understanding, which was one of the things Claire loved about him. On the other hand, one of the things she hated about him was the endless meetings he was called to. Especially lately. People who said teachers had it easy with short days and long holidays had no idea, she thought. So many meetings.

"Did you know him? The boy in the news?" She asked as much to steer herself away from troubling thoughts as anything else, suddenly wondering if, in fact, the news might have upset her son. Had he been a friend? *Shit!* Should she have recognised him? Tony's scornful snort reassured her that he was not unduly grieving.

"Everyone knows Clayton Kerry," Tony said. "I mean, I don't *know* him. *Didn't* know him. He's two years ahead of me, but I knew him. Y'know."

"That makes no sense at all." But Claire was relieved.

Tony lowered his book. "He's a thug, Mum. A really nasty piece of work. Him and his gang of cronies make life a misery for the kids. And teachers."

"*Was* a thug, love."

"Well yeah, right. Sorry. Thing is, though, I don't think that many people are going to miss him." Tony raised his graphic novel again as a shield against any more discussion.

Claire sighed and returned to her paperwork. The moment had gone. Still, it had been good while it had lasted. She felt an unexpected twinge of sympathy for the parents of the dead boy. There'd be no more moments like that for them, would there? Ever. Tony had said no one would miss Clayton Kerry, but there had to be someone. How must they be feeling right now? She forced herself to concentrate on the tedious printouts in front of her. She couldn't imagine it. She didn't want to.

From out in the hallway came the sound of the front door opening and Ian's traditional laconic, "Hello?"

Tony immediately got up from the sofa. "You don't have to go yet, love," Claire said.

"Bedtime. Tired. See you in the morning. Night." Tony left the living room, via the kitchen so he didn't have to bump into his stepfather.

Ian walked into the living room, came over to his wife, and pecked her on the cheek. "How's it going?"

Claire pushed aside the papers she was working on. "It's not. And you're late."

"Yeah. More to do than expected."

"There's some lasagne in the fridge. You can zap it if you want."

"'S okay." Ian dropped onto the sofa so recently vacated by Tony. "I've been grazing all day. Don't mind me. You carry on. What's on the box?" He reached for the remote control.

Claire sat with her dining table covered in forms and photocopies and didn't touch any of them. She sat, looking at her husband while he lay looking at the television, flicking through the channels searching for something interesting. *So many meetings lately.*

Chapter Two

"Morning, Tony."

"Morning, Dave."

"DS Lyon," Claire corrected as she and her son got into Dave's car. It was done without commitment as she knew her son wasn't listening, and her sergeant never seemed to mind the informality anyway.

"Have a good evening?" Claire asked as she fastened her seatbelt and they pulled off, first to drop Tony at school and then on to Foregate Street.

"Yes thanks. You?"

"Okay, ta."

It wasn't often that Claire played the *what-if* game. *We don't have no time for much of that,* as her Pontypridd maternal grandmother would have said. But mornings like this did make her wonder. At one point in the not so distant past, it had seemed a done deal that when she got her promotion to DI, she'd be taking her oppo and best mate Jenny Trent up the ladder with her. But then Dave Lyon had appeared on the scene, summoned up from seemingly nowhere (in actual fact, Redditch) by a well-intentioned equal opportunities initiative both of them had hated. And suddenly, she'd had an unknown man at her side instead of a well-known friend. He was a good man, a good *police*man, too, no doubt about that, and Claire was coming to accept that she couldn't begrudge him his promotion or regret his posting to Foregate Street. Except maybe on mornings like this when instead of the entertaining flood of gossip Jenny would have given her, all she got from Dave was *Yes thanks.* He was gay for Pete's sake. Didn't that mean he was out every free night he had, having meaningless sexual encounters he could then describe to her the next day in shocking detail? Once they'd dropped Tony off, of course. Claire gazed out of the car's side window and watched the houses and shops pass by. Apparently, it didn't.

"Big crowd outside the school, Tony," Dave said.

Claire was roused from her woolgathering and looked out through the windscreen. Past the front gates of Monastery Grove High, the road led to a large, grassed roundabout in front of the school's main doors. Each morning, parents' cars and school buses slowly circled it, pausing only to drop off their respective loads. Claire expected to see the usual snail's pace circulation of vehicles on the road and pupils on the bordering pavement. Instead, the flow of traffic was stopped and up ahead of them she could see a crowd of people milling around the glass entrance doors which seemed, unusually for a school morning, to be closed. Claire peered more closely. More adults than children, too, which was definitely odd for that time.

"Is that a television van?" Dave asked.

Claire followed the direction he was pointing. "Of course. One of the kids was killed in an accident yesterday."

"Ah, right. I saw it on the news." Dave glanced up to the driver's mirror and the reflection of their passenger. "Did you know him, Tony?"

"Not really," Tony mumbled.

"Don't know why reporters have to be here though," Claire said. Her thoughts were already turning to the delay getting into work that this was going to cause. With her reputation for lateness in the morning she could really do without it. "He was killed over at the old brewery, wasn't he?"

"Yes, but you know how it goes with telly reports. Footage of the grieving parents and a sound bite from the headmaster saying what a great kid he was and how he's going to be missed."

From the back of the car came a derisive noise. "I don't think the head's going to find it easy to say anything good about Clayton Kerry." Tony looked quickly down into his lap to avoid his mother's frown.

Up ahead of them, events seemed to be playing out as Dave had outlined. A man in a suit stood at the top of the small flight of stone steps that led up to the doors. Claire was fairly sure he was the headmaster. She'd seen him once, over two years previously, at a meeting to greet new parents to the school. In front of him was a woman dressed mainly in black holding something out in front of her. From this distance, Claire couldn't make out what it was, but she guessed it was a microphone given that at the woman's side stood a much less formally dressed man with a camera over one shoulder.

"Hope this doesn't take long," she muttered. "Don't they know some of us have got jobs to go to? And what are all those parents hanging around for? They can't all be part of the boy's family, can they?"

"Rubberneckers, I guess. Although…" Dave leaned forward. Wondering what he'd seen, Claire did the same.

Three of the crowd had mounted the step below the headmaster who was raising his hands as if to ward them off and retreating until his back was up against the glass doors. Normally these would have automatically slid open, but now, for some reason, they were staying closed. The interviewer was still thrusting her microphone into the headmaster's face, but her companion was focusing his camera on the three figures just one step below him. Letting the window down, Dave and Claire caught shouts, undeniably angry exclamations, and even the sound of what could have been booing.

"Something's up," Claire said, reaching for her seat belt buckle.

"What are you doing?" Tony exclaimed, as Dave killed the engine and undid his own seat belt.

"Back in a minute. Stay here."

"Wait!" Tony yelled. "My friends are out there. They'll see you."

Dave grimaced sympathetically at the lad who was twisting himself into knots at the thought of what his mother was about to do to him. When it came to opportunities for embarrassing your kids in front of their mates, no one had it better than a copper. "Sorry, Tony. All in a day's work. I'll make sure she doesn't get hurt."

"That's not what I'm worried about." Tony slouched down deep into the back seat. He appeared to be praying that no one would see him there.

Dave closed the car door and followed his boss.

As Summerskill and Lyon drew closer to the crowd, the words being shouted out became clearer. "Shame!" and "Resign!" were the most often repeated though the occasional "Wanker!" and "Tosser!" added colour.

"Not like any parent teacher meeting I remember," Dave said.

"You didn't go to school in Pontypridd. All right." Claire raised her voice to crowd control level. "If you'd excuse me. Ladies. Gentlemen. Police. Please make way. Thank you. Thank you." Holding out her ID card in front of her, Claire forced her way through the small crowd and climbed the steps to stand at the same level as the headmaster, the interviewer and her cameraman, and the three others.

"DCI Summerskill," she said, making sure everyone in the small group could see her card. "And this is DS Lyon." Dave had taken up his position on the step below her, so that he could face down the small crowd on the steps and beyond, but Claire knew he was also keeping an eye on the small hoodied group on her level for which she was grateful. "Now, would someone mind telling me what is going on here? Please?"

From a distance, Claire had assumed that the three figures confronting the head, dressed alike in jeans and hoodies, were all teenagers. Now, however, the one leading pulled back his hood, revealing a face worn by hardship and ravaged by grief and fury. "My son's dead!" he yelled, his voice thick with anger, and he jabbed a finger at the suited man in front of them, seemingly unable to say more.

Claire's eyes automatically went to the man being pointed at. Tall, silvered hair, quite distinguished looking in a senior civil servant sort of way. His face was familiar to her from the school's prospectus and that new parents' meeting. *But what's his name? I ought to know. My son goes to his bloody school!*

"If I could just..." the headmaster began.

"And this bastard...!" the distraught father yelled, cutting him off before tailing off himself, clearly so choked with violent emotion he couldn't speak. By his side, the taller of the two figures who still had their hoods up reached out a hand and rested it on his upper arm, muttering something Claire couldn't make out.

"Please. If we could all just calm down a minute. Mr...?" Claire waited for the man to give his name, but he was still too caught up in his passion and she doubted whether he had even heard her.

"Kerry," said the figure at his side, his hand still on the man's arm, consoling or restraining. Maybe both, Claire thought. *Of course. The name of that boy who was killed.*

"Thank you." Claire glanced at the face beneath the hoodie. Late teens, early twenties perhaps. Hard to tell with that typically fashionable beard. She looked to the other person in a hoodie but caught only a glimpse before he turned his face away from her. Younger than the bearded lad, and much more of his father in his face. But there was something else, too, someone else he reminded her of. With a stab of guilt and a flash of anger at her own stupidity Claire realised who it was. Of course, he looked so much like that picture of the dead boy. This had to be his brother. She faced the tall lad again. "And you are...?"

"I'm Mark. And this"—indicating the other young man—"is Caleb." Caleb raised his head just long enough to scowl at Claire before looking down again fixedly at his worn trainers.

Not a family comfortable with the police. Not the younger brother anyway. Claire quickly squashed the thought as unworthy at this time.

She turned back to the starkly contrasting figure in the suit. "Mr...?"

"Blake."

Of course! "Mr. Blake. Yes."

"My son is dead," Kerry shouted again.

"I know, sir," Claire said. "And please believe me, Mr. Kerry, I am truly sorry for your loss. But this really isn't the time or the place to be...dealing with it. Now, I'm going to ask if we can take this somewhere else, somewhere a bit more suitable and private. Mr. Blake, is there perhaps some meeting room or space we could use? Inside?"

It was clear from the headteacher's expression that inviting this man into the sanctuary of his school was the last thing he wanted to do, but before he could reply two things happened with an explosive speed, catching him and both police officers unawares. With no warning, the lad Mark yelled out and threw himself at Claire, sending her flying as he crashed into her. At the same time, a blurred something, the size and shape of a rugby ball, flew past them from the back of the small crowd and smashed into the glass door behind them. Someone screamed.

Claire's first thought was that Mark had snapped for some reason and attacked her. Quickly, though, she realised that, far from assaulting her, the young man had just saved her, pushing her out of the way of whatever had been flung at them. "Did you see who threw that?" she yelled at Dave as she scrambled back to her feet. Dave shook his head. "Right. Enough is bloody enough. Call for backup." Claire stepped forward decisively in front of Mr. Blake and raised her arms, hoping with all her might that no one was going to throw anything else at them. "Listen to me," she shouted. "My name is Detective Inspector Claire Summerskill and if I have to I will..."

Her words were cut off by the urgent blare of police sirens as two squad cars raced up the school drive. "That was quick."

"Not me." Dave indicated the reception office window near the doors and the agitated pair of middle-aged women within. One of them was still clutching a phone and nodding with relief as she spoke into it, presumably acknowledging the arrival of the cars.

"All right!" Claire stepped forward to take charge of the arriving uniforms. "I want these people cleared away. And you—" she turned back to Mr. Kerry, softening her tone with a considerable effort. "I would like a word with you, sir, down at the station."

"I didn't chuck the fucking brick."

"I didn't say you did, sir." Claire took a second to collect herself, all too aware that she was still acting on an adrenaline rush. *Well, someone lobbed a bloody brick at my head, didn't they?* But the man in front of her had just lost his child. And he was right: he hadn't thrown the object. "I'd still like a word, sir."

"Are you arresting me?"

Now there's interesting. Something in the way Kerry had said that tripped her police instincts. More challenge than question. *Oh, come on. Give the man a break,* her conscience protested, even as her professionalism filed the observation away for future consideration. "No, sir," she said in as soothing a tone as she could manage. "I am inviting you to the station so that we can have a word in...calmer surroundings. I really would appreciate your cooperation at this moment."

She watched as Mark, the young man who had pushed her out of the way, leaned into Kerry and whispered something in his ear, giving him a reassuring pat on the shoulder as he did. Kerry's shoulders sagged as if he was accepting there was no point protesting. "Thank you," she said. She turned to the other man. "And to you, too, for pushing me out of the way just then."

"No problem, officer," Mark said, with a broad smile. He certainly didn't seem to share either his family's looks or temperament. Caleb, at his side, gave her another glare from within his hoodie.

"Right, well, Mr. Kerry, if you would be so good as to go with this officer." She didn't recognise the constable who had stepped up to them. He had to be one of the station's recent batch of new recruits. She groaned inwardly, remembering the personnel reports she hadn't finished reviewing last night. Presumably, his details were in there. She looked round for the rookie's oppo—someone so new should be partnered up with a more experienced officer—and sure enough found reliable Sergeant Chris McNeil, a way off, calmly listening to some woman's angry protests and gradually defusing the situation. The newbie seemed capable enough though. With a nod of her head, Claire indicated that he should escort Mr. Kerry to one of the waiting cars. "Thank you. PC...?"

"Jones, ma'am." The new recruit stepped forward smartly, reached out, and put his hand on Kerry's shoulder. "If you'd come along with me, sir."

Kerry bridled instantly at the touch. Summerskill frowned at the young PC and shook her head. Jones immediately dropped his hand but stood his ground. Kerry glared at both of them before stalking off to the police car, Jones following quickly to keep up with him. *Rookie error*, Claire thought. *But that's what rookies do.*

"I don't suppose you'll be wanting us as well, will you, officer?"

Claire turned round to face Mark again. "I don't think so." Easier to deal with Kerry on his own. "Unless you'd like to come along as well to, you know, support your father?"

Caleb Kelly raised his head as if he was about to say something but ducked his head down again quickly when he felt her eyes on his face.

"He's not my dad, officer," Mark said. "He's, like, my uncle, but thanks all the same. C'mon, mate." He put his arm protectively over Caleb's shoulder. "Let's get you home." The pair of them turned and walked off in the same direction as the other, now fast-dissipating protestors.

Dave came and stood beside her. "You okay?"

The scene apparently well in hand, Claire took a moment to consider whether she was in fact okay. There were some slivers of glass in her hair and on her coat but otherwise she'd been untouched by the brief instance of violence. "I'm fine. Are you all right, Mr. Blake?"

"I suppose you could say that I am *all right*. Yes. Yes, I am, thank you." The tone of his voice suggested that he was very far from happy. Considering the wreckage of his school's front door and the fact he had been verbally and almost physically abused on the steps of his own school, Claire could hardly blame him. She doubted many school days started like this—even in Pontypridd they'd been rarities.

"I'm assuming, sir," Dave said, "that your school has some form of CCTV coverage?"

"Of course."

"Good," Claire said. "Then if I may, I'll be sending along a couple of officers a little later to review the cameras covering this area. I would very much like to see who threw whatever that was at me."

"Large stone, ma'am," Dave said, holding out a plastic evidence bag in which could be seen the rounded grey rock that had done the damage. "There was a pile of them back there where most of the people were standing."

"It's a Japanese Zen garden," Blake said. "A Year Seven project. Designed to foster calm and tranquillity."

"Yes, well, you might like to rethink that," Claire said. "When they come, the officers will also be taking statements."

"Statements?"

"Yes, sir. At the least this is a case of criminal damage. And even before someone smashed your door, it looked like that man and some of the other people here were threatening you. I don't know about what yet, and I believe there may be...extenuating circumstances, but we still need to investigate what went down before we can see what, if any, charges need to be brought."

Blake's lips thinned. "I see. But I doubt that will be necessary. I know I personally won't be pressing any charges."

Claire frowned. "I can understand you might be reluctant to pursue a course that could give the school some bad publicity, but really, I would advise you..."

"Mr. Blake? Mr. Blake? Are you all right? Have you been hurt?"

A woman had managed to evade the work of the uniformed police in clearing the scene, and was now thrusting herself between Summerskill, Lyon, and the headmaster. She shoved something into the latter's face causing him to jerk back in alarm. Instinctively, Claire went to push the object away before seeing the weapon for what it actually was. A microphone. Of course. She had forgotten about the reporters. And her partner's camera was pointed unwaveringly in their direction. *Shit!* Claire hated being filmed.

"Mr. Blake?" the woman repeated. "Sarah Moody, *Midlands Now*."

"I remember who you are, Miss Moody." The headteacher's tone was undeniably cold.

Completely unfazed, Sarah Moody pushed her microphone into Mr. Blake's face. "How do you feel?"

Claire knew how she'd feel if someone shoved something practically up her nose like that. Now she watched as the headteacher took a second to collect himself before carefully answering. "I am, of course, disappointed by the events of this morning. But I am sure matters can be sorted and everything can get back to normal." He paused and when he spoke again his voice had a slightly more rehearsed tone to it. "The people we should be thinking of at this time are, of course, the Kerry family, and, as I have said before, our sympathies are with them at this difficult time.

Now, if you'll excuse me, we have a busy school day ahead of us." He pointedly turned his back on both camera and reporter to address Summerskill and Lyon. "Inspector, sergeant. I will tell Reception to expect your officers later. Thank you again for your help here this morning."

He left them, his shoes crunching over the pebbles of reinforced glass the door had largely disintegrated into, and strode through the empty doorframe, back into his school.

"Guess you don't get to be a head these days without knowing how to handle the media," Dave said, softly enough that the reporters would only just be able to hear him.

"Inspector?"

Claire turned to find the reporter, Sarah Moody, addressing Dave. "*I'm* Inspector Summerskill," she said.

For a second, Claire wondered if the reporter was going to dispute the fact that she, the small blonde woman, was a higher ranked police officer than the man. Moody, however, recovered her television composure in a beat and launched into her reporter's shtick. "How do you feel?"

Really? That's the first question you're going to ask the senior police officer on the scene? Claire wondered if it would have been the first question she'd have asked Dave. "I'm happy to say that what seems to have been quite a minor incident has been cleared up without too much difficulty."

Behind Moody's back, holding a stone missile in a plastic bag and standing in broken glass, Dave mouthed the word, *Minor?* Claire ignored him.

"Do you have any further comment about this incident, and do you think Mr. Kerry will be able to bring charges?"

Claire began to reel off a standard response which could more honestly have been paraphrased as, *I have nothing to say. You know I have nothing to say. There will be an official statement later,* but then the actual sense of the reporter's words sank in and she stopped. Would *Kerry* be pressing charges? What for? Claire realised she might be the senior officer on the scene, but she still had no idea of what the situation had really been about. "It would not be appropriate at this point for the police to comment but as soon as it is, we will release an official statement," she said, and then she assumed her official stone face, the one that had just enough of a threat in it to deter all but the most insistent and stupid hack. Moody, it seemed, was not stupid, though Claire did see her glance briefly at Dave as if weighing up the chances of getting a good quote from him. Dave also assumed the official face, and Moody was professional enough to know when she was beaten.

She turned to face her colleague's camera. "Sarah Moody from Monastery Grove, Worcester. And now, back to the studio."

"C'mon," Claire said to Dave. The two of them walked back to Dave's car.

Tony, they discovered, was still mortified. "Can I go now?" he demanded with all the truculence of a young offender in a holding cell.

"Yes. And if a reporter called Sarah Moody tries to stop you for an interview, don't tell her I'm your mum."

"Like I would!" Tony slung his sports bag over his shoulder and set off up the school path. "I'm gonna be late," were the last words she caught from him.

"You and me both."

Chapter Three

"You're late."

"And you're old. But tomorrow I'll be on time."

From behind his desk, DI Rudge grunted. "With age comes wisdom, girly."

"And arthritis. And Alzheimer's. And gout. And..."

"I suppose you think you've got a good reason to be waltzing in at this time of the afternoon?"

Claire threw her coat over the back of her chair in the office she shared with her former boss and their sergeants. "The school run from hell."

Rudge grunted again. It was his default form of communication. "Mob of angry villagers baying for blood at the school gates?"

Rudge was a good detective, but this seemed positively supernatural. "Kind of. How'd you know?"

Rudge jerked a thumb over his shoulder at the tiny room the station laughingly referred to as its Video Lounge. "You're a daytime TV star."

Claire signalled to Dave who had followed her in. "C'mon you."

"I thought we were going to be starting with the kid's dad. Desk sergeant says they've taken him to Interview Three."

"I reckon you ought to check out the news first," Rudge said, adding without looking up from his paperwork, "always good to know what you're letting yourself in for."

The two of them left Rudge to his admin and third coffee of the day—he'd have been in for over an hour by then—and crossed the corridor to the Video Lounge. From within came the sound of voices and, unexpectedly, laughter. A female voice was saying, "And if you freeze it there, it looks like she's just sat on something."

Claire pushed the door open and strode in. "Cracking cases or downloading porn?"

DS Cortez had the grace to look slightly embarrassed. WPC Jenny Trent had no such inhibitions. "Morning, Claire. Day got off to a flying start I see."

Puzzled, Summerskill and Lyon looked past their colleagues to the screen. At that moment, it was a paused head and shoulders shot of Claire, and the expression did indeed look like she had just sat on something extremely uncomfortable. "Did I really look like that?"

"Not all the time," Dave said.

"Local telly news," Jenny explained.

"Shit, that Moody's quick."

"Well, this does have to be the most exciting thing that's happened of a morning for weeks," Jenny said. "When you consider the second most exciting thing was a suspected outbreak of foot-and-mouth in Hereford you can see why they'd rush it out. They'll be showing this on the hour every hour for the rest of the day." She handed the remote to Claire. "I've recorded it for you, though, just in case. Enjoy," and she and Cortez left the room, their laughter only slightly muffled by the door closing behind them.

"Popcorn?" Dave asked as he sat down in the seat nearest the screen.

Claire scowled, rewound the clip to its start, and remained standing as she pressed play. An establishing shot of the front doors of Monastery Grove panned across to one of Sarah Moody speaking directly to camera.

"Last night we reported on the sad news of the death of local schoolboy Clayton Kerry, a pupil here at Monastery Grove High School in the heart of the city. Almost immediately, however, that tragic event was overshadowed by the social media storm that broke out in response to remarks made by Mr. Alun Blake, headteacher of the school where Clayton had been a pupil for over four years."

The picture changed to show an interior scene, an office in which Alun Blake was sitting at a desk much larger and neater than any desk Claire was used to at Foregate Street. At the bottom of the screen a caption came up giving his name and position. "We were very sad to hear of the death of Clayton Kerry," Blake said. "It is always a tragedy when a young life is cut short before it has the chance to realise its full potential."

Cut to a shot of Moody, eyes furrowed in concern. "And how are you feeling right now?"

"Jesus! Has she only got the one question?"

The question might have been lazy, but the response wasn't what Claire had expected. She'd been braced for the sort of bland expression of sadness and dismay Dave had earlier identified as appropriate. Instead, Blake's lips thinned again in that expression of near distaste she'd seen less than an hour previously when he was dealing with Moody for a second time on the steps of his school. "It's very sad," he said again.

The screen cut back to Moody's face, her eyes narrowing as if she was focusing on something that needed teasing out.

"They're called noddies, y'know," Dave whispered.

"What?"

"These shots of the reporters responding to interviewees. They're often shot after the interviews have taken place and then intercut."

Well, that would explain the air of artificiality Claire sensed about this piece. Or maybe that came simply from the dislike she was feeling for the interviewer.

"Was Clayton a good pupil?" Moody was asking.

"What's that got to do with anything?" Claire demanded.

"I didn't teach the boy myself," Blake replied, "but I speak on behalf of those teachers here who did who are all very saddened by this news."

"But as the headteacher you must have been aware of what kind of pupil Clayton was."

Claire frowned. "Why is she making such a song and dance of this? She's got the head saying how sad it was. Job done, move on."

Dave shook his head. "But he's not done the full job, has he? Not said what an angel Clayton was, how he was full of fun, kind, loved by all, etc., etc."

Claire recalled what Tony had told her last night. "That could possibly be difficult."

By now, the camera had moved in so closely Blake's face was practically filling the screen. "And why're they doing that? That's the sort of shot they use in documentaries on serial killers. Get up that close and you could make my old mam look psychotic."

Blake was now obviously weighing his words. "Clayton was...a challenging young boy," he said. "He came from...a difficult home background. We had worked closely with him and his parents to help him make the most of his opportunities during his time with us."

The camera remained fixed on Blake's face, Sarah Moody's insistent questioning coming from somewhere out of shot. "But you had recently expelled Clayton, hadn't you?"

"The term usually used these days is 'excluded'," he replied stiffly, "but yes, Clayton had been excluded."

"Permanently?"

"Subject to the usual procedures, including any appeals from the family, and after a meeting of the Governors. But yes, Clayton's exclusion would almost certainly have become permanent."

"But," Moody pressed on, "it would be fair to say, wouldn't it, that if he hadn't been 'excluded', he would have been in school and so this tragic accident could not have occurred?"

Blake looked directly into the camera as he replied. "The school cannot be held responsible for anything that happens to its pupils when they are not on our premises or under our direct care."

"But he wasn't on your premises, was he, Mr. Blake, or under your care because you had refused to teach him? As a headteacher, are you aware of a recent government report which said that one of the major contributory factors to teenagers becoming involved in crime is exclusion, either temporary or most especially permanent, from schools?"

For a second, Claire thought she saw something at the corner of one of Blake's eyes, a tic or brief tightening. Blake's voice, though, when he spoke was commendably calm and level. "I don't think that is really an appropriate direction to pursue at this moment in time, do you? All I will say now, once again, is that our thoughts and prayers are with Clayton's family. Thank you."

The clip ended and the screen returned to its menu. Claire threw the remote on to the table in disgust. "Talk about hatchet job."

"I don't know," Dave demurred. "All he had to do was say the expected things."

"Passing over the inconvenient truth that they'd had to kick the kid out for being a little shit?"

"Maybe I'd have focused more on the work they'd done with the family rather than the actual kicking out bit."

"You'd have made a good headmaster. Or politician."

"Never a headmaster," Dave said quickly, partly to cover any reaction he might have shown to the word "politician". "Can't stand kids."

"You're okay with Tony," Claire said, heading for the door.

"We have a lot in common."

"Yeah, you're both too up yourselves sometimes."

"I was going to say we both struggle with dominating women. And you know what that leads to."

"Successful men. Now get a move on. I want to get this interview over with so I can crack on with some real police work."

*

Outside Interview Room Three, they saw again the young copper who had escorted Kerry to the station. "Ma'am. Sir." Dave smiled at the way the new PC almost stood to attention. He wondered how long that would last. He also wondered why Jones looked slightly embarrassed, until he spoke again. "I was—er, just going to get Callum a cup of tea."

"Callum?"

"Mr. Kerry. That's his first name."

"Oh, right. Good idea." Jones visibly brightened at Dave's praise. "He been giving you any grief?"

"No, no. Not at all. Dead quiet in fact. I tried getting him to talk a bit but, well, he doesn't want to know. Only to be expected I suppose."

"Quite. Good work. Jones, wasn't it?"

The young uniform smiled broadly. "Yes, ma'am. Joseph Jones. Joe."

"Welsh?"

"No, ma'am. Brummie."

"Can't be helped. Bring the tea in when you've got it. One for me too. White, no sugar. And a black coffee for Sergeant Lyon."

"You know he'll only get something disgusting from the machine," Dave said after PC Jones had scurried off round the corner.

"I know. But I like seeing young men fetch and carry for me."

"Do tell. And even I could tell that was a Birmingham accent not Welsh."

"Roots, man. I was going by the name."

Dave went to respond to that but a surprising impulse of political correctness and the fact that Claire had already opened the door into the interview room held him back Maybe he'd return to that at a later date. They entered the room.

Interview Room Three was, by custom, the room used for what were semi-jokingly called "the friendlies", the interviewees called in for a "chat" rather than for something more formal that would probably be the first step towards something altogether more permanent. Rumour had it that was why the room was painted in a slightly less disgusting shade of light green than the others and boasted a desk and chairs of marginally higher quality than was the norm. To Claire's eye, the only real difference between this and the station's four other interview rooms was that it was fractionally less worn and battered—probably because visits by "friendlies" were far and away less common.

Kerry was sitting hunched over one side of the desk. He raised his head when Summerskill and Lyon entered, only to let it fall back down again when he saw it wasn't PC Jones and his cup of tea.

Dave took in the crude tattooed skulls and snakes across the backs of both hands and the Roman numerals on the side of his neck. (Dates perhaps? Children's birthdays? Was one of them Clayton's?) They'd met guys like this before in the interview rooms and would meet many more. But few were as sunk in misery as this man was now, and Dave couldn't help wondering if Claire had done the right thing bringing him in.

"Mr. Kerry," Claire began. "Callum."

"You recording this?" Kerry jerked his head at the recording apparatus set into the wall by the desk.

"No. Definitely not. As I said, this is not an arrest. It's not…"

"So, I'm free to walk out if I want to?"

Dave watched Claire weigh her words carefully. "Yes, you are. But I really hope you won't. I think it would be better for everyone if we could sit and talk about what happened today."

They waited. The seconds ticked by. After ten seconds, Claire took his silence as consent to continue. She sat down and Dave took the seat next to her. "First of all, Mr. Kerry," she began, "may I say how sorry…"

"Don't!" Kerry's eyes were riveted on his hands, his fingers pulling and tearing at loose bits of skin around the nails, teeth gritted. *That has to hurt,* Dave thought. "That's all everyone's fucking saying, isn't it? 'We're sorry. We're all so fucking sorry.' Well, you can shove it. All of you. It doesn't… It doesn't help," he finished, his voice almost inaudible.

"Mr. Kerry."

Don't say it, Dave thought. *Don't say you understand. How can you? How can any of us?*

"Why were you at the school this morning?"

Kerry squinted as if the question had taken him unawares. "I always takes my girl, don' I?"

"But…"

"An' *he's* always there, in't he?"

"Mr. Blake, the head, you mean? But why…?"

"Standing there," Kerry said, as if Claire hadn't spoken, "all smiles for the parents and saying hello to the kids, like he cares. Like he even knows them. Never used to say hello to me, though, did he? Never used to say, 'Good morning,' to Clayton or his brother or sister. Oh no." Once again Kerry's voice was rising, and now he finally looked up from his hands at the two officers, eyes red-rimmed and wet.

Dave tensed in his seat. A quick glance at Claire and he saw her brief frown, the small shake of her head. *Stay put.* He gritted his teeth but stayed ready.

"Why was Clayton excluded, Mr. Kerry?"

Why are you asking that now?

"For nothing!" They waited. "Nothing," Kerry said again. "Kids' stuff, that's all."

"Fighting?" Claire suggested.

Kerry glared at her and she met his eyes steadily. "He weren't an angel, all right? I know he weren't. But there's worse up at that school. And them teachers were always picking on him, bullying him because he wasn't the brightest. Well, I don't care. He were as good as any of them. And now he's... Now he's..." Kerry smashed both hands on the desk and went to shove his chair back, but the fixed legs held firm. He slumped forward again, face down and invisible to both officers.

"Tea?" PC Jones re-entered the interview room with a tray bearing three plastic cups.

"Thank you," Claire said, glad of the diversion. "It's only from the machine, Mr. Kerry, but it's wet and warm as my mam used to say." Kerry neither moved nor spoke as Claire took the cups from the tray and set them on the table. "Sugar?" She put three packets next to Kerry's cup. "Thank you, constable." She indicated for him to leave and then sat back down and picked up her cup. Dave followed suit and for the next few seconds both pretended to drink.

Kerry reached out, took his cup, and swallowed a mouthful. "Tastes like shit."

"You're not wrong," Dave said. Summerskill and Lyon both put their cups back down.

"Mr. Kerry," Claire tried again. "What I'd really like to know is what was going on at the school this morning?"

Kerry stared down into his cup of tepid tea. "It was...it was because of what he said."

"Mr. Blake. The headmaster?"

"Yeah, him. He could have said something good, y'know? He *should* have said something good. Clayton was a good lad. But he didn't. He made him sound bad. He made us, his family, sound shit. And it were on the telly."

Claire thought of that clip she and Dave had just seen, tried to imagine how she would have felt if that had been Tony the headteacher had been talking about. "What," she began, struggling to get in this man's head, "what did you go there to do? What were you hoping to gain?"

Kerry raised his head, and Claire saw the answer in his eyes before he spoke. "I dunno. I didn't know what else to do. What else *could* I do?"

*

"Good start to the day, Chris?"

Sergeant McNeil grunted. "Thought closing time at The Arms was bad enough. Now it's civil disorder on the school run."

Jenny Trent laughed. "New kid okay, was he? Didn't reach for the riot shield and pepper spray?"

"Joe? No. Handled it well he did. Good lad. Don't think there's going to be any problems there. We'll see about the others. Early days yet."

"Great. Then neither of you'll have a problem going back to the school and getting a few statements?"

McNeil groaned. "Couldn't Community Liaison take it?"

"Totally tied up with that fire at the Youthie."

"Fantastic. All right then. We'll go. Not as if there's any proper policing to do."

"It'll be good for the rookie," Jenny said briskly. "Show him what he's got to look forward to. Start off with the head, only politic, then go on to the Reception ladies and any other staff who were hanging about at the time. Shouldn't take long. Then any CCTC footage they've got. Claire is very keen on finding out who threw the rock at her."

McNeil chuckled. "I'll bet she is. Pity the poor sod when she does. Okay. No problem. I'll round Joe up and head over there now, get it out of the way."

Jenny handed over the folder of interview forms they'd need. "So, what's he like then, the new kid? Apart from being okay when it comes to handling mobs?"

McNeil smiled knowingly. "What do you mean, what's he like?"

"Just asking, y'know. Fresh blood in the station."

"Fresh *meat*. You mean?"

"Po-tay-to, po-tah-to."

"We're talking about meat, not veg. Good-looking meat too."

"Really? I hadn't noticed."

"Bit young for you, eh Jen?"

"You old git!" Jenny pretended annoyance to cover the fact that she really was annoyed. "He's not that much younger. Simply welcoming him to our little community."

"You are so public-spirited."

"Yes. Yes, I am. So?"

"What?"

"Hobbies? Interests? Likes? Dislikes?"

"You mean, married or single?"

"Well, that as well."

McNeil shook his head and smiled as if at some private joke. "I've only known him a couple of days, Jen, so I haven't got down to his shoe size and inside leg measurement yet." He went to leave, adding just before he did, "I can tell you, though, you're barking up the wrong tree with young Joseph."

"What do you mean?"

Chapter Four

The library had been closed for some meeting or other. The benches behind the science block, out of sight of the main building, had been overrun by Year Seven girls claiming them as their territory. Every other place was way too close to cameras, teachers, or kids she hated or who hated her. That left only this place, just through the back gates and off the path through the small patch of no-man's-land behind the school. Technically out of bounds, of course, but then she couldn't care less about that. Unfortunately, neither could the four lads who'd snuck out for a smoke, and who now found themselves with a bit of ready-made entertainment too.

"Clayton's dad's going to fucking kill your dad."

Her eyes darted nervously from one to the other of the boys and to the path behind them leading back to what had now, ironically, become the sanctuary of the school. There was no way she could get past them. She bit her lip and waited.

"Fuck-ing kill him," the leader said again with brutish relish, holding out his mobile phone in front of himself like some sort of talisman.

She saw the screen was lit but couldn't read it from that distance. She guessed it was probably the social media page that had sparked off that morning's disturbance outside the school. Maybe the death threat was there too. "What do you mean? I don't…"

"My dad says he'd do the same," the boy went on. His mates muttered agreement. "No call for it, he says. You don't treat lads like that. Not around here."

Another of the lads stepped forward for his share of the fun. "My dad says, like, your dad would get it if something happened, like, to his little girl." The four boys laughed. She took a step back. A tree blocked any further retreat, a branch sticking hard into her back. Her heart raced in her chest. Should she call out? Would anyone hear her? Would that just provoke her tormentors?

The leader took a step towards her. His menacing proximity was like a physical force pushing her back into the tree. "Think he'd like that? Think he'd like to find his darling girl all fucked up under some old brick wall? Think he'd find something nice to say about you? Or would he say you were a scumbag loser like he did Clayton?" He thrust his snarling face into hers. "Say something!"

"Now, why don't you all just fuck off back to school, like good little boys?"

All four lads swung round to the sound of the new voice coming from the path behind them. "All right, Mark?" the leader said uncertainly.

The young man smiled. "Fine and dandy, mate," he said, but he didn't move. It was clear he was waiting for them to do what he had so emphatically suggested. "It's Alex, isn't it? And Owen. Pedro." He squinted as he came to the last one. "And Ryan, yeah? Time to be moving on, lads."

"She…" Alex began. Mark took one step forward. Alex took two back. From the distant buildings came the high-pitched beeping that signalled the end of morning break.

"You don't want to be late for lessons now, do you, Alex?" Mark said.

Caught in conflicting impulses, the outcome was never really in doubt. "Later," Alex said to the girl. "C'mon," he ordered the others and stalked off. His mates followed, the one called Owen even daring to run ahead, snickering as he went. Alex punched him.

Her tormentors gone, the girl hugged herself, her nails digging into her arms. She knew she had to move, too, had to go and rejoin the hateful pushing, shoving, faceless kids pointing and mouthing and whispering about her. But she couldn't. She couldn't even put one foot in front of the other.

"You all right, Annie?"

"Anne," she whispered. Mark held out his hand. She flinched. Mark kept his hand out. Reluctantly she stepped forward, but she didn't take his hand.

"Okay. It's okay." Mark moved in and gently stroked the side of her face with the back of his hand. "It'll be all right, Annie."

Anne hugged herself, and under cover of the action, dug her fingernails deeper into her arms, using the biting pain to wipe out the even fiercer pain inside.

*

"Working late?"

Dave checked his watch. It was three minutes to six. "Technically, no. Leaving early?"

Claire let herself drop into the chair in front of her sergeant's desk. "Technically, yes. Though as I was up half last night doing reviews and will doubtless be doing the same again tonight, I suppose I'm not really."

Dave grunted wry agreement and returned to his own work at his computer. Gradually he became aware that Claire was still sitting in front of him. She was looking at him in a way he was coming to recognise. "What?"

"Nothing." But she smiled when she said it.

In his head, Dave hurriedly ran through the latest long list of "to do" tasks his boss had given him. Practically everything in the "urgent" category had been done. The only thing not quite complete, the thing he was in fact working on now, was an analysis of the monthly budget audit which, given Summerskill's dislike of matters financial, was bound to be the last thing she'd check up on anyway. "No, really. What?"

Claire picked up a pen and toyed with it as she spoke. "No station news? Gossip? Scuttlebutt?"

"What on earth is scuttlebutt? Sounds like an STI."

"You are hopeless, y'know? I mean the new recruits."

"South, Dennison, and Jones?" Dave said immediately. "No. But then I haven't been able to see their reviews yet, have I, because you..."

"...haven't finished them yet. Yada yada, yes, I know. I mean, specifically, PC Jones. You remember, the lad who helped out this morning at school. Brought in Kerry? Made tea?"

"No. Early onset Alzheimer's means I am blessedly untroubled by events that happened so long ago." Reluctantly, Dave accepted that he wasn't going to be able to get any further with his work until he had found out what was on Claire's mind. He pushed his keyboard to one side. "All right. What about him?"

"He's on your team."

Dave's expression settled into the stone face they'd both used to such good effect earlier that day. A suspicion was forming as to what Claire was driving at. "My team? Is this some new operation I haven't been told about?"

"Very funny." Claire sat back and folded her arms, a maddening smile on her lips. "I mean, he's gay."

"You thought he was Welsh. You were wrong about that."

"I *hoped* he was Welsh. I *know* he's gay."

"And how do you *know?*"

"He's told Chris who told Jen who's told me."

"Ah. WPC Trent," Dave said. He might just as well have added, *Of course.* He checked his watch. "I suppose I'd better go and find him then and have sex."

"Oh c'mon."

"Well, what do you want me to say?"

"Aren't you pleased?"

"Why should I be?"

Claire searched for the right thing to say. "Well, now you're not the only gay in the village."

Dave gave the hackneyed catchphrase the evil eye. "If you mean in the station then I very much doubt I have been anyway."

"Really?" Claire leaned forward again. "So, who else do you reckon?"

"I am not speculating on our colleagues' private lives. If they've chosen not to put it out there, then I'm not going to pry."

"We're police. It's what we do for a living. Not that we had to with you, of course. I mean, you did kind of 'put it out there', didn't you? With that photograph on your desk of your 'boyfriend'." Claire made air quotation marks with her fingers. "And the message."

"Ah. That." Dave had indeed put a photograph of a man on his desk when he had first arrived at Foregate Street, with a loving inscription to him written on it. But it hadn't been of the man he was seeing at the time. It hadn't even been of a past boyfriend. It had been a fake, the picture chosen, after careful and lengthy research, from the internet. "That was different." Claire arched an eyebrow. "I'd been posted here to fill a quota. Everyone knew that. I didn't like it but I'm a sergeant, not," he said with heavy emphasis, "a rookie plod. So, I wasn't going to go around apologising for what I am or looking like I was trying to hide it. It seemed the most efficient way to—" He searched for the right phrase. "nail my colours to the mast."

"There's a joke there about rainbow flags, isn't there?"

Dave shook his head wearily. "There really isn't."

"You could just have said."

"Why should I? Is everyone expected to give a potted history of themselves on their first day?"

Claire shrugged and glanced around at the four desks in the office. Three of them had framed pictures on them: hers and Jim's were pictures of their respective families; Terry's was of him and his statuesque girlfriend Debs, a selfie at one of the many exotic locations they got to visit through Debs's job as an air stewardess. There was no photo on Dave's desk now. "Shame you got rid of it," Claire said. "He was very easy on the eye."

"It did its job," Dave said. They both knew, of course, that was only half the story. Dave had had to rescue that picture many times from the floor or the bin where it had been knocked or thrown by person or persons unknown. While he'd have replaced it a hundred times over if it had been of a real partner, the effort had come to seem misplaced once it had been there long enough to do its job. Besides, the irony of using a lie to convey a truth had begun to irk. He could, he supposed, have used a rainbow flag, but quite probably many of his colleagues would have then taken him for some kind of eco-warrior. Plus, it would have been way too camp.

"So, you really didn't get a vibe?"

"What?" Dave dragged his thoughts back to Claire's annoying probing.

"Any feeling?" she persisted. "From Jones. Any hint, suspicion, sympathetic vibration? When we saw him this morning?"

"I think," Dave said slowly, screwing his eyes up and looking into the middle distance as if trying to recall events, "I was too busy making sure no one was going to smash your head in with a rock." He brought his focus back to her. "And..."

"I know. I know. There's no such thing as gaydar." She sat back in her chair and folded her arms. "Well, I thought there was something."

"Perhaps it was his Welshness."

"Funny." Claire looked thoughtful for a moment. "You know, if there was such a thing as gaydar and if I had it, y'know who'd I'd have down as gay?"

"Me?"

"Almost certainly not. No. Terry. He's got an eye for his clothes, looks after his body, and grooms a bit too much, if you know what I mean."

"I think I stopped knowing what you mean when you started this conversation," Dave said. "And you do realise, don't you, that you've just strung together a whole load of offensive stereotypes?" What Dave would have denied even under torture was that, at first, he had wondered, and hoped a little, about the handsome Sergeant Cortez. But that had been simple physical attraction to a good-looking guy not some semi-mythical sixth sense. Hadn't it?

"I'm a detective. I can call it profiling."

"Well, you might like to add Sergeant Cortez's girlfriend to your profile." Dave waved at the photograph on Cortez's desk. "Rather undermines your case, doesn't she?"

Claire wrinkled her nose in disappointment. "Ah yes. Debs."

"And the..." Dave stopped.

"And the what?"

"Lack of irony."

"Now who's trotting out the stereotypes?"

Dave gave a small shrug as if conceding the point but the word he had really been about to say had been *homophobia*. Maybe that wasn't fair. Certainly, he and Terry Cortez hadn't struck up anything like a friendship, but that could be down to any number of reasons. There was no law that said you had to like your colleagues, especially if they were so different in background and temperament. But of course, sometimes what blocked a friendship was the most obvious difference after all. And maybe, just maybe... Dave shook his head. He'd torpedoed once again Claire's wishful thinking about gaydar. He wasn't about to get her started on the cod psychology of internalised homophobia. He reached for his keyboard. "I have got to finish this analysis."

"Not interrupting, am I?" Sergeant McNeil was standing at the office door.

Claire shook her head. "Just reviewing this morning's little adventure. What can we do for you, Chris?"

"Just to let you know, we went back to the school where you had your run-in this morning. Had a chat with the head, those secretaries, and a couple of the other teachers who'd seen what was going on. All backs up what you got from Kerry. He was upset about his lad, angry that it had happened because he wasn't in school and then pissed off when the head dissed the family in his telly interview. Went off on a rant on social media then took it to the school in person, drawing in a bunch of his Facebook 'friends'. I don't think he'd thought as far ahead as actually doing anything. Might have been that nothing would've happened, if..."

"...if we hadn't shown up."

"I think that might have been a bit of a catalyst," McNeil said tactfully. "A police officer was just too much of a tempting target for one person."

Claire's eyes narrowed. "You found out who threw the rock?"

McNeil grinned. "Turns out the school's got a bloody good CCTV setup, and a lady in charge who loves her job. Spends most of her time catching kids smoking in the loos and vandalising lockers so she was well up for something a bit juicier. She'd got footage and printouts before we even got there."

"And?"

"It was a kid. A Year Seven lad. That's eleven in old money," he added helpfully.

"I know what Year Seven means, sergeant."

"Course you do, ma'am. Nothing to do with the Kerry family as far as we can see. Just a lad with an attitude who saw an opportunity for mischief. Got himself quite a record at school for bad behaviour but not on our radar yet."

"Well, he bloody well is now, the little shit."

"Don't worry, ma'am," McNeil said happily. "I put the fear of God into him."

"And what about Kerry. Is the head pressing charges?" Dave asked.

McNeil shook his head. "I think he wants to put all of it behind him as quickly as possible."

"That's very big of him," Claire said.

"More like diplomatic," Dave said. "Schools are all about PR these days. Probably thinks Monastery Grove's had quite enough bad publicity for the moment without drawing it out."

Claire nodded but Dave noticed she was looking at McNeil as if she had something else on her mind, and surprisingly it wasn't hanging, drawing, and quartering the young rock thrower who had nearly kayoed her. Dave had an uncomfortable feeling he knew what it was. "Well, if that's all, Chris..." he began.

"Did you take that new lad with you, Chris?" Claire asked with an innocent ease that didn't fool Dave for a second. "Jones was it?" She pretended not to notice Dave's look of disgust at her fake uncertainty over the new PC's name.

"Yeah, and actually, that's the other reason I've dropped in now."

"Is there a problem?" Claire asked quickly.

"No, not at all. It's only we're having a drink like, tonight, to welcome the new recruits and I was looking for Jenny and maybe Terry to see if they wanted to come along."

"Great idea," Claire enthused with, Dave thought, more gusto than was necessary. "We'd love to come. Wouldn't we, sergeant?"

"Right," said McNeil. "Good. I didn't think... I mean. Right."

"And what about the kids?" Dave asked. "You know, the two children you have at home who call you mother. You remember them?"

"It can be Ian's turn to look after them tonight," Claire declared after a moment's thought. "God knows he owes me."

"And the performance reviews?"

"Will be even more accurate once I've got to know the new recruits better."

"All of them?"

"Of course, all of them." She turned back to McNeil. "Where and when, Chris?"

"Eight o'clock at the Farrier's."

"We'll be there. See you then."

"And the plans I had for this evening?" Dave asked as the door closed behind the constable.

"The ready meal can stay in the fridge and you can record whatever documentary you were going to watch when you were eating it for tomorrow."

"So, we're going to a pub just because there's going to be another gay copper there?"

"It's got to be an incentive, hasn't it?"

"He's a rookie uniform for Pete's sake. I'm older and senior. We're not going to be friends, or anything else, just because we're both gay."

"Oh, I'm hoping for a lot more than just friends. No seriously," Claire added quickly when she saw Dave's scowl. "It'll do you good to socialise. You need to know the people you're working with. Mix with them socially. And you can't back out of it now. You've been invited."

"*I* wasn't invited," Dave said. "And I don't think *you* were on the guest list, either, until you gate-crashed for both of us."

"Yes, well, like you, everyone knows I've got kids to get home to. Most of the time. And you...well, you're just a bit...spiky sometimes."

"Spiky!"

Claire stood up to leave. "That's right. Like that. Spiky. But tonight, Cinders, you are going to the ball. And that's an order."

Chapter Five

"Night, Mr. Blake."

At his desk, Alun Blake didn't look up from his papers as he waved one hand and made a vague sound that could have been a reply.

Dan Barnes, chief school caretaker (or *"Premises Manager",* as he'd remind anyone who did, or didn't, care) closed the door to the headteacher's office, flipped the occupant a finger below the level of the frosted glass, and went on his way. He'd worked for three headteachers during his time at Monastery Grove and hadn't got on well with any of them. But then he didn't like most of the rest of the staff either. Or any of the kids. It went, or so he believed, with the territory.

As he made his way along the corridors from the administration area of the school which contained the head's office to the exit that led back to his own small bungalow in the school grounds, Barnes passed the main entrance in the foyer. In place of the glass door shattered that morning was now a large sheet of thin wood. "Bloody tendering," Dan muttered to himself as he walked past it. That was what happened when every job had to be hawked out to the company that would do it the cheapest. It took bloody ages to get anything done. And he'd bet they'd let the brat who'd smashed it get off with just a slapped wrist. Dan would have given him a damned good hiding. Or at the least, something to think about the next time he went to heave bricks around. Now when he'd been a lad…

Trailing bitter memories, Dan wandered down the corridors and left through an exit some way from the foyer. Five minutes later, just long enough to ensure he was a safe enough distance away, the flimsy wood blocking the shattered door began to bulge, the cheap nails holding it in place giving up easily to the pressure from outside.

*

In his office, Blake looked up. Had that been Barnes a minute ago? He glanced at his clock. Gone seven. At that time, it must have been Barnes.

Not likely to be many other members of staff still around putting in the hours. He turned his attention back to his work, the printout of an e-mail from the new parent governor he had deliberately left until last. He read again the question it was asking.

"Do you think that permanent exclusion was, in the long term, the right course of action to pursue with such a vulnerable and needy member of our school community?"

Blake picked up the silver pen awarded him for services to his previous school from its stand on his desk, depressed its button, and slowly and deliberately crossed out *"vulnerable and needy"* again and again, only stopping when the pen's point had ripped right through the paper and was in danger of scoring his desk's surface. "Yes," he said softly. "Yes, I bloody well do."

The door to his office flew open, slamming into the filing cabinets on one side so hard it sent a pile of box files crashing to the floor.

Blake leaped to his feet. Standing at the door was a figure in a dark-blue hoodie, hood up to cover the head, a scarf wrapped around their lower face and baseball cap under the hood pulled down low to conceal all but the eyes. In the intruder's hand was a baseball bat.

For a second the two men stood, facing each other. Blake's eyes darted to the telephone on his desk. He held out his hands, palms down. "All right. Look. We don't keep any money in this office." He took a step towards the phone. "There's really nothing..."

The hooded figure leaped across the room and brought the bat down hard. The telephone shattered across the desk. Blake threw himself backwards, away from the vicious impact, and fell into the bookshelves behind him, sending still more files and folders cascading to the floor. Slowly, the eerily silent hooded figure circled the desk, slapping the baseball bat down into his gloved hand as he did. Once. Twice. Three times. Blake, too, circled backwards away from him, snatching fearful glances at the floor, wary of tripping over one of the fallen books or folders and leaving himself completely helpless.

With a sudden, vicious scything motion the intruder swung the bat sideways, sending a row of framed photos and trophies on a bookcase flying in all directions.

Shielding his eyes with his arm from the showers of debris, Blake flung himself towards his office's door. Barnes! If he could just find Barnes. Dear God, let the miserable git not have locked the exit doors!

*

The Farrier's Arms was, Dave decided, on the whole, not an absolute dump.

That was the best thing he could find to say about it.

Its location, only a couple of hundred yards down the road from the Foregate Street station, made it ideal for off-duty coppers (and, at one time, for those on duty, too, if DCI Rudge's tales of "the good old days" were to be believed). But the dismal décor and out-of-date furnishings now left Dave feeling that the pub's identity as a police watering hole was something it had resigned itself to rather than embraced, lying back and accepting its decay, like a drag queen who'd wanted to be Marlene Dietrich in *The Blue Angel* but ended up as Bette Davis in *Whatever Happened to Baby Jane?* Even if the presence of so many police wasn't enough to deter anyone with a dodgy record or guilty conscience, the seventies carpeting and wallpaper and the overall beige and sticky ambience were bound to do the trick.

Dave wondered if that was why he felt more uncomfortable here now than he had done in any of the half dozen or so other godforsaken watering holes he had been in over the last couple of months during his half-hearted wanderings through the torture of app "dating". Or maybe it was the prospect of being expected to play nice with a wet-behind-the-ears baby cop, just because he also happened to be gay. He found himself beginning to dislike young Joe Jones (*daft name*) but checked the impulse as unfair. Why couldn't Claire have let him find out for himself about Jones? Why did straight people—straight *women* in particular—go into frantic matchmaker mode when two gay guys came into sight? Maybe they just wanted to spread the misery of commitment.

That bitter thought revived an uncomfortable recent memory. While Summerskill and Lyon had been investigating a series of murders based around local gyms, a charismatic businesswoman, Susan Green, had tried to set him up with a guy. That had turned out to be just the smallest example of her control-freakery, the more significant examples being the stitching up of her ex-husband on a very nasty charge of underage sex, and the very strong suspicion that she had been accessory after the fact in at least one case of murder. Dave smiled grimly. "Susie" Green had been a manipulative cow, but the courts were even then picking her game-playing past apart piece by piece, and Dave was hopeful of her receiving a suitably rewarding stretch in prison.

On the other hand, the guy she had set him up with had been Sean Cullen.

Hardly a match made in heaven. There was obviously no future in it. They were completely different people, and Cullen had given no sign that he was interested in anything other than the sex. Which, it had to be said, was great. And that was really all Dave was looking for at this stage in his life. Wasn't it? If Cullen was home then Dave could be with him now, in his bed, trading sarcastic comments, making love. It'd be good. Well, the sex would be. All it would take would be a quick text to confirm. Better than sitting in this retrograde fleapit.

Of course, afterwards there was always that awkward small-talk-while-I-put-my-clothes-back-on-and-get-out scene to play. Not that Sean seemed to find it particularly awkward.

Dave squared his shoulders and faced up to reality. It wasn't as if he had a choice. Summerskill would give him hell if he left before he'd even said hello. The best he could do would be to keep it brief and get it over with as quickly as possible.

"Move it, Lyon! I've seen funeral processions move faster. And look more cheerful."

Claire's voice in his ear and her elbow in his back jogged Dave out of his introspection. "I was lost in thought contemplating the range of ales," he said, indicating the two pumps at the bar.

"Well, go and get yourself a piña colada, and a gin and tonic for me then come and join us over there. Hi, Jen," and Claire strolled happily over to their colleagues.

There were about a dozen men and women in the Arms, two small groups of hardened regulars and then the welcoming party that Chris had gathered: Terry Cortez, Jenny Trent, and, of course, the newbies. When Dave joined them a couple of minutes later with his pint and Claire's G&T, Chris raised his glass to him. "Glad you could join us, sergeant."

"Dave," Claire said, accepting her drink. "We're all off duty. Chris has been doing the introductions," she continued. "This is Baz South, who's from the north so get your jokes out of the way now." She pointed to the thin, pale young man who seemed almost to be trying to sit to attention in the presence of so much service seniority. Dave raised his pint in greeting. "This is Becky Dennison." The dark-haired girl sitting, looking rather uncomfortable Dave thought, next to Jenny gave Dave a nervous smile. "And this," Claire concluded with what to Dave felt like a flourish, "is Joe Jones who you already know. From this morning. Here you are. I've saved you a seat." Claire patted the spot on the bench seat she had made next to her. She had also made sure it was right next to PC Jones.

Dave raised his pint again, first to Becky and then to Joe who raised his own in acknowledgement before returning to a lively chat he was having with Chris.

"So come on, you lot," Claire declared, turning to the rookies. "Fill us in. We might as well get all the dirt on you now rather than wait for Jen to fill us in later."

"Time was you'd have got the lowdown before any of us, Claire," Jenny declared.

"Time was I didn't have so much bloody paperwork to do."

"Drawbacks of rapid promotion."

"Not *that* rapid."

"Did I hear you say you were from Birmingham?" Dave asked Joe quickly. There was a surprised silence around the table, and Dave realised he had spoken too quickly and too loudly, and so had promoted himself from least interesting new arrival to centre of attention.

"Er, yeah," Joe said. "Northfield. You know it?"

"No."

"Me neither," Claire said. "What a coincidence."

"Nor me," admitted Becky, a second or two later.

There was an embarrassed silence.

"We used to be a lot rowdier in my day," said a voice from the main door.

"Jim!" Claire shouted. Dave thought she could just as easily have exclaimed *Thank God!* "Get over here, you miserable old sod. How come you're out at this time of night? Rose finally thrown you out?"

Chief Inspector Rudge grunted with unusual amiability as he made his way over to the table. "I have put my foot down with a firm hand and made it clear that there are times when a man's natural urges have to be acknowledged and he should be given free rein to wander and indulge himself in whatsoever fashion he does choose."

"She's at her mother's, isn't she?"

"For the next three nights," Rudge said, clapping his hands and rubbing them together happily. "I may even go fishing on the Saturday. But—" he spread his arms wide in a gesture of generosity at least as unusual as this expansive good humour—"not before I treat the assembled crowd. What will it be, ladies and gentlemen?"

"Make the most of this moment," Claire said to the table. "You'll not see the inside of this man's wallet again before you make sergeant." As Rudge took the orders she leaned sideways into Dave. "Well, that was smooth," she said out of the side of her mouth. "What next? *Do you come here often?* I know gay guys are supposed to cop off quick, but I still thought they'd have time for better chat-up lines than that."

"That was not a chat-up line! I was just trying to be less...spiky. And I was also trying to put a lid on Trent's moaning."

"Jenny? What do you mean?"

"All that guff about *rapid promotion.*"

"She didn't mean anything by it."

"Right!" Dave took a pull at his pint.

"And if she did, so what? It's just a joke."

"She does it all the time: lots of little digs about how you got promoted and she didn't. I don't get how you don't see it."

"She's my friend."

She's not mine.

"Jenny doesn't begrudge me my promotion."

She damn well begrudges me mine.

"And, okay," Claire continued, choosing her words carefully, "I know she can appear a bit...prickly..."

"Not spiky?"

"...at times, but you did get the job she would have got..."

"*Might* have got."

"So, you've got to expect some tension. At least to begin with."

"It's been three months."

"And maybe it's just one of those things that comes with climbing the promotion ladder. Suck it up, sergeant. Use tonight as a chance to get to know her better. Y'know"—she swirled the ice in her G&T—"I think at least part of the problem is the fact that you're so good-looking."

"What?"

Claire took a sip of her drink. "And unavailable. Jenny's just not used to that."

Dave tried to process that, and the fact his superior officer and immediate boss had just told him he was good-looking. Was that even appropriate? "You would make such a shit counsellor. Ma'am."

"All right, which one of you lazy buggers is going to give me a hand getting this lot back from the bar then?" DI Rudge demanded.

"That'll be me, sir," Joe said, going to stand, Baz giving him a slap on the back as he did.

"You stay there, Joe," Claire said quickly, getting up herself and pushing the young man back into his seat. Jones looked surprised but clearly not ready to argue with an inspector. "Tel, come and give us a hand, too, will you?" She made what Dave thought was an unnecessarily big show of squeezing past him. When she gave him a decidedly forceful shove, pushing him into her vacated spot, he understood why and saw the fullness of her awful plan. "And cwtch along, you," she said, "so I can just plonk myself on the end here when I get back rather than push past you again." With the skill of a chess grandmaster, Claire had moved him into position right next to Joe Jones. He glared at her as she made her way to the bar. Over her shoulder, Claire mouthed something that might have been, *Go on!*

Another uncomfortable silence fell around the table. Dave realised unhappily that he was now the most senior officer there. Did that mean it was up to him to keep the conversational ball rolling? It didn't seem fair given that they were all off duty. On the other hand, the sudden silence was speeding rapidly past uncomfortable and smacking into downright painful. "So," Dave looked straight past PC Jones sitting right by him to address WPC Dennison, "where do you come from then?" Even to his own ears the words sounded more like the start of an interview room interrogation than an invitation to a friendly chat.

"Er, I..."

"We've already done that bit," Jenny Trent declared. "Becky's from Exeter, Baz is from Leeds, and Joe...you've already asked. So, come on, let's move on to the interesting stuff." She folded her arms and addressed Joe. "How you finding the scene here in Worcester? Not as lively as back in Brum I'm guessing?"

"It's...not so bad." Joe smiled uncertainly. "I mean, when you say *scene,* do you mean...?"

"Hard to compare Worcester and Birmingham," Dave said quickly. "They're very different places."

"Gay scene," Jenny said. "'Cause you are gay, right?"

"Right," Joe replied cheerfully.

"I mean, you told Chris, didn't you...?"

"Amongst other things," McNeil cut in. "I mean, it just came up in the conversation. And I didn't run around telling everyone..."

Joe laughed. "Hey, it's cool, y'know. No probs."

"No point in being in the closet, is there?" Jenny said, waving her vodka and orange in the air. "Not these days."

"No point at all," Joe agreed.

Jenny put her glass on the table. "So. What kind of guys you into then?"

"I don't think..." Dave began, but Joe had already started to answer.

"You first," he said. "Could be awkward if we find out we're both after the same kind of guy."

"I don't think there's much chance of that," Jenny said. "And by the way, you might like to keep a lid on this kind of talk around DCI Rudge. Bit old school if you know what I mean?"

"Oh. Okay."

Jones looked puzzled, Dave noted, whether it was by the warning about Rudge or by Jenny's closing down a conversation she had determinedly opened in the first place. For his part, Dave was fuming. What the hell gave Jenny Trent the right to grill this guy about his private life on practically a first meeting? She didn't seem to have any interest in learning about the other two newbies. Was Jones's sex life fair game just because he was gay?

"Talking of scenes, anyone know any good clubs roundabouts?" Baz South asked breezily with just a touch of that desperate-to-change-the-topic tone of voice.

"Gay clubs are cool," Dennison added, looking at Joe as if she'd just given him a compliment.

"Some are," he said.

Dennison lowered her voice and glanced at the bar as if to check that DCI Rudge couldn't overhear. "I love gay clubs," she said in a conspiratorial whisper. "You can have a good time but feel really, y'know, safe. Good to hang out with people your own age too. I mean this is okay"—she waved her white wine at the Arms in general—"but, no offence." She gave Chris, Dave, and Jenny a thin smile. "Y'know."

"None taken," Dave said. *Take that, Trent,* he thought, enjoying Jenny's obvious irritation at not being counted as one of the "young, cool kids".

"There's Pharos," Joe said, "though I've heard it's only gay once a week. Kind of like a guy I knew once." Becky laughed, though Dave could tell she didn't quite get it. "And Vagabonds seems pretty mixed. Haven't had time to check out the rest yet." Dave noted the research the young PC had already put into his new stomping ground, and the fact that he didn't lower his voice in the slightest as he shared his intel.

"And there's always Gallery 48," Jenny said.

What? Gallery 48, the achingly trendy and definitely gay bar where he had met Sean Cullen. Twice. Did Jenny...?

Joe guffawed. "No way. That is definitely for your A gays, that is. Not for your piss-poor plods. Maybe when we're inspectors, eh?" He raised his glass to his fellow new recruits who all raised theirs and laughed ruefully at the distance of that prospect.

"Or sergeants at least," Jenny said quietly. "You mentioned mates," she went on quickly. "Anyone special in your life? Got a boyfriend?"

"Jeez, this is like Interview Technique 101. Have you?"

Touché. Dave smiled into his pint.

"Not yet," said Jenny, "but the night is young."

Joe tipped his glass to her. "And so am I. So, if anyone happens to know any good-looking guys, preferably young, rich, and single, feel free to slip them my way."

"Well, maybe..." Jenny began.

"Drinks up." Claire reappeared at the side of their table bearing the first tray of Rudge's round. "Nibbles too." She pulled a couple of packets of nuts out of her coat pocket and threw them down on the table. From the other she pulled out a packet of crisps and lobbed them at Dave. "Salt and vinegar," she said. She leaned in more closely as she came to sit down. "To match your face."

"Thank you, inspector," Dave said loudly. "Here you go." He stood up and conspicuously ushered Claire back into the spot next to PC Jones she had so recently vacated. "I've kept it warm for you."

"Only just," she muttered as she sat down.

In short order, Rudge and Cortez returned with the rest of the drinks, and they and Jenny were soon deep in conversation. McNeil chatted gamely with the new recruits for a while before getting up to join some other, older mates at a different table, leaving the newbies to chat amongst themselves. Dave had little doubt they were already thinking up their excuses to get out of this geriatric rest home of a pub, probably so they could go and find one of those gay clubs Becky was so keen on. Would he feel more comfortable in one of those, he wondered. Somewhere he could be himself? He drained the pint he'd been nursing and reached for the new one he'd been bought. But then, who was he when he was himself? Wasn't it when he was being a police officer? Then he was in the right place, wasn't he? And wasn't that a depressing thought? Or was it when he was having sex with Sean Cullen? And was that even more depressing? He regarded his drink with mild surprise. A pint and a bit in and he was already getting maudlin.

"So?" Claire said.

"Mm? So what?"

"Get anywhere?"

"If you mean, did I make a move on the new uniform in our station then no, I'm afraid I didn't. Perhaps I'll wait until I get him alone in a patrol car, maybe when we're on a stakeout or in a car chase."

"Did you let him know you're gay?" Claire said, refusing to recognise his sarcasm.

"No. Did you let him know you're straight?"

"He is cute, though, isn't he?"

Dave winced. "Are you trying to 'talk gay'?"

"Okay, good-looking then? In a boyish kind of way? Is it okay to put it like that? C'mon, if we were two women checking out the new recruits, we'd talk about what they looked like. Or," she added quickly, seeing that glint in Dave's eye, "if we were two guys eying up the new female recruits. Or two lesbians checking out..."

"All right, all right. You don't have to go through all the combinations." Despite himself, Dave finally couldn't help a small smile. "I surrender." He leaned back and took a moment to look at the people around the table. Colleagues. Hardly friends, even the ones he'd known for a few months now. Except maybe for Claire, and could you ever really be friends with your superior officer? He didn't know. Summerskill and Rudge seemed to manage it, even though the older officer treated her with a patronising sexism Dave was sure she would have killed anyone else for.

He studied the two groups for a moment: the rookies beginning to bond, and the older, established group of Foregate veterans. Both groups were joking and laughing, completely at ease with themselves it seemed. Why then did Dave feel so on the outside? Okay, so he hadn't known

Rudge and the others for anything like as long as they had known each other, and his age and rank both set him aside from the rookies, but was that all of it? Did he also feel an outsider as a gay man in a notoriously "macho" environment? That didn't seem to be bothering PC Jones one bit.

For the first time, Dave let himself really look at Joe. Claire was right. There was something boyish about him, though what did you expect from someone in his early twenties? A shame that boyish didn't really work for him. Joe was probably just a bit shorter than him, too, which didn't help, though he definitely had broader shoulders. He'd probably fill out quite nicely in just a few years, especially if he kept up the gym work. Dave had little doubt there was a trained gym body under that simple white shirt. Joe's narrow waist wasn't just down to youth. And his jawline... If there was something Dave liked it was a strong jawline. Surprising really, considering the amount of smiling and laughing Jones was into. In Dave's experience the two didn't usually go together. No, he thought, still considering the young man, Joe really wasn't his type. And if he had to sum up that type, he guessed he'd probably have to reach for the cliché and say "strong and silent".

Like Sean Cullen?

Dave thought about that for a minute. Strong? Definitely, yes. Silent? Definitely, no. Sarcastic? Definitely, definitely. So, was Sean his type these days? And what did that say about him?

Dave dragged his mind away from that disturbing thought and back to Jones. Good teeth, too, he thought, as Joe gave a quite dazzling smile. And a strong five-o'clock shadow on that jaw. He wondered what Joe would look like with one of those hipster beards that were so fashionable at the moment. He wondered...

With a start he caught Jenny Trent watching him, watching Joe. Dave swiftly knocked back the rest of his drink. "I've got to go."

"What?" Claire demanded. "Now look here, Dave..."

"And I—aye—aye—will always loooove you—ooh ooh!"

"Still got that ringtone, Claire?" Jenny jeered. "That is such a crap song."

"It's the station," Claire said shortly. She cupped her phone to her ear with one hand. The message was short.

"What's up, girlie?" Rudge asked.

"It's that bloody school again. Monastery Grove. Someone's broken in and assaulted the head."

"Serious?"

"He's shaken but unhurt. He's at the station now giving a statement."

"I'll go and give a hand," Dave cut in.

"Jenkins can deal with it for now, and you can get on the scene and CCTV tomorrow," Rudge said.

"Sorry, sir. Don't want to give the new recruits the wrong impression. Strike while the iron's hot." Dave was already standing.

"Yeah, right," Claire grumbled, getting to her feet, too, and knocking back the last of her G&T. "All right, all right, hold your horses. I'm coming with you. You got any mints in the glove box? See you lot tomorrow. Terry, get in a round from me. Charge it to Jim. Night all."

The assembled coppers variously waved and said their goodbyes as Summerskill and Lyon left the pub.

*

"He's keen, isn't he?" Joe Jones commented as the door closed behind them.

"Oh, he's very driven," Jenny said. "You like that in a man, Joe?" Joe laughed. "Are you blushing?"

"Course not."

But it was hard to tell.

Chapter Six

"Why aren't you stopping where we normally stop?" Tony asked.

"Because today, we are parking in the visitors' car park," Claire said. She waited for her son's next question.

"Why?" asked Tony, suspicious and on cue.

"Because today we're going into the school to have a meeting with the head."

"What?" Tony was incredulous. "Again?"

"Yes. Sometimes police matters aren't all sewn up in one go. And last night, someone had a go at your head in his office with a baseball bat."

"Sounds like the worst game of Cluedo," Dave said.

"Was he hurt?"

"That was just a touch too eager, my lad," said Claire, "and no, of course not. If he had been, we wouldn't be going to talk to him in his office now, would we?"

Tony sank back in his car seat. Couldn't you drop me off here, like?" he suggested. "I can walk from here, easy."

"It's no bother."

A minute went by. "How about here? It's actually quicker for me from here."

"Anyone would think you didn't want to be seen with your old mam."

"You know I don't!" Tony protested. "Not when my 'mam' is going in as police. It's not cool, is it?"

"I thought you weren't bothered about 'cool'? I thought only the 'lame' kids worried about being 'cool'.

"Aw c'mon. It's bad enough having a stepdad who's a teacher. If even my mum is a copper…"

"What do you mean, 'even'?"

"Dave," Tony pleaded, appealing to the other male in the car.

"Sergeant Lyon," Claire corrected.

"Just following orders, Tony," Dave said.

Tony collapsed back into his seat, a muttering knot of teenage resentment. "Even the Nazis weren't allowed to use that excuse."

Dave considered pointing out that the Nazis hadn't had to take their orders from DI Summerskill but decided that was pushing the morning's banter too far.

"And you know if you don't like coming into school with your old mam then you can pull your finger out and get up earlier to go with Ian."

"No thank you."

Dave glanced up at the driver's mirror. There'd been something in that reply more than the usual teen truculence, but Tony was deliberately looking out of the window avoiding eye contact with anyone, and when Dave looked back at Claire, she was doing the same. Dave focused on his driving. *Domestic. Nothing to see here. Move along.*

They pulled into the visitors' car park, and Tony was out of the car and gone before his mother could do anything that might cause him excruciating pain, like say goodbye, wish him a nice day or, God forbid, kiss him.

*

Summerskill and Lyon made their way into the school buildings. "Well, we know how your son feels about his mum coming into school. How about your husband? What does Ian think?"

"Not a lot," Claire said shortly. She had in fact told Ian that morning she'd be going into school and why. Out of curiosity, she'd also asked him about his opinion of the head.

"You know, don't you? I've said it often enough." Claire waited, reluctant to admit that these days she generally zoned out when Ian went into one of his diatribes about the school and its management. "He's a bastard. They all are: SLT, the senior leadership team, the lot of them. Get promoted out of the classroom as quick as they can and then spend every hour God sends heaping work onto the poor sods lower down the chain of command." And that had been it, as Ian had been rushing to be in school early to get some preparation or report writing out of the way before the day proper began. It was just another short, snatched conversation. Like most of their conversations these days.

Summerskill and Lyon were shown to the head's office where the solitary SOCO who had been dispatched first thing was already packing up ready to leave. "Nothing that's going to give you any leads," he said. "Your best bet's CCTV."

Claire thanked him and stepped into the office. Broken plastic crunched underfoot. Dented silver trophies lay scattered around on the floor and burst cardboard box folders had strewn papers everywhere. The telephone on the desk was a twisted wreck of broken plastic. "The times I wanted to do this to my headmaster's office," Claire said. Dave's warning cough came too late.

"Good morning, inspector."

Claire whirled round. "Good morning, Mr. Blake."

"I hope this won't take long, inspector. I really did say everything I had to say last night, and I do have several important meetings today that I cannot afford to postpone."

Do teachers actually do any teaching these days, or is it all nonstop meetings?

"We'll try not to keep you longer than we possibly have to, sir," Claire said. By the time Summerskill and Lyon had turned up at the station the previous night, the duty sergeant had done most of their work for them, and there had been little more to do other than to confirm they would see Blake again the next day at the scene of the crime and review any CCTV footage they had. *("See, you really could have stayed longer at the pub," Claire had said. "No, I really couldn't," Dave had replied.)* Now, Alun Blake was clearly more than ready to move on, and as she considered him in his fresh suit and impeccable grooming, Claire felt more as if she was dealing with some successful businessman, the head of some small corporation, rather than the head of a school. But then that was what headteachers had to be these days she supposed. She contrasted Blake with her own husband, every inch a typical teacher and no nearer senior management level now than he had been when he had started. She wondered if that was the reason for at least some of Ian's antipathy.

"You asked to look at our CCTV footage, again. This is Abbi Sharpe."

A cheerful young blonde woman, her jeans and T shirt a surprising contrast to Blake's corporate look, stepped forward to shake hands, juggling a laptop she was carrying to do so, and, in Claire's opinion, holding on to Dave's hand just a bit longer than she needed to. "Abbi's one of our technical support staff," Blake said. "And has recently been given overall responsibility for our CCTV setup."

"Yes, we've heard about you, Miss Sharpe. Thank you for your help last time."

"No worries," Abbi declared, wasting no time in sitting herself at the head's desk and sweeping the remains of the phone to one side to make way for her laptop. "Before I got this job, I was mostly restringing guitars for the Music department and photocopying worksheets." Her face was bent close to her screen as her fingers worked away at the keyboard. "But now I get to do this as well. I fucking love it."

Dave came and stood behind Abbi, looking over her shoulder at the screen as she scrolled through menus with impressive speed. "Do you get to do this much?"

"All the time. The buggers are always up to something. Smoking in the toilets. Pulling handles off the doors. Setting fire to the science labs."

"That was just the once," Blake said quickly.

"It was me who nailed the little bastard who threw that stone at you. I can see fucking *everything*!" It had been a while since Summerskill and Lyon had seen someone so happy in her work. Across the room, Mr. Blake's lips thinned.

"I'm glad they didn't have a setup like this when I was at school," Claire murmured.

"I'll bet," Dave said. "There!" He pointed suddenly at the screen, even as Abbi stopped speeding through a file and punched the air in triumph.

"Got you, fucker!" she declared.

"Miss Sharpe!"

Ignoring the head's obvious unhappiness, Claire stepped forward to join her sergeant and the school techie, and together they looked down at the laptop and the images Abbi had uncovered.

The camera they were downloading from was positioned outside Blake's office, looking down on the door. Abbi had frozen the image at fourteen minutes past seven o'clock the previous evening. Now, she pressed play and together they watched as a hoodied figure threw itself through the door and into the room. A minute passed, then another during which time they couldn't see anything, then there was a blurred flurry of activity and there was Blake himself flying through the door. "Two minutes," the head said softly, reading the digits at the bottom of the screen. "It felt longer."

Through the door they caught glimpses of more movement, a silver cup and a couple of box files falling to the floor, and then the intruder was in the frame again, head down as he rushed out. "Freeze it, please!"

Dave said but Abbi was already on it. They all leaned in again even more closely, but despite Abbi's moving the picture frame by frame, back and forth, they couldn't make out the features of the hooded figure.

"Have you got any other cameras on the way in and out?" Claire said.

"Hang on." Within a minute, Abbi had keyed in another couple of screens. "These are the best shots." she said. Again, the face was just a blur in the dim evening light. "I keep telling them they ought to get better cameras than this shit, but they don't listen."

"Miss Sharpe!"

Claire studied the static images closely. "I think we might have enough to be going on with," she said. "Thank you very much, Miss Sharpe..."

"Abbi."

"Abbi. For what you've done today and for finding that little...person who threw the rock at me the other day."

"Any time," Abbi said, cheerfully closing her laptop and rising to leave. "Better than tidying out all the shit in the Drama store cupboard."

"Ever thought of working for the police?" Dave said, semi-seriously. "I know we've got some serious tech needs down at Foregate."

"Nah. I need the school holidays. Besides, I'm not sure the police could put up with my language."

"And on that topic. If you'll excuse me one moment, officers." Blake held the door open for Abbi, followed her as she walked through, and closed it behind them.

"I think she'd fit in just fine," Dave said.

Claire's expression was thoughtful. "No prints," she said, "and no face pics. But..."

"But."

"The build. The hoodie?"

"The motive?"

"The motive."

"Angry dad."

"Yeah. Mr. Kerry."

"So? We going to bring him in for questioning?"

Claire considered, remembering the last time they'd had Mr. Kerry at the station, "No. Let's go to him this time."

Dave gestured to the devastated office. "I know he's grieving but this is still pretty extensive damage to property. And who knows what he might have done to Mr. Blake if he hadn't managed to get away?"

"Can't prosecute a man for what he might have done, sergeant. And we haven't got anything approaching hard evidence. So, let's go and talk to him this time. Come on. We'll get the address from Reception."

*

According to the school secretary, the Kerry family lived smack in the middle of one of the more disadvantaged parts of the school's catchment area. Their house itself was an ugly 1930s utilitarian construct which looked as if it had had precious little done to it since the day it was built. It was surprisingly large, but even so, they were told, it was hardly big enough to accommodate the number of immediate family members, distant family members, and associated hangers-on who seemed to live there or who passed through at indeterminate intervals. "Our social welfare officer has had to make a number of visits to that particular house," the secretary told them. "The meetings have not always been...easy."

Two children, a boy and a girl aged probably about eight and eleven respectively, were playing in a pile of old cardboard boxes on the patches of dried earth at the front of the house as the police officers approached. He seemed to think they constituted a spaceship: she was under the impression they were in a palace. Both of them stopped their play and arguments and stared openly and fiercely at Summerskill and Lyon as they made their way up the garden path to the front door. Their faces were mirrors of the features and the hostility the police officers had already encountered in their brother Caleb and their father. "Daaaad!" the boy screamed, as they both abandoned their cardboard construction and ran round the side of the house to alert those inside to their visitors.

Summerskill and Lyon still had to wait on the doorstep for a good two minutes after knocking before the front door was finally opened to them. "Yeah?" A woman in a faded T-shirt and tracksuit bottoms stood there, struggling to keep hold of a wriggling, crying baby. She looked like she was in her mid-fifties. Claire suspected she was actually a good decade younger.

"Hello. Mrs. Kerry? I'm DI Summerskill and this is DS Lyon. We're looking for Mr. Kerry. Your husband?"

The woman stood, dealing with the baby's struggles while looking from one to the other of the police officers. "What for?"

"If we could just have a word with him please, Mrs. Kerry?"

Mrs. Kerry turned her back on them and walked down the hallway. "He's in there," she said, using an elbow to indicate a door on her left, shushing to no effect the baby in her arms as she carried on down the hallway, through a door, and out of sight.

"I think that was an invitation to come in," Dave said.

The two of them stepped into the house, picking their way past discarded toys and more cardboard boxes, shoes, and discarded clothes until they reached the door Mrs. Kerry had indicated. Claire knocked on the door and gingerly pushed it open. "Mr. Kerry?"

The living room was dim, the curtains almost completely drawn, and the air thick with stale cigarette smoke, the sourness of sweat and another, earthier smell. Two battered sofas lined two of the walls in a large L shape, bracketing an enormous television in the far corner. On the screen, men and women dressed much as the Kerry family were sat on plush armchairs and shouted and swore at each other, the worst of their cursing beeped out, egged on by an unctuous presenter pretending to keep control. The studio audience bayed and heckled, the whole cacophonous row blaring out of a large soundbar on the floor at the foot of the screen.

Sprawled at one end of one of the sofas was Mr. Kerry. Claire was pretty sure he was wearing the same clothes as the ones he'd had on when they had last seen him except for the hoodie. His eyes were even redder than before and his cheeks thick with greying beard. At the other end was Caleb. The boy lounged back, looking at them through the pale smoke of the joint he had just pulled on, his eyes challenging them, daring them to say something. He was wearing the hoodie his father had worn on the school steps. The hoodie Summerskill and Lyon believed they had seen on the school's CCTV. Claire looked more closely. Was that a bruise on the side of his face? For a moment, she wondered. Blake definitely hadn't said anything about hitting his assailant but maybe... Caleb shifted and she wasn't sure after all if what she thought she'd seen had been a bruise or just a shadow in this damn fuggy, darkened room.

"Could we have a word, Mr. Kerry?" Claire said, raising her voice to compete with the racket from the television.

"Wha' about this time?" His words were slurred. He frowned as if trying to bring the two officers into focus.

"I'm sorry, but could you...could you please... Could you please turn the television down for a moment?"

For a second neither father nor son moved, and Claire wondered whether they were both so out of it they hadn't heard or understood her or if they were perhaps simply going to ignore her. Finally, Mr. Kerry nodded to his son who reached for a remote and with provoking slowness reduced the volume of the onscreen reality show to a level that made conversation possible if not comfortable.

"Thank you. Mr. Kerry, I'm sorry to have to intrude again at such a difficult time but could you tell us please what you were doing last night between about seven p.m. and nine p.m.?"

"Don't tell 'em, Dad." The younger Kerry was now sitting up, his joint momentarily forgotten. "You don't have to tell 'em anything. They haven't got a search warrant or nothing."

"This isn't a search, Caleb. It's not a raid—" and Claire looked pointedly at the cigarette between the boy's fingers. "So, we don't need a warrant. We're just asking a few questions and it would be really helpful, for everyone concerned, if you could answer them. In fact, if you don't want your dad to tell us where he was, maybe you could tell us where you were."

"He was with me, inspector."

The two officers turned to face the new arrival in the room. The young man who had been with Caleb and his father on the steps of Monastery Grove the previous day smiled openly back at them. "Ah, hello there. It's Mark, isn't it?"

"That's right."

"Mark...Kerry?"

"Smith." He came into the room, walking over to the older man on the settee. "Here you go, Uncle Callum." He swung across a plastic bag that landed in Kerry's lap. Kerry pulled out a linked six-pack of beer cans, broke one from its plastic ring, and opened it immediately, grunting a thank-you. Caleb quickly rose from his seat to pull another can from its binding and take it back to his position on the sofa. Mark turned to regard the police officers. "Can I help you, inspector?"

"Okay. Could you tell us please where you were with Caleb last night?"

"Sure. No probs. Birmingham. We went clubbing."

Dave frowned. "Caleb's just lost a brother," he said. "And you went clubbing? That hardly seems appropriate."

"Well, I guess we all deal with things in different ways, officer." His eyes darted first to Callum Kerry and his drink then to Caleb and his joint. "Some worse than others, yeah?" He took a step closer to Claire, lowering his voice. "Seriously, though, I really think it was for the best, you know what I mean? Caleb needed the break. He had to get out." He inclined his head very slightly in the father's direction. "Not the most chilled of guys at the best of times, I think you know what I mean."

Claire wondered again about that mark on Caleb's face. "And would you have anyone who could verify that, Mark?"

"I'm sure I could find some guys."

"And you, Mr. Kerry," she said to the father. "Where were you?"

"Here," he said thickly. "Ask anyone. Ask the kids."

"That won't be necessary, thank you." She doubted the man could have got up from his sofa now if he'd tried, and she suspected he'd have been much the same for most of yesterday too. She considered Mark Smith's not-so-veiled hint about his temper. Perhaps keeping Mr. Kerry anaesthetised with cheap booze really was best for all of them, at least for the moment. What else was he supposed to do? How did you even begin to cope?

"Right, well, thank you for that. It was just something we needed to confirm. We won't take up any more of your time. Sergeant."

Dave went to follow his boss but then stopped as if suddenly remembering something. "You don't happen to have a baseball bat, do you? Any of you?"

Callum Kerry was squinting at him, trying to bring him into focus. "Course I haven't got a fuckin' baseball bat. Do I look like a fuckin' baseball player?"

Dave looked to Caleb. "No," the boy snarled.

"Er, yeah. I do." Mark Smith had a slight frown on his face. "I can fetch it if you want," he said. "I bring it round sometimes just to play around with the little ones." He gave a sudden grin. "Want to borrow it? Good for keeping rocks from hitting you in the head, know what I mean?" He mimed swinging a bat, clicking his tongue to indicate the hit.

"Thank you. That won't be necessary. Sergeant." Summerskill and Lyon left the house.

*

"Was he just taking the piss?" Claire said when she and Dave were back in the clean air of their car.

Dave started the engine. "I don't think so. Seems a decent enough guy. The good cousin every family should have. Didn't yours have one?"

Claire considered. "I think that was me."

Dave sniffed. "I am going to have to have these clothes dry-cleaned to get the reek of weed out."

"Use your normal detergent but add a cupful of vinegar. Usually does the trick. What? Didn't you have a life before you became a cop?"

"And you were the *good* cousin?" They drove off. "Still think the dad did it?" Dave asked.

"Smash up the head's office? No."

"Think it was the boy? Caleb?"

"Almost certainly."

"Right. And there's not a thing we can do about it, is there?"

Claire shook her head. "Did you see how many kids were wearing hoodies just like that one as we drove onto the estate? All we've got are some blurred CCTV pictures. No way."

They drove on. "We could get him for possession," Dave said.

"He's not dealing. At least, we didn't see him dealing. You know he'd only get a slap on the wrist and then it just looks plain vindictive on our part."

Dave nodded reluctantly. "Nice lad that Mark Smith," he said, thoughtfully.

"He did push me out of the path of a rock."

"Everybody makes mistakes. No, I meant going out and buying booze for his dear old uncle. Not the cheap stuff either."

"Really? I hadn't noticed. You've got bloody sharp eyes, you know that?"

"Nice TV setup they've got there too. Expensive."

"Noisy."

"And did you catch that watch young Caleb was wearing? Surprised he can tell the time, but that apart, you don't see many kids these days wearing watches, do you? Unless it's one of those new blingy numbers."

They drove on for another mile. "No," Claire said finally. "I see where you're going with this. There's more money being splashed around back there than you'd expect but that's probably because there's more going down the old man's neck than into the kids' mouths, and I'm not going to be party to running in a grieving family because they've got a feckless father or they're doing a spot of black market labouring or similar on the side. This is running away with us. We are not taking this any further. It's one case of vandalism..."

"Potential aggravated assault. Menacing with a weapon."

"And one guy who got shook up and who maybe, just maybe, deserved it. And if you ever quote me on that I'll have your arse in a sling. And not in a fun way. No. We've got a family in shock here after a particularly horrible accident, and they need space to grieve. If the break-in of Mr. Blake's office was linked to the death of the Kelly boy, I say *if,*" she repeated in response to Dave's feigned amusement, "then I've a feeling it was a reaction that's spent itself. I'm not saying we won't hear again from young Caleb, and probably in the not-too-distant future I'm guessing, but I don't think it will be because of anything to do with Clayton's death. Without a shred of concrete evidence, I say we leave it there." She looked at Dave as if daring him to disagree. Wisely, he kept his eye on the road. "And wind down your window, will you? I don't want to get back to Foregate high."

"Experiencing a flashback, ma'am?" Dave did as he was told.

"And before we arrive," Claire said, settling back into her seat, "you can tell me what you thought of Joe Jones last night?"

*

"Anne? Anne? It's dinner time. Come down now, please."

Anne lay on her bed, staring up at the ceiling. She made no movement or effort to reply to the voice coming up the stairs but began a countdown in her head. She had reached forty-five before her bedroom door opened and her father stood there, arms folded. She'd thought she might have got to fifty. "Anne, your dinner is ready."

"I'm not hungry."

"Don't be silly. You have to eat. I'm not going through this again."

"I said, I'm not hungry."

"And I've said, it's ready. I'm going back downstairs now and I'm going to serve it up. And it will stay on that table until you eat it. Whether you eat it hot or cold is up to you. Do you understand? I said, do you understand?"

"Yes, Daddy."

"Don't be long." Her father went away, leaving her bedroom door open for Anne to follow.

Anne lay there and waited and counted in her head again, and this time she did reach fifty before she got up, crept softly across the bedroom, and closed the door again before returning to the bed and slowly lying down so as to make as little noise as possible. She screwed her eyes tight shut and dug her fingernails into her arms, teeth clenched tight against the pain. It was that or scream. That would only have brought her father up again. She knew from experience he would not be patient with her a second time.

On the table by her bedside her phone chirruped the arrival of a message. She snatched it up and switched it to silent mode so that the sound couldn't carry downstairs. She waited, straining to hear. When she was sure her father wasn't coming, she opened the message.

Fancy a trip to Brum? Take your mind off things.

She flung the phone to the floor and then hugged herself into a tight ball, bracing herself for the response from her father that her furious reaction would be bound to provoke. She shouldn't have, but she just hadn't been able to help herself. Rocking back and forth on her duvet, Anne dug her fingers still deeper into her flesh, a thin rivulet of blood beginning to seep from under one nail. On the carpet by her bedside the mobile phone lay, face up, its glowing screen mocking her with the name of the message's sender.

Mark.

*

Downstairs, her father heard the thump of the phone hitting the floor and then silence. He knew his daughter would not be joining him. Forcing himself to breathe deeply and slowly, he took the cover from a china tureen and helped himself to the potatoes inside. He counted them out onto his plate. One. Two.

With a yell of fury, he threw the cover across the table and into the far wall where it smashed into pieces. With his other hand he swept the tureen onto the floor, scattering potatoes across the dining room floor, before bringing both fists smashing down onto the table, sending glasses and cutlery toppling.

For a moment he sat, staring at the mess he'd made, not really seeing it. Waiting for the red mist to fade. He took a breath, that's what he'd been told, wasn't it? Take a long, deep breath, then hold it, hold it, then let it out slowly. He did it again and then again.

Damn the girl. Damn her!

He recovered his glass from the floor where it had tumbled but fortunately not broken, picked up the wine bottle from where it was lying on the centre of the table, unscrewed it and filled the glass. One more deep breath, and then he threw the drink back, barely registering its taste. He reached for the bottle again.

Mechanically and with no pleasure at all, Alun Blake worked his way through the wine while the food cooled and congealed on the table and the floor. It was clear his daughter was not going to join him. Well, she could clear this mess up in the morning.

It was all her fault.

Chapter Seven

"It's Christmas again."

"You have got to be kidding me! I haven't finished the last lot yet."

"Yeah, and about those." Jenny Trent laughed as she dumped the latest enormous pile of folders on Claire's desk. "Madden wants them on his desk tomorrow. Or he'll have your lungs. Or heart. One of those things."

Claire swore under her breath. Jim Rudge had warned her, the further up the promotion ladder you climbed, the more paperwork they dumped on you, until you hit and broke through what he called "the paper ceiling" and became someone like Chief Superintendent Madden. Then it became your job, and pleasure, to shower paperwork down on the poor sods scurrying up the ladder below you. The old git had never made it clear how much paperwork there would be until that golden moment, and just how far away that bloody paper ceiling was. "Thanks," she said out loud.

"You're most welcome," Jenny sang, and headed for the door and the next happy load she had to deliver.

"Hey, Jen."

"Yeah?" Jenny leaned back into the office.

"It was nice the other day, meeting up at the Arms. It's been too long."

Jenny looked mildly surprised. "Yeah. It was. Like old times."

"We need to do it again, soon. Not with the guys though. Just a girls' night out. Like we used to."

"Uh huh." Jenny leaned against the door frame, clear scepticism on her face. "Claire, I've lost track of the number of times you've said that, but every time I've suggested a date you've said you've got too much work to do.

"Yes, well…" Claire began indignantly, about to gesture to the paper avalanche Jenny had just dropped in her lap. She stopped, guiltily aware that her friend was right. "All right then, name a night," she said. "And we'll do it."

Jenny grinned. "Tonight."

Dammit! "All right. You're on."

"Really?" Jenny glanced down at Claire's desk. Claire refused to do the same.

"Yeah. Why not?"

"Well, all right then. The Arms?"

"God no! The Feathers?"

"Closed down last month. Where have you been lately?"

"The Flamingo?"

"Have you seen the crowd there lately? We are not seventeen any more, girl."

The options narrowing, the two women considered.

"You could always come round to my place," Claire suggested. "Bottle of wine? I'll cook us a meal. We can have a good old catch-up." To her surprise, Claire realised she actually did want that: an evening with an old girlfriend. Someone she could really talk to. Someone she could...open up to.

Jenny's look of scepticism returned. "A girls' night in? At yours? With your husband? A boy. No, really. And your two sons. Also, less controversially, boys?"

"Ian's...out a lot. At meetings. Sam'll be in bed, and I can always bribe Tony to make sure he leaves us alone."

"Forget it. Come round to mine. But I am not cooking. We are having a takeaway from the local pizza house which comes with a cute delivery boy we can go cougar on."

"Okay. Want me to bring that bottle of wine?"

Jenny laughed scornfully. "Only if it comes with two of its friends."

*

Running late. Meet me at G48 @ 8.

The text had really annoyed Dave on so many levels. Sean had texted earlier in the day. That message had been similarly terse—*My place @7?*—but the time was good for Dave, and the intention obvious—and welcome—so Dave had answered yes. Now, although the promise of Cullen's bed hadn't been ruled out, it had definitely been delayed. Not only that, but Cullen had chosen the chichi gay bar that made Dave want to jump back into the closet and close the door after him every time he went there. And he'd framed his message in teenage text speak. *OMG!*

It was with a mixture of feelings, therefore, that Dave stepped through the gilded doors of Gallery 48 at precisely two minutes to eight. He noted that the plastic palm in one corner was looking even dustier than the last time he had seen it, and that the bartender on duty was the same one who had half-heartedly tried to pick him up the first time he had been there. Scanning the room, he spotted Sean at a table chatting to two young men in suits. Cullen waved, rose, shook hands with both men and kissed one on the cheek before strolling over to join Dave at the bar. For a second Dave wondered if he would kiss him. Sean did not. "Good to see you again," he said as he settled on the barstool next to Dave. Dave thought it sounded like something he might have said to a constituent at a constituency surgery.

"You too. Friends?" he asked, indicating the two men Cullen had just left, wishing he could have taken the question back almost the moment it was asked. He'd sounded almost jealous. Cullen's crooked smile told him that was what he thought too.

"Yin and Yang? Purely work, Dave, I assure you. That's partly why I asked you to come here, so I could touch base with them first and tidy up a bit of business."

"Partly?"

The bartender had come over and Sean ordered a pint for Dave and a scotch and soda for himself. Dave didn't know whether to be irritated that Sean didn't bother to ask him what he wanted or impressed that he remembered exactly the ale Dave preferred. The bartender gave not the slightest indication that providing beer hadn't once been the only exchange of fluids he'd been interested in.

"Yes," Cullen said smoothly, swinging round on his barstool to face Dave again. "I'm certainly not averse to taking the time out now and again to spend some quality time with an attractive man whose company I enjoy."

"Is that what this is?" Dave said cautiously. "Quality time?"

Sean leaned in a little closer. "I hope so. And you know, as I may have mentioned before, it can do you no harm at all, detective *sergeant,* to be seen out on the town on...good terms with someone as well-placed as myself. Which I'll admit does make me sound as if I'm blowing my own trumpet. If you'll excuse a slightly risky double entendre."

Before Dave could question exactly how far *out on the town* Gallery 48 was supposed to be and who precisely was supposed to be here to profitably notice Cullen's patronage, the bartender returned with their drinks. "Oh, hi again," he said with a truly heart-stopping smile, as he put their drinks down in front of them.

All right, Dave thought, *so you've finally remembered me, have you?* "Hi," he said. Maybe he could use flirtation to make Cullen a little jealous, to dent that insufferable self-confidence just a fraction. Turnabout was fair play, yes? Not that he *had* been jealous of course. But then he noticed that Sean wasn't looking at him but over his shoulder and past him. As was the beautifully smiling bartender. Dave swung round on his barstool.

"Hi," said PC Joe Jones to the bartender. "Oh, and hi to you, too, sergeant."

*

"God, are you still drinking this old rotgut?"

"You like it. *We* like it."

Jenny grimaced as she accepted the bottle off Claire. "Maybe I was expecting something a bit posher, now that, you know, you're in the money."

"Yeah right," Claire said. "And I'm still waiting for the bottle of champagne you said you were going to crack open when I got my promotion."

"Saving it now for my own stripes," Jenny called back over her shoulder as she took the bottles of white off into the kitchen. "I'll just put this in the fridge. There's one on the table already open."

Claire hung her coat up in the hallway and stepped into Jenny's small lounge. She smiled at the familiar pair of stuffed penguins in one corner, a fairground prize from a former beau, and the large framed collage of photos over the mantelpiece of Jenny and her friends, almost all gurning for the camera and almost always brandishing drink of some description. Some of the pictures included Claire. Nothing had changed. But then, she reminded herself, it hadn't exactly been years since her last visit, had it? Surely not long enough for this slightly weird feeling of nostalgia. How long had it been? With a twinge of guilt, she reckoned it must have been about four months. Where had the time gone?

"You're losing your touch, girl," Jenny said as she came back in.

"What?"

"You've been in a minute and you haven't helped yourself to a drink. C'mon, let's get this party started."

Claire let herself fall back onto Jenny's familiar, comfortable old sofa and reached for the bottle and glass on the coffee table in front of them. "I can't get too rat-arsed," she said. "I've got a shit load of reviews to finish, and Madden's going to eat me alive if I don't get them finished tomorrow."

Jenny took the bottle from Claire, poured at least as much again into Claire's glass, and then poured herself an equally generous measure. "Tell him you *have* finished them, even if you haven't. He's not going to get round to checking them for at least the next three days, trust me. But tonight, let us eat drink and be merry for tomorrow..."

"...we must lie. Cheers." The two friends clinked glasses and drank deep.

I've missed this, thought Claire.

*

"A friend of yours?"

Dave tried to judge the tone of Sean's question, and to read that bloody irritating crooked smile. He thought he'd covered his surprise at finding a station plod behind him (and not just any plod—PC Joe bloody Jones) but he should have known that very little got past the professional politician. "Not exactly," Dave said carefully. "PC Jones, Joe, has just joined the station."

"A new recruit! Excellent." Sean held out his hand to Joe. "Sean Cullen."

With a nervous glance at Dave that might almost have been a request for permission, Joe took Sean's hand. "Hi. How d'you do?" He peered more closely at Sean's face. "I'm sorry. Have we...?" He clicked his fingers in pleased recognition. "You're the MP guy, aren't you?"

Sean nodded with a modesty that Dave knew was completely feigned. "Can I rely on your vote? Only joking," he added at Joe's look of slight alarm. "No elections in the offing. None that I know about anyway. And we're all off duty here, aren't we?" He glanced at Dave.

"Right, yeah," Joe said with obvious relief. "Not that I wouldn't vote for you," he added hastily. "I mean..." He ground to a momentary halt.

"Actually, I wouldn't vote for you," he admitted. "Sorry, but strong Labour family and all that. No offence."

"And absolutely none taken," Sean said, and for all his faults, Dave knew that was almost certainly the case. A thick skin didn't even come close to describing Sean Cullen's impregnable ego. Cullen waved his hand at Dave. "So's the sergeant's family."

How did he know that? Dave tried to remember if he had ever told Cullen as much. The longest conversations they'd had so far had all been in bed, and family hadn't been one of the subjects uppermost in either of their minds then.

"Gotta say, though, that's not how I recognised you," Joe went on. "I knew you from your sports work."

"Ah yes. Fitness First."

"That's the one. I've seen you on the telly talking about it. And some clips of you rowing before that. Really impressive stuff."

"Thank you."

"That was a while ago though," Dave said. Sean was practically purring. It really annoyed him.

"Right, well, I'd better be getting on then," Joe said.

"Meeting someone?" Cullen asked.

"Er, yeah." Joe ducked his head, momentarily embarrassed, and then inclined it in the direction of the bartender who was still standing by them. "Eddie."

"Edward." Cullen couldn't have sounded more pleased if Joe had said he was wanting tips on how to become a Tory councillor.

So that's his name, Dave thought.

"But you don't get off for, what, another fifteen minutes do you, Edward?"

"'Fraid not."

Cullen stood. "Then there's plenty of time for young Joe here to come and join Sergeant Lyon and me in a drink, yes? What will you have, Joe?"

"Oh, I don't... I mean, I..." Joe looked to Eddie, but the bartender gave a resigned smile and moved off to serve another couple of guys at the far end of the bar. *Get used to that,* Dave thought, burned once before by Eddie's cavalier manner.

"I'm guessing you're a lager man," Cullen said, holding out his arm in an invitation to move to one of the tables by the nasty plastic palm tree,

"I'll have...a pint of that," Joe said pointing randomly. "Thank you."

"Oh. Same as the sergeant," Cullen said. "Good choice. I think I'll join you. Edward." He pointed to the pump Joe had chosen. "When you're finished over there, three pints please. We'll be over here."

*

"Oh God, d'you know how long it's been since I've had a pizza like that?"

"Deep pan Hawaiian, extra ham, extra pineapple, no mushrooms," Jenny said, happily quoting Claire's traditional order. "You're not still on that diet, are you? Give it up, girl, it's not going anywhere."

"Thanks very much for the encouragement. And no. It's not because of the diet. Not entirely. Ian's been on this massive health kick lately. And I can't deny I'd like to see him losing a few pounds. And it's good for Sam, too, if we eat healthy. And Tony of course, though he can eat anything, you know what teenagers are like."

"I'll take your word for it." Jenny held out her glass and Claire obliged by refilling it, neither woman making much of a pretence any more to keep to moderation. "And talking of tubby hubby—how are things with Ian these days?"

Claire paused, last slice of delicious pizza halfway to her mouth. "What d'you mean?"

"Well, y'know. The last time we talked about stuff like this you said things were getting...boring?"

"I did not say *boring*." Claire paused, all too aware of how defensive she sounded. "Routine, perhaps. Maybe overly comfortable."

"I distinctly remember the word boring being used."

"Yeah well, remind me not to let you take any witness statements in the near future."

"You get a better conviction rate from my statements."

"I did not hear you say that."

Jenny reclined on her sofa, eying her friend over her wineglass and refusing to let her off the hook. "So?"

"So what?"

"Don't even try that, Claire. Something's wrong. I know it is. I know you." Jenny put her glass down and leaned in towards Claire. "And I can tell when things aren't really going right. Even when you're not talking to me."

"I've not not been talking to..."

Jenny waved the protestation aside. "So?"

Claire reached for her own glass. There'd been a time, not so very long ago, when she would have opened up in an instant to Jenny. Now, absurdly she found herself thinking of pulling rank, of saying something stupid like it wasn't appropriate for them to talk about personal matters like this, that they ought to keep work and home separate. "Okay, so things were getting a bit...dull. In the relationship I mean. But for Christ's sake that's only to be expected, isn't it? We've been together for over ten years now. And we're neither of us exactly spring chickens any more. We're bringing up two boys. We've both got demanding jobs. And..." Claire took a deep gulp of her wine before looking up to meet Jenny's level gaze. "...I think Ian might have been seeing another woman."

Jenny nodded slowly as if this was simply confirmation of something she already knew. "One of the teachers at his school?"

"How did you know?"

"He's a married teacher, *detective*. When is he going to find time to gallivant about with another woman anywhere else? What's her name? Mrs or Miss."

"Miss, I think. They're all Miss, aren't they, even the married ones. Grant, anyway, is her name. And Ian's not been gallivanting."

"Then what has he been doing?"

"Nothing. Not really. I mean... I don't think so." Claire took a drink from her glass. "It was Tony who started me off, wondering. According to him all the kids at school were talking about how his dad was having it away with this Miss Grant." She smiled sadly to herself. "Got himself into a couple of fights over it, he did."

"So? Rip his balls off, did you? Ian's, I mean, not Tony's."

Claire shook her head.

"Okay. Why ever not?"

"Because it was just a bunch of gossiping schoolkids. They talk shit. We did when we were at school."

"But...?"

"But...there were other things. Personal things. And all the bloody meetings."

"So, you asked him, right?"

Claire nodded. "He said no. He said there was nothing going on."

"And you believed him?"

"He still has his balls."

"Seriously, Claire."

"Well, why shouldn't I?" Claire said with sudden fire. "Kids talk crap. They say much worse things about teachers these days. Remember that guy we had to take in for questioning and who ended up on the front page of the local rag? The two girls who said he'd been feeling them up hadn't even been in school on the days they claimed he did it. They can be vicious little shits sometimes."

Jenny raised an eyebrow at her friend's vehemence. "But you still think something's going on, don't you?"

Slowly, Claire nodded. "I dunno. Maybe he's just tired. Maybe I'm tired. Maybe this is just what happens when you've got two kids and two mad jobs. But he isn't... We're not... And there are all these bloody meetings he goes to."

Jenny put her glass down and for a moment Claire thought she was going to hug her. She raised her glass as if to drink but really to use it as a kind of shield. She didn't want hugs.

"Claire. You've been carrying this around on your own when you didn't need to. You need to talk about this with someone. You can't just bottle it up and keep it to yourself."

Claire gave a watery smile. "Well, Dave knows."

Jenny stiffened. "*Dave Lyon knows?*"

*

Was it impressive, Dave wondered, or just bloody annoying? Sean Cullen had the professional politician's ability to talk to anyone and he was using that talent now on PC Jones. Bumping into a junior officer in a gay bar should have been embarrassing for absolutely everyone concerned, but Sean was chatting away with Joe, asking about his family, his background, hobbies, and interests as easily as if he was on a campaign trail working to win voters' hearts and minds. If there'd been a baby there, he'd probably have kissed it. Or maybe, Dave thought acidly, it wasn't babies he was thinking of kissing right then. Maybe it wasn't good-looking Joe Jones's heart and mind he was after.

Dave could see that Joe also was uncertain about what exactly was going on, but Sean's effortless bonhomie was winning him over enough so that he relaxed, answering Sean's questions easily, holding his own in the conversation. Occasionally, though, he'd glance at his superior officer, sitting there with his drink and conspicuously saying nothing. It was when Sean asked, "And how do you see your career progressing, Joe?" that Dave sat up and began to pay closer attention.

"Wow. Er, well, I'm not really sure," Joe admitted.

"Do you think you could be happy as a policeman on the beat for the rest of your career or do you have ambitions for some...higher position?" Cullen waved his glass in a direction that might have taken in Dave.

"That's rather a loaded way of putting it," Dave said. "Some people get real job satisfaction from working the beat, as you put it. They enjoy that level of communication with the public, actually helping at grass roots level."

Cullen chuckled. "David, you're sounding like someone on a TV recruitment ad."

Dave didn't respond, partly because he did not want to be drawn into a friendly conversation on first name terms with a junior member of his station present, and partly because he knew Cullen was right.

"Back to you, Joseph," Cullen said. "Where do you see yourself, say, when you're the age of the sergeant here?"

"Well, that's not really so far in the future, is it?" Joe laughed and then took a pull from his pint to cover his embarrassment. What had been meant as a joke had come off like clumsy flattery. "No, well, I reckon I'll just take it slowly, to begin with. Find out what the job's really about. Find out what kind of cop I am. Then decide where I want to go. One day at a time." And he raised his glass and drained the rest of his pint.

Cullen smiled. It was, Dave noted, the smile he used for his publicity shots, not the real one. "A good answer. And a good policy. I wish you every success with it." His expression sobered momentarily. "But if I could play the old mentor just briefly, don't wait too long. Opportunities don't always hang around, and before you know it you can find yourself stalled while others pass you by." He raised his own glass to Joe. "And never forget, it doesn't hurt to have friends along the way."

"And talking of friends..." Eddie the bartender had come up and was standing by their table, jacket slung over one shoulder. He put a hand on Joe's shoulder. "Ready to go, Joe?"

"Ah, shift finished, Edward? Time to let you go then, PC Jones." Cullen adopted an avuncular tone. "I'd ask you what your plans are but that would just be prying, wouldn't it?"

Eddie the bartender grinned broadly.

"Well, actually," Joe said, "I think we're just going for a drink. Somewhere else. 'Cause that wouldn't be, like, work for Ed, y'know?"

"Of course. We understand. Have a good night, both of you."

"Good night, Mr. Cullen. Pleasure meeting you."

"Sean, please."

"Right." Joe turned to Dave, obviously unsure still how to address his superior officer. "Sergeant," he said in the end.

"Constable."

The two young men withdrew leaving Sean and Dave alone at their table. Cullen was running a finger around the rim of his now empty glass and smiling to himself.

Dave gave him ten seconds before he spoke. "All right. What the hell was all that about?"

*

"Yeah, Dave knows," Claire said. "Why shouldn't he?"

"Why *should* he? I mean, okay, I could understand if you'd told Sheila over in traffic. God knows she's been through this kind of thing enough times."

"This isn't *this kind of thing...*"

"Or maybe even Carole in admin. She's got that whole Earth mother, eighties feminist thing going on. Shit, even Eileen in the canteen. But Dave Lyons!"

"I told you. He bumped into Tony when Tony had bunked off school."

Jenny nodded. "Right, yeah, I remember that. So, what had he done? Wandered off into the woods? What was Sergeant Lyon doing there?"

Claire gave a sad smile. "No, the daft sod had gone into town where he was bound to be seen by someone."

"Kids today, eh? In my day we'd have been down the woods having a quick fag and a snog. That's where I was most geography lessons. So, Lyon found him and dragged him back to you?"

"No. Dave took him for a coffee. They talked."

"There's cosy."

Claire frowned, not liking her friend's tone. "Tony likes Dave."

"Someone has to." She laughed. "Sure there's nothing you need to be asking Tony?"

Claire felt the warm fuzziness of earlier begin to chill and fade away. "No, Jen, there isn't."

Jen sobered slightly. "Only kidding. Right, so Tony opens up to Lyon about how his stepdad is carrying on with another teacher, and Dave runs back and tells you all about it?"

"Is that what you would have done?"

"Yes, I suppose so. Though I can't see Tony opening up to me like that."

"No. Me neither. And no, that's not what Dave did. Tony swore him to secrecy. I only found out when Tony told me himself a couple of days later."

"So. Your sergeant keeps family secrets from you?"

"It wasn't like that," said Claire, covering up how it had seemed exactly like that to her at first. "He was respecting my son's confidence. And I respected him for that."

"Well, good for him," Jenny said facetiously. "And, when Tony did finally tell you what was going on, did you have it out with Ian?"

Claire wasn't sure now whether they were changing the topic or getting back to it. "Course I did. I asked him straight out if he was having it away with this other teacher."

"And?"

"He said no."

"And?"

"That was it."

"You going soft in your old age, girl? You believed him?"

"Yes actually, I did."

"Right. And what did Sergeant Lyon have to say about that, then? I presume you told him?"

Ah, back to the real point of this discussion. "Yes, Jen. I told him. We didn't discuss it or share our problems over a glass of wine or while we were plaiting each other's hair. I *told* him. End of story."

"Not quite one of the girls then," Jen said softly, almost to herself.

Claire put her wine glass back on the coffee table in front of her. She did it very carefully as, in spite of the good intentions they had expressed earlier, both she and Jenny had worked their way through nearly two bottles already and her hand wasn't quite as steady as she would have liked. Her growing anger wasn't helping that either. "Jen," she said, "don't be such a bitch."

The two women regarded each other across the sofa.

"My bad," Jenny said eventually. "I didn't realise you two had grown so...close so quickly."

"He's my sergeant, Jen. And he's a good man. I've told you how he got caught up in this and I've told you how far it's gone, though God knows I don't have to justify myself to you." Claire forced herself to calm down a little, not wanting her temper to lead her to say something to this woman, whom she still thought of as one of her best friends, that she would regret. "That's all there is to it."

Jenny lifted her glass and took a drink before answering. "Fair enough, Claire. Though, if you want my opinion, I think you ought to go carefully."

Claire's eyes narrowed. "With Ian?"

"With Dave Lyon. He might be gay, and you might think he's all touchy-feely, but he's still a man. An ambitious man. I wouldn't trust him as far as I could throw him."

Damning the wine fug in her head, Claire struggled to process what she was hearing from her friend. "The very last thing Dave Lyon is is touchy-feely. And how do you even begin to imagine he's going to use what Tony told him to further his career? And what the hell do you mean by saying he *might* be gay but he's *still* a man? Of course, he's a bloody man! That's what gay men are. That's why they like each other so bloody much!"

Jenny held her hand up in the face of Claire's rising vehemence. "Hey, okay, okay."

"No, it's not okay, Jen. You've been out to get Dave from the day he started at Foregate. Now I want you to tell me why. Why don't you like Dave Lyon?"

Jenny contemplated the glass in her hand before setting it down on the coffee table next to Claire's. When she spoke her answer came quickly, like something well-rehearsed that she had long been waiting for an opportunity to voice. "I think he's uptight, arrogant, and smug, and he walks around as if he's got a stick up his arse. Or would like one."

Claire forced herself take a few seconds before answering, made herself react like a police officer dealing with some arsey civilian, not her supposed best friend. "That's pretty damn homophobic, don't you think? You realise it's technically a hate crime."

"I thought we were off duty. You've said as much, if not worse, about other guys at the station."

"I'm not saying I haven't. But Dave's..."

"Gay. I know. God, we all know! What, so criticism is off limits? Another perk of the sisterhood. Along with rapid promotion of course."

"Dave's promotion has hardly been rapid."

"Then I refer you to my previous comments: uptight, arrogant, and smug. That's not going to make you many friends. Well, maybe not in police circles anyway."

There was something about that last comment, some layer of meaning Claire could sense but didn't fully understand. For the moment, though, she had enough to deal with given what she *could* understand. "Dave's a sergeant. *My* sergeant. What kind of a boss am I if I let everyone take cheap shots at him, for whatever reason? And okay, he may have been posted to Foregate as part of some bureaucratic quota system. I didn't like that. But *he* didn't like that either. And since he's been here, he's done a bloody good job that leaves me in no doubt at all that he deserves his stripes."

"And I didn't?"

"Is that what this is really about, Jenny? That he got promoted and you didn't?"

"You tell me, Claire. Does he get to be your friend now because he's got the stripes and I get the odd night in with a glass of wine when you've got the time?"

"You're talking like someone Tony's age. Grow up, Jen. It's the nature of the job. We're in each other's pockets hour after hour, day after day. You know how close that brings people. I mean, how many affairs have you seen between straight male and female coppers for that very reason, eh? We used to take bets on who would end up copping off with who. At least you know that's never going to happen with Dave and me."

"A *safe* man, then, is he?"

"What is wrong with you, Jen? Why do you keep trying to bring everything round to his sexuality?"

"Are you saying that makes no difference at all?"

The denial was on the tip of her tongue, but... When she and Dave had started working together, still not so very long ago, she had found herself watching and wondering. *Did he say that because he was gay? Did he do that because he was gay?* Then she'd stopped. She couldn't remember when, but it had been pretty early on. It had all come to seem pretty pointless. She and Dave struck up a good working relationship. She felt *comfortable* with him. Was that because he was gay? If the truth were told, she realised, she still wasn't sure. "No," she said out loud, "it doesn't matter."

*

"What was all what about?" Cullen asked with studied innocence.

"You, drinking beer and chatting up one of my uniforms."

"I'm fairly sure he was off duty and therefore not in uniform." Cullen looked thoughtful for a moment. "Though I must admit, the thought of seeing him in uniform, and then out of it, is quite an appealing one. Have you got a uniform, Dave? You must have, mustn't you?" Cullen continued without waiting for an answer. "And I was hardly chatting him up. He is one of my new constituents, remember? It's what MPs do. It's important to know the people you're paid to represent and to forge links, particularly in certain areas."

"Because you never know when it might be handy to have a police officer to help you out?"

"And, as I have said before, that vice is versa. You scratch my back..." He smiled. "Which you do so well by the way."

"It's...awkward mixing socially with new recruits."

"Really? I thought you said you all went for a jolly policeman's knees-up, at, where was it, The Farriers Arms, just the other day?"

"That was different."

"How?" Cullen assumed a hurt expression though the laughter behind it was clear. "Is it because you don't want to be seen with me? A known homosexual. And a Tory to boot? I'll admit the politics might have bothered young PC Jones a little, but the sexuality obviously didn't."

"Maybe it's because I don't want to be seen out with someone who came within a hairsbreadth of being implicated in a grubby little sex scandal and murder."

Cullen tutted and wagged a finger. "Be careful, David. *Implicated* is a very strong word. My friendly support for Susan Green, who, need I remind you, remains unconvicted of any crime at all up to and including the present time, can hardly be construed as implication in any crime, let alone a murder. You know that. Otherwise I very much doubt you would have allowed yourself to have become as...friendly as you have."

Cullen was, of course, right. Dave also knew that Claire Summerskill wouldn't see it that way.

"Or is it that you're worried what that fiery little Welsh dominatrix of yours will think?"

Dave nearly choked on a mouthful of his beer, not just at the image of Claire Summerskill as a dominatrix, but at the uncanny knack Cullen had of seeming to read his mind.

"She won't always be your boss, Dave," Cullen said smoothly. "That is, she doesn't have to be. Come on." Cullen finished off the last of his drink and stood, his mood suddenly brisker. "Enough games. Let's go back to my place."

Dave stayed seated. "Is that what all this has been about? Games?"

Cullen leaned down. "David. I'm not the easiest of men to get on with. I know that. I also make no apologies for it whatsoever. I think life is there to be enjoyed, and I fully intend to enjoy it for as long as I am able." His voice lowered as he leaned in even closer to Dave, so close Dave could feel his breath on the skin of his face. "That doesn't mean I don't take some things, some...relationships, seriously." He straightened again, the crooked smile back on his face. "And right now, I seriously want to get you back home. Coming?" He held out his hand.

Dave didn't take it. He did stand, however, and together the two men left the club.

Chapter Eight

"Are you all right, Anne?"

"Fine."

"Will you be okay getting home today after school? I've got that governors' meeting till five so I can't take you straightaway, but if you want to wait in the library I can come along and pick you up at..."

"It's fine. I can catch a bus."

Alun Blake nodded. "All right. Good." He drove on, just one more parent on the school run with his daughter. How many more like him would be doing just that in the city right now? Hundreds, he supposed. How many would be fathers though? It should be the mother's job really, shouldn't it? And how many would be headteachers? Blake mentally ran through how many of the local headteachers he knew who had teenage children themselves. There was only the one as far as he could recall. Geoff Cooper over at Chapel High had a boy just started in Year Seven this year. Blake blasted his horn at some doddery old fool who was taking all day to turn out of a side road. Cooper didn't know how lucky he was. Boys were a damn sight easier to deal with than girls. Certainly easier than his girl, or at least the girl she was turning out to be. Just like her mother.

Blake reached down to turn on the car radio. Radio 4's usual morning chorus of doomsayers and bleeding hearts was as irritating as ever, but at least it drowned out the black thoughts circling in his head and filled the silence between father and daughter.

Up ahead of them was the pedestrian bridge that crossed the road just a hundred yards or so from Monastery Grove. Two minutes, three at the most and Alun could drop his daughter off and take his place in his office again. At least at school people did what they were damn well told. Or if they didn't...

Glancing in the driver's mirror he saw his daughter looking at her mobile phone. How many times had he told her to put the damn thing away? "Anne," he began.

The windscreen just inches from his face exploded into thousands of glittering shards. His daughter screamed.

*

Both preoccupied by the events of the preceding night and their consequences, Summerskill and Lyon's own journey into work had been remarkably similar in its silence.

The minute they were in Foregate Street station both made a beeline for the day's desk sergeant. "After you," Dave said to Claire, though he had been marginally ahead of her.

Claire pulled a face at the unwonted chivalry. "Age before beauty, or pearls before swine?" Without waiting for an answer, she addressed the desk sergeant. "All right, Andy? Have you seen Jenny anywhere yet?"

"Canteen, love."

"Cheers. And call me love again I'll have you up on sexual harassment."

"Sound," Andy said, giving a thumbs-up.

"Your turn," she said to Dave, and headed off to the canteen.

"So kind." Dave waited until she was well out of earshot before turning back to the desk. "Is PC Jones on duty today?" He was uncomfortably aware of something in the officer's expression. "Knowing" would probably have been a good description. "I have to run through some reports with him," he said. The desk sergeant's knowing look became even more pronounced. "Today if possible."

"Down in the car pool, getting ready to go out with Sergeant McNeil. Sir."

"Thank you, Sergeant Rowland."

"You're welcome, Sergeant Lyon." The two men stood, looking at each other. "They'll be leaving in one minute."

Shit. "Thank you again." Dave turned and walked purposefully in the direction of the car pool. He wasn't going to run. He *couldn't* run, not while Rowland was watching. There was no way he wanted to make it look like he was chasing after young Joe Jones. But the instant there was a door between him and the front desk he did run for it, as fast as he safely could down the corridors leading to the outside door to the car pool.

*

"Jenny."

Jenny Trent looked up from the conversation she was having with another WPC. "Inspector," she said stiffly.

Claire stood to one side of the table. "Can I have a word?" She waited pointedly until the other woman got the hint. "Catch you later, Jen," she said, got up, and left. Claire took her chair. "Look about last night..." She ground to a halt. All through the night and throughout that morning's journey into work she had been turning over and over in her mind what had happened between them the previous evening. She'd been seriously angered and worried by some of the things Jen had said, but, at the same time, Jen was one of her oldest friends in the service. She couldn't just pretend it hadn't happened.

"It's all right, Claire. You don't need to worry. I can be perfectly *professional* about this."

"I think we need to talk it through."

"Oh, I think we said everything that needed to be said last night."

"Jen, I..."

"Inspector?"

The two women looked up to the source of the interruption. WPC Dennison, nervous and slightly out of breath, was standing by the table. "Sorry to butt in but Andy, Sergeant Rowland, said you'd want to know this right away. Seems that headmaster you've been dealing with has been attacked again. Something about a car crash."

*

Dave found PC Jones just as the young copper was getting into a police car with his mentor. "Chris. Chris!"

McNeil wound the driver's window down. "Sergeant?"

Dave walked over to the police car, taking the time to recover as much of his breath as he could so that it did not look like he had been running at all. "Could I just have a quick word with PC Jones, please? It won't take a minute." And there it was again. That bloody *knowing* look. Did everyone assume that just because he was gay, he'd go running after Jones? Even though, admittedly, that was exactly what he had just done.

"Sergeant wants a word with you, Joe," Chris said. "I'll just drive round to the front and wait for you there."

"Okay, Sarge." Joe got out of the car and Chris drove off, leaving him facing Dave. "Morning, sir."

"Good morning." Dave paused. What had sounded so sensible and reasonable in his head this morning seemed now suddenly stilted and open to all kinds of misinterpretation. "Look, about last night." He stopped, aware there was something about the young officer's face. Was he...? Was he trying not to laugh?

Joe sobered quickly, seeing Dave's expression. It obviously took a bit of an effort. "Yes, sir?"

"I think you were put in something of an...awkward situation." Joe said nothing. Dave realised he was waiting for something more. "It's perhaps a little unusual for new recruits and senior officers to find themselves socialising quite so soon in the job." *Unless they're having a bloody let's-all-get-acquainted party organised by one of the station's bloody senior officers.*

"I guess it probably is, sir," Joe said.

"It is, and I'm sorry if..."

"It's no biggie really, sir," Joe interrupted. "Just two guys, out on the town. Bound to happen sooner or later in a small town like Worcester." He gave a smile that vanished quickly before Dave's sergeant face.

Later rather than sooner would have been better, Dave thought. *And never would have been best of all. Just two guys?* Was he annoyed that this new recruit was assuming an easy familiarity? Or was he rather envious of Jones's naiveté? And it hadn't just been two guys, had it?

"In an ideal world, yes," Dave said. "But even so, I think it would be...politic not to mention it, not to let it get around, if you know what I mean?"

He watched as Jones digested what he'd said. "Ah right, sir," Jones said. "I think I'm with you. Jenny, that is, WPC Trent said there were one or two less up to date members of the force here."

"Yes. Yes, that's it." Dave took it for granted Jones was referring to DI Rudge. "And it's also probably best not to...involve members of the public as well."

"Sir?"

Dave groaned inwardly. How to persuade Joe not to mention Sean Cullen's name without actually mentioning it himself?

"Sergeant Lyon?"

Dave was distracted from the problem at hand by the arrival of WPC Dennison, looking, though he didn't know it, even more out of breath than she had minutes earlier. "Inspector Summerskill wants you, sir," she gasped. "It's about that headmaster. From Monastery Grove?"

Damn. "What's happened now? Someone taken a bat to him again?"

"No sir. A breeze-block."

*

"This," Dave muttered, as he poked at the shattered windscreen of Alun Blake's car, "could have been very nasty indeed."

"What? Like this isn't bad enough?" Claire asked, gesturing at the crumpled front of the car with its frosting of granular safety glass.

Dave straightened. "I mean, if Mr. Blake had swerved left instead of right. And if the traffic had been moving any faster."

"It wasn't, though, was it? It was the school run. What better time...?"

"...to drop a concrete block through a headmaster's windscreen." Dave flipped his notepad closed. "You're saying this wasn't just some mindless yobs taking their pet brick for a walk and accidentally letting it fall on any old car?"

"The car of someone who had his office trashed only the day beforehand. What do you think?"

"Inspector Summerskill." Stalking towards them was Alun Blake, clutching a handkerchief to his head and ignoring the protests of the medic in the ambulance drawn up on the grass verge. "You've got here very quickly. I hope this time you'll be as quick catching whoever did this. Unlike the dangerous criminal who attacked me in my own office."

"You really should get that seen to properly, Mr. Blake," said Claire, indicating his forehead. Behind the headteacher she saw the medic's *Good luck with that* expression.

"Do you have any idea who did this, sir?" Dave asked. "Did you manage to see who it was on the bridge there?"

"Of course, I didn't! Firstly. I was watching the road. Then, when the bloody thing was dropped on my car, I had flying glass in my eyes and was trying not to crash into anyone."

Claire looked across to the ambulance. A young girl was sitting in the back where the second paramedic was shining a light in her eyes and testing her reactions. "That young lady was with you, sir? Your daughter?"

"Yes, yes," Blake said impatiently. "She's fine."

"Did she see anything, sir?" Dave asked.

"She's a young girl, sergeant. She had her nose down in her mobile phone."

"Even so, perhaps if I..."

"I said she didn't see anything, sergeant."

Dave glanced at Claire who gave a small shake of her head. He flipped his notepad shut and shoved it back in his jacket pocket.

"If that thing had gone an inch the other way..."

Claire took in the chunk of rock resting on the sill of the head's car, half in, half out of the cabin. He was right. An inch either way and the driver or the passenger might have been lying in that ambulance, not sitting or walking around.

"How old is your daughter, sir?" Claire asked, as much to give herself a little thinking time as for any real desire to know the answer.

"She's in Year Ten. That's fifteen."

"Yes. I do know. And she goes to Monastery Grove?"

"Yes."

Always trust a butcher who eats the meat from his own shop, Claire's gran had used to say. She didn't think it would be a good idea to quote the old lady now, and she wasn't sure it really applied to teachers and their kids anyway. "Right. Well, would you mind telling me, as best as you can recall..."

"If you could bear with us, sir," Dave said, "it really would be helpful."

Claire saw the visible effort Blake made to keep his temper in check. Fair enough. He'd just had a nasty shock.

"I was proceeding along the A44 towards the school," Blake began. Dave looked up from his reopened notepad. Was this stilted style some kind of piss-take of a stereotypical police statement? Blake's humourless expression persuaded him it was not. "We had just passed the garage on the right and were about to move under the pedestrian bridge that goes across the road when...well, I'll admit my very first thought was that I must have hit someone. I knew there hadn't been another car in front of us so I thought a pedestrian must have walked out in front of us, or a cyclist had come up on the inside. I don't know. It was all so sudden."

"That's understandable, sir," Dave said. "That's how everyone reacts to situations like this. It's one of the reasons we ask you to tell us about it again—in case something comes to you once things have had a chance to settle a bit."

Blake gave him an irritated look but carried on. "So, I jammed the brakes on and cut the ignition. I was covered in glass from the windscreen and so was my daughter. Luckily, I only had a couple of small cuts to my face. I don't think Anne was cut at all."

You don't think? Claire thought but said nothing.

"And did you then get a chance to look outside of the car to see what had happened?"

"No. The next thing I knew, cars were pulling up behind and to one side of me. Someone was at my door, banging on the window, and someone else was on the other side, opening the passenger door and pulling my daughter out." Blake frowned. "I'm afraid Anne is...highly strung at the best of times. In the confusion, she wasn't sure what was going on and may have, well, she did scream a bit. I was able to calm her down, though, and we both got out and stood on the grass verge in the centre of the road and waited for the police and ambulance which someone had called. It was only then that I got a good look at my car and saw the brick or block or whatever it is and realised what must have happened. At first, I couldn't believe anyone had been able to throw something that large but then I realised we'd been passing under that bridge and it must have been dropped from there."

"So, you looked up at the bridge?"

"Of course, but obviously by then there was no one there."

"Did you see any of your kids around about, sir? I mean, pupils from the school?" Dave asked.

Blake's lips thinned. "We call them *students*, sergeant. Why do you ask?"

"Witnesses, sir. We'll see what we can pull from any CCTV there might be in the area, but a good witness is just as good if not better. Any...students who might have seen something would be a great help."

"It seems unlikely that there wouldn't be any of your kids around at that time of day, Mr. Blake," Claire added. "In their parents' cars, walking or cycling to school. And we will of course be able to identify any of them from any camera footage we can locate."

"I see. Well, as I said, inspector, things did happen rather too fast for me to take in but, yes, I could see a couple of uniforms. You'll have to forgive me if I can't name every student in the school. We do have over thirteen hundred, you know, but I do remember one. Greg Reader in Year Ten. I'm afraid the name sticks in my head because we have had a few...dealings with him in the past. A lad who needs to find his way, shall we say. But I think we can rely on him to say if he saw anything. Or anyone."

"And maybe your daughter saw some of her mates and could pass on their names," Dave suggested.

"My daughter doesn't have *mates*, sergeant," Blake said. His tone had been sharp, and he took a second as if to collect himself. "I very much doubt she could pass on any names. I'd be grateful if you could just allow her to rest and recover and not bother her."

"I agree with Sergeant Lyon," Claire began. "It really would be a good idea if..."

"Inspector," Blake said firmly. "Sergeant. Perhaps you don't understand." Claire stiffened at the suggestion and Dave reacted as if he hadn't noticed. She knew there were times when he found her temper unfortunate. And then there were times like this when he actually appeared to be impressed by her self-restraint. "It's difficult enough at the best of times being the daughter of an ordinary teacher at the school you go to. But when your father is the headteacher... I would appreciate it if you could keep my daughter's involvement in any identification to a minimum."

Claire frowned. *Overprotective or what?* she thought, but she nodded. "We'll send someone along to talk to this Greg Reader and anyone else he might turn up, and we'll have a look at the CCTV situation. But if that gets us nowhere, we may still have to talk to your daughter."

"A shame your young technician, Abbi was it, hasn't got any cameras out here," Dave said. "She'd get us something in a jiffy."

Claire hadn't thought Alun Blake's expression could get any sourer until then.

*

"You know, I think he actually shuddered when I suggested their techie got involved."

Claire had noticed and she had been amused. Now, though, even as she and Dave walked back to their car, she was running through in her head who they could actually spare to do the necessary spade work. "McNeil's babies."

"What?"

"The new recruits. They can go and do the interviews. Good experience for them. South, Dennison, and who was the other one?"

"Like you don't remember."

Claire smiled sweetly. "Oh yes. Jones. How could I forget?"

"How indeed?"

Chapter Nine

"You were lucky."

"You were *fucking* lucky."

"They should be scraping you off the fucking pavement right now."

"Next time..." Alex took another step that brought him so close to Anne she could smell his breath. It made her want to throw up. "Next time," he said again, "I think..."

"What's going on here?"

The knot of boys who had Anne Blake pinned against a wall didn't move but the situation had changed. Their power over her had evaporated in an instant. Anne could tell they knew it, even as she saw from their failure to step back away from her that they were going to try to tough it out. Idiots. The contempt she felt for them was so strong it almost completed the task Alex's bad breath had started and made her sick.

"I said," the teacher repeated, putting more impatience into her voice, "what is going on here?"

Alex stepped back from Anne with provoking slowness. He turned to face the teacher. She was two inches shorter than him, probably weighed two stone less, but she didn't give a damn. "Nothing, Miss Grant," he said in a singsong imitation of a younger child.

"Good." The teacher blithely ignored the insolence. "Now go and do it somewhere else. Preferably nowhere near my room."

For a moment, none of the four boys moved but all concerned recognised it for the token gesture it was. "C'mon, lads," Alex said finally. "We've got better places to be than this."

Alex's cronies delivered the obligatory sneering laughs and moved off with a swagger that was meant to suggest the exit was all their idea.

*

Cassie Grant stood watching the four boys disappear round a corner and shook her head. "If they put half as much effort into actually trying to learn something, they'd be geniuses." She looked back to the girl. She'd only caught a fraction of what had been said but had a feeling she had just rescued Anne Blake. *It would be her, wouldn't it?* "You all right, Anne? You weren't in registration this morning, were you? I heard you were in some kind of accident." She looked at Anne more closely, searching for any sign of injury. "You sure you should be here?"

"I'm fine, Miss."

"You don't look it." *She should be at home. Why isn't she?* Cassie sighed. She had a pretty good idea why not. Their beloved headteacher's *show must go on* attitude. Well, okay, if *he* still wanted to come in after a near fatal accident that was fine by her. If he really thought the school couldn't cope without him. But he could have cut his own daughter a bit of slack. Especially after...

"I wanted to see you, miss," Anne said.

"Oh right." Despite herself, Cassie's heart sank. Wednesday. *It would be Wednesday, wouldn't it?* Five lessons teaching, a breaktime duty she'd just done, and a meeting after school. There was just this one, brief five-minute window when she could have snuck in a coffee and slice of rye bread. And now Anne Blake wanted to talk to her. "You'd better come in then." Maybe she could at least put the kettle on while the girl was talking. That wouldn't look too insensitive, would it? It probably depended on what Anne was going to say. She leaned past and used her fob to unlock the door to her room.

Anne didn't move. Cassie could tell she was struggling with something, trying to come to a decision. "Come on, Anne. Chop-chop." As soon as she spoke, Cassie knew she had made her impatience and desire to get this interview quickly out of the way too obvious. She could practically feel Anne close up in front of her.

"It's all right, miss," Anne said. "I can ask you later. When you've got more time."

"No, wait a minute. Anne," Cassie called after her. "Anne!" But the girl was gone. "Damn."

When you've got more time. The words cut like a knife. Adolescent passive aggression. Cassie recognised it for what it was, but that didn't lessen the sting of guilt. "Damn, and...bloody damn." The swearing didn't help, especially when you always had to moderate it on school property. You never knew when little ears could be listening.

Mentally beating herself up, Cassie entered her room and made for the store cupboard at the back where she kept her supply of much needed caffeine and crackers. The second her hand touched the kettle the bell rang to signal the start of the next lesson. "Bloody, bloody damn!"

There was a knock at the door. "Anne?" Cassie's tone was one of mingled annoyance and hope. "Come in!"

A male teacher stuck his head round the door. "'Fraid not. Still welcome?"

Cassie let her *I'm here to help* expression slide into a combination of relief and pleasure. "Ian. Come in. Better still, come in and stand against the door so no one else can get in. At least until I've had a cup of bloody coffee."

Claire Summerskill's husband grinned, walked in, and closed the door behind him.

*

A dozen yards down the corridor, Anne ducked into one of the girls' toilets and slammed the bolt closed. She waited, with eyes screwed tight shut, for the noise and commotion precipitated by the lesson bell to die down, signalling that all kids and teachers were safely in their designated rooms for at least the next hour. She prayed no other reluctant learner had the thought of bunking off in the loos too.

Eventually silence fell. Anne slid the door bolt back and peeked out. No one in the main toilet area. She withdrew again into the cubicle, safe even from the prying eye of the CCTV camera. She pulled out her mobile phone. Another breach of school rules. *Yeah, fuck that, too, Daddy.* With shaking hands, she entered the preset number and waited, hugging herself, rocking back and forth on the toilet seat. *Please answer. Please answer.* He'd be there of course. He was always there, on the end of his phone. It was where he lived, wasn't it, where he worked. But would he answer?

"Hello, Annie?" That eager-to-please tone. How hollow that seemed now.

"Mark!" Anne struggled to keep her voice under control, alarmed that her inadvertent cry might have given away her hiding place.

"Hey." In her mind she could see his face, that concerned frown. Mark loved everyone, that was the joke, wasn't it? "What's up? Are you getting grief again, Annie? Want me to come round and sort it for you. Annie? Annie?"

Hot, furious tears flowed down Anne's cheeks, the muscles in her throat so constricted she could hardly breathe let alone talk, her grip on the phone so tight she actually thought she might break it. When she could get the words out, her voice was a strangled whisper.

"What's that? Annie love, I can't hear you. Speak up. What's the matter, darlin'?"

"I can't go on," she gasped. "I just can't go on, Mark."

*

"You seen this?" Dave angled his computer screen so that Claire could make it out from where she was sitting at her desk.

She craned her neck to see better. "Catch-up of local news?" Dave nodded. "You've got to show me how you get that on your computer."

"I have. Twice."

Claire waved dismissively. "So's Tony, three times. Play."

Dave clicked and the familiar face of their local TV news anchor began to speak.

"Traffic today was brought to a standstill on the A44 northbound as vandals dropped what is believed to have been a large breeze-block from an overhead pedestrian bridge onto moving traffic below, hitting a car passing underneath. The driver of the car struck was Mr. Alun Blake, headteacher at Monastery Grove. Both he and his daughter, who was in the car with him, were shaken but uninjured when the stone block smashed the windscreen of their car causing them to swerve onto the grass verge at the centre of the dual carriageway. Any further accidents were prevented by speedy intervention from drivers of other passing vehicles before the eventual arrival of the police."

"Eventual arrival!" Claire was scornful. "It was only up the road. We were on it practically as soon as it happened." She leaned forward. "Oh no. Why are they showing that?"

"This is what I thought you'd want to see," Dave said.

To one side of the newsreader on the screen had been inserted the head shot of Clayton Kerry that Claire remembered from when the boy's death had first been reported. "Alun Blake has been at the centre of a social media storm in recent days," the anchor continued, "since the recent death of Clayton Kerry, a former pupil of Monastery Grove High where Mr. Blake is headmaster. Mr. Blake had excluded Clayton the day before his death, a move which some have seen as putting a vulnerable young man at risk, and when Mr. Blake was questioned about this after the boy's death, he made comments that many people found disrespectful and upsetting."

The picture cut to the footage of Monastery Grove's entrance with the angry parents, Mr, Clayton, his two companions, and Claire and Dave trying to impose order.

"Not that shot again," Claire pleaded. "Dammit."

The scene played out just long enough to show everyone ducking from the flung Zen garden rock before cutting once again to a head and shoulders shot of someone both police officers recognised.

"That's right, Gary," said Sarah Moody, the reporter who had been on the school steps that day. The camera pulled back to reveal that she now seemed to be at the old Fitzmaurice brewery. "And here at the site of Clayton Kerry's tragic death, the reaction to Mr. Blake's comments seems to have inspired people to show their feelings even more than usual." The camera pulled out further to reveal an astonishing mass of flowers by the side of the collapsed wall that had killed the boy. As the officers watched, a self-conscious youth in a T-shirt walked up to the tributes with his own bunch of flowers, clutching them with an awkwardness that suggested bouquets were not something he routinely dealt with, and that possibly even this one had come as a bit of a surprise to him. He threw the flowers, rather unceremoniously Claire thought, on to the heap of other offerings, looked sideways quickly into the camera with what she would definitely have described as a smirk, and then walked out of shot. The brief glimpse of pixel-blurred T-shirt suggested that he had come to show his feelings of grief while sporting an obscene slogan.

The camera zoomed in and panned along the piles of flowers and the messages of condolence attached to them.

"Is it wrong to notice the bad grammar and spelling?"

"Yes," Claire said.

The pan came to a stop, the camera focusing on one single rose that had been placed a short distance from the rest of the floral tributes, holding the image for a couple of seconds before returning to a head and shoulders shot of Moody. "And the Oscar for cinematography goes to..." Claire muttered.

"The question that people are asking," Moody said with professional gravitas, "is, was the attack on Mr. Blake's car some mindless act of vandalism or was it in fact connected with the sad death of this young man? This is Sarah Moody, for *Midlands Now*, Worcester."

Dave shut the widow on his computer and sat back

"Oh, so that's the question people are asking, is it?" Claire fumed.

"Isn't it?"

*

The kid's a natural, McNeil thought and then chided himself for thinking of PC Jones as a kid. *Getting old, Chris*. But PC Jones *was* good with kids.

Dispatched once again to Monastery Grove, a school he was definitely beginning to feel he had seen too much of recently, McNeil had taken Joe with him. First, they had addressed the pupils in a series of year-group assemblies, introducing themselves, explaining why they were there, impressing on the kids the seriousness of what too many of them undoubtedly saw as a bit of amusing, anti-teacher mischief, and encouraging them to come forward if they had any information. Then they had set up in what he assumed was an unused art room. (He could think of no other reason why a school room would have in it a life-sized mannequin, spray-painted silver, sitting on a bright yellow sofa, and a papier-mâché head of a Chinese dragon.) There, they waited for the kids to come to them. For the first two hours they were undisturbed by anyone apart from the school's CCTV expert Abbi who, having heard where they were and now seeing herself as something of a police liaison officer, kindly brought them some tea and biscuits. "Hope you catch the little fuckers," she said.

When morning break came, McNeil and Jones went for a wander around the school's yards. His recent glut of visits to this school aside, Chris had visited Monastery Grove several times in the past, doing the community bobby bit of talking to kids on a variety of topics. When he'd started doing that, the talks had mostly been about the dangers of jaywalking or larking about on rail tracks. Lately, he'd had to talk about knife crime and even what to do in the event of a school lockdown because of a terrorist attack. This also made him feel old.

It did mean, however, that he knew the score. Most of the younger kids, eleven to twelve years old, still had a quite sweet naiveté, and either looked shyly at the two police officers from a safe distance or came bouncing up for a chat that had nothing to do with the reason Chris and Joe were there. Common gambits were, "You came into my junior school once. Do you remember?" and "My brother's so-and-so. Do you know him?" This last, often with an edge of challenge to it.

A year or two older and attitudes changed, often along gender lines. The girls tended to clump together, still keeping a distance with several of them nudging each other, giggling and pointing at PC Jones. (*Not at me,* Chris thought. *Not any more. Old.*) The interest shown by some of the older girls was a lot more overt. Chris couldn't help tutting and shaking his head at the brazenness of it and at the uncanny (and disturbing) way they could make a school uniform look like some sort of provocative nightclub outfit. For his part, Joe seemed blissfully unaware of the effect his good looks were having.

And then there were the older boys. "Wankers!" came the shout from behind the corner of one building. "Pigs," from another, and then the sound of jeering laughter and scarpering feet.

"*Counting coup*," Chris said.

"Sorry?"

"It means they've got to show who's got balls by poking us and getting away with it. Rite of passage. Doesn't mean anything. Didn't you do anything similar when you were that age?"

"I guess," Joe said uncertainly. "So, we let it go?"

"You want to chase after them, be my guest. It's not really worth it, and it doesn't do our job at this minute any good, does it? We're here to be approachable today, so we play the bigger men." He stared off thoughtfully in the direction their abusers had fled. "Course, if they'd run off into a dead end, I'd have gone in and given the little shits what for."

By the time break was nearly over, the only real contact they'd had with any of the student body had been a short chat with a small knot of earnest twelve-year-old boys who had been eager to know about the guns you could use when you were a policeman and were deeply disappointed that McNeil and Jones weren't armed right then.

As the bell was ringing, they were approached by a girl and a middle-aged woman who was looking very embarrassed. The woman was being pulled along by the girl who was holding her hand. The girl was very small even by the standards of the youngest kids milling around them. Chris was surprised. You didn't tend to see kids holding the teachers' hands in a high school. The pair came closer, and Chris began to understand.

"Excuse us," the woman said, with apparent reluctance.

"Hello." McNeil and Jones smiled openly.

"I'm Mrs. Bevan, one of the TA's."

"That's teaching assistant sir," Jones said.

"I know, constable."

"They told us you were looking for anybody who might have seen anything to do with that incident this morning. You know, with Mr. Blake's car."

"That's right."

The woman gave the hand of the little girl by her side a squeeze. "This is Shameena. She...she said she saw something."

Joe knelt so that his face was on a level with the little girl's. "Hello, Shameena."

Shameena's face lit up with a broad smile. She giggled, and Chris nodded to himself. *Poor mite. Back in the day she'd have been in a special school. Nowadays, it's all about "inclusion", isn't it? Is she really included?* he wondered, seeing the little girl attached to her adult support without any of the other children showing any interest in her.

"Shameena," Mrs. Bevan began, obviously uncertain what to say with the child there in front of them.

"No probs, Mrs. Bevan," Joe said, looking up. "I knew a girl like Shameena at my school." He turned again to the girl. "How are you today, Shameena?"

Shameena giggled again, and pulled Mrs. Bevan's arm round herself as if it was a scarf she could wrap herself up in and hide.

"Did you want to talk to us about something?" Joe coaxed. Shameena nodded. "Was it about what happened to the headmaster's car?" Shameena nodded again; a big bounce of her head which was just that fraction larger for her body than it should have been. Her face was almost split in two by her huge smile.

"Shameena thinks," Mrs. Bevan began.

"It's all right, Miss," Joe said. "Sorry, Mrs. Bevan. Shameena can tell us, can't you Shameena?" More enthusiastic nods. "All right then. You tell me and Sergeant McNeil what you saw."

"I saw the ghost!" Shameena shouted delightedly, clapping her hands with glee at her own cleverness. "I saw the ghost drop the brick on Mr. Blake's car."

*

"She meant Caleb, didn't she?" Dave said.

McNeil nodded. "We're pretty sure, yes. Got to admit, it was young Joe here who cottoned on straight away. I thought we were in some weird *Sixth Sense* setup at first. And then I thought that the girl had, well, you know, imagined things."

"Well done, constable," Claire said.

"Well, it was like I told Chris, Sergeant McNeil," Joe said. "We had a girl like Shameena at my school. Happy little soul, but she didn't... Well, she didn't live till she was very old. But Shameena recognised someone who looked like Clayton Kerry, and that has got to be Caleb. I mean most of that family look like they've been made by the same cookie cutter."

"Including the father."

Claire shook her head. "That man has had a hard paper round. Would even a kid like Shameena mistake father for son?" Jones looked doubtful. "And she'll have known Clayton's face from around school probably, if not then possibly from the television reports. God knows they keep showing them often enough."

"Bottom line is, Shameena said she saw a ghost," Dave said. "I think we can all imagine how well that would go down in a courtroom."

"And no one else in that entire school came forward to say they'd seen anything?" Claire asked. Jones and McNeil shook their heads. "Right." Claire's disbelief was evident. "In that case, I don't think we have any choice. We bring Caleb Kerry in for questioning."

"Inspector?" WPC Dennison stood, looking nervous. Dave was beginning to think she always looked nervous. There was, however, something more now—the look in her eyes of a young woman beginning to suspect she was out of her depth. "Jenny, WPC Trent sent me," she began.

Seeing Claire's look of exasperation, Dave went over to the young officer while his boss discussed with Chris who would be best to take with them to the Kerry house. Dave was back with them within a minute. "Bad news, ma'am. There's been another death over at the Fitzmaurice brewery."

"Shit! Another accident?"

"No, ma'am. This one's definitely murder."

Chapter Ten

"I remember this," Claire said, looking down at the rose at her feet. "It was on that bloody awful news report." She looked over to the heaps of floral tributes marking Clayton Kerry's place of death. They'd lost their freshness but weren't rotting yet. "It stood out because it was apart from all the others."

"And didn't have a misspelt card attached?"

"Time and place, sergeant. Time and place." Claire picked up the rose. It seemed fresher somehow than the piles of other flowers, though it was broken now, muddied and spotted with blood. No need to ask SOCO whose blood. Only feet away the police screens concealed a body as the forensic officers went about their business, taking photos, samples, documenting the last scene of a young man's all too brief life. Claire held the flower for a moment, suddenly unsure what to do with it. Simply dropping it to the ground again seemed wrong. Carefully, she laid it back where she had found it. When she stood up again, she scowled at Dave, daring him to make some snarky comment.

She stepped back and surveyed the old brewery site. Two small, single-storey buildings right by where they were standing and a variety of others beyond, some as tall as three storeys. A few of the windows sported scanty remnants of glass. Most were gaping holes in a crumbling brickwork overgrown with ivy and briars. Everywhere was the painted logo of the old Fitzmaurice brewery, the large, stylised F and M, once jaunty in bright red and yellow, now faded and peeling, like scabs on the stone. "Will someone tell me exactly why this place hasn't been sealed off?"

"It's as sealed off as it was before Clayton Kerry got killed. There are fences, signs, you name it, but if someone wants to get in here badly enough, there's really not a lot can be done to stop them." Dave thought back to his conversation with Cullen. "Kids have been doing it for ages."

"Then someone needs to put a rocket up the arses of the owners! Maybe a writ of criminal liability."

"Oh no."

Claire frowned. "What?"

Dave pointed in the direction of the flimsy tape barriers that had been put up to keep rubberneckers at bay. "Trouble."

Showing complete disregard for the police tape, two figures were heading towards them at speed, or at least at the most speed one of them could manage burdened by a camera, and the other in heels that were definitely unsuitable for the boggy grass and fractured concrete now covering most of the old brewery site. "Inspector Summers! Inspector Summers."

"Summer*skill*," Claire said through gritted teeth.

Sarah Moody, the reporter who had covered the fracas on the steps of Monastery Grove, strode up, clearly out of breath. Her shoes were obviously not the only things unused to such activity. Her companion raised his camera and focused on Claire. Claire stiffened, knowing her first thoughts about unflattering freeze-frames were unworthy, but unable to help herself.

"Inspector. We understand there has been another...incident here today? Can you confirm that, please?"

"I'm afraid there has. Yes, that is so."

"And the victim is...?"

"As I'm sure you understand, we are unable to comment at this point in time."

"Of course."

The two women eyed each other. *If she asks me how I feel I will shove that microphone up...*

"But are you able to comment on whether there were any...suspicious circumstances?"

Like the bloody gash across the top of the thigh and the knife in the guts? "As I'm sure you understand..." Claire repeated in a monotone.

"Of course. But," Moody persisted, "this is the second death in less than a week in the same place, isn't it? Would you say that is beginning to look like some kind of pattern?"

"Actually," Dave, said, "two incidents could at most be correlation, but more likely coincidence. It would take three..." He stopped, suddenly aware that his impulsive comment had drawn him to the attention of not just the reporter but also her cameraman.

That'll teach you, Claire couldn't help thinking.

"A coincidence?" Moody said, her perfectly pencilled eyebrow raised in a very telegenic arch. "Isn't that rather a flippant comment, Inspector Lyon?"

So, you've remembered his *name have, you?* Claire thought sourly. *Even if you have promoted him.* "I can assure you my sergeant intended no flippancy," she said, with just a touch of emphasis on Dave's rank.

Moody switched her focus back to Claire. "Inspector, are you able to say whether there is any link, any *correlation,* between the two deaths that have happened here?"

Give me a break. Why don't you just ask me how I feel and then sod off so we can get on with our jobs and maybe find that out? "As I'm sure..." she began.

*

Frank Aldridge, the chief medical officer assigned to Foregate Street police station, was a snob, a misogynist, and almost certainly a homophobe, although, in his defence, that was largely due to an absolute conviction of his own superiority to all other human beings, male, female, gay or straight, rather than to any actual prejudice. He was also very good at his job, which was annoying as it left Summerskill and Lyon feeling guilty for their dislike of him. Sometimes.

"...straight across the femoral artery," Aldridge concluded. "Not instant, but quick. He would have bled to death in a matter of minutes. That also, of course, accounts for the large quantities of blood at the scene of the crime. The following thrust of the knife into the lower abdomen was completely *de trop.* That's *too much,*" he added with a patronising smirk.

Claire nodded, determined as ever not to give this man any indication of the revulsion she felt at the memory of the bloodshed. "Are you saying then that this was done, the slicing of the artery at least, with some degree of skill? By someone who knew how to handle a knife?"

"I'm saying," Aldridge replied with dogged and annoying literalness, "that it cut across the femoral artery. That is all I can say. I can say that the ensuing thrust into the lower abdomen seems to suggest otherwise as it was far less likely to have ensured certain death and was, in any case, completely unnecessary by that point."

"So, either the first cut was lucky, or the second cut was vindictive?" Dave mused. "Maybe both?"

Aldridge's expression made clear his low opinion of "amateur" interpretation in his field of expertise. "I can say that the angles of both cut and insertion are unusual. I don't need to tell you, we're seeing more and more knife crime amongst kids and young adults these days, but even so, the majority of wounds in such cases are slashes or cuts that come from up high and stab downwards, like so." Without warning he mimed a downward plunge of a knife into Dave's chest. Dave instinctively jerked backwards. "To have slashed and stabbed in this way, the killer would have to have been very short. Or on his knees."

"Thank you for not demonstrating that, doctor," Dave murmured.

"Oh, I was fairly sure you could imagine a man on his knees in front of you, sergeant."

Dave gave a very tight, cold smile. "Just never you."

Claire considered the body on the autopsy room's table. In his preliminaries, Aldridge had described him as five ten. "It's got to have been someone on their knees."

"Probably," Aldridge agreed breezily, "though not necessarily. They're stabbing each other younger and younger these days, aren't they? They'll be doing it from high chairs soon. Could have been a child I suppose."

"But unlikely," Claire insisted.

"Yes, unlikely," Aldridge agreed, with apparent disappointment.

"And the murder weapon?"

"Ah yes, that." Aldridge brightened, and with a typical flourish, produced a plastic evidence bag. Claire studied it before handing it over to Dave. "So much for our recent knife amnesty," she muttered.

Dave scrutinised the object through the plastic. "It's a...nice one," he said. "Not your customised, bargain shop bread knife. Actually looks like it would have cost a few pennies."

"Mother-of-pearl inlay and finest Sheffield steel," Aldridge confirmed.

"Not something you'd gut fish with."

"Not something any boy would do anything with," Aldridge said. "This is most definitely a girl's knife. I'm sorry," he quickly added in pretend apology, "I mean, a *woman's* knife. I don't want to offend any homicidal maniacs of the female persuasion, do I?"

"No more than you usually do," Claire muttered.

"No self-respecting young thug would try to establish his credentials with such an effeminate weapon," Aldridge continued as if he hadn't heard the inspector. "Not even..." He looked at Dave. "Well, not anyone," he concluded.

"No matter how provoked?" Dave asked.

"And the marks on the inlay?" Claire asked, pointing to the pale-grey handle and the series of lines scored into its surface.

Aldridge sniffed. "Artistic vandalism. Someone spent a reasonable amount on this little beauty and then defaced it with a load of clumsy scratches."

"Presumably, it meant something to someone."

"Perhaps a tally of the owner's victims?"

"I don't think so, doctor. These two here and here," Claire indicated, "look more like arrows."

"Both pointing the same way," Dave agreed.

"Which brings us," Claire said.

"As it always does."

"To prints," Claire concluded.

"Of which there are none," Aldridge said.

"As there so rarely are," Dave said.

"Not even the victim's?"

"No, which is unlikely as almost the first thing you're likely to do if someone sticks a knife into you is to take a hold of it with a view to pulling it out."

"So, it was wiped?"

"Well enough to do away with any immediately detectable prints." Aldridge took the bag back from Dave. "Needless to say, I shall now go and run some more thorough tests but even if I can, through the appliance of science, lift some fragment of a print or crumb of DNA I don't suppose it will do much good, will it? If this is another of those random youth stabbings we keep hearing about in the news, you're unlikely to have the murderer on your databases, are you? Unless, of course, those marks on the knife *are* tallies in which case he stroke she, and I draw your attention back to the daintiness of the weapon, has killed before and left his stroke her genetic fingerprints all over the scene of the crime. And in *that* case," he said, drawing to a triumphant conclusion, "what we might have here is a ser..."

"Don't say it," Claire growled. "Don't even think it."

"As you wish. I have to say, though, I'd have thought some madman murdering to a giveaway pattern would have lifted the heart more than a one-off, random killer leaving no helpful telltale trail of clues."

"If it is a one-off," Claire muttered almost to herself.

"What?"

"Nothing. Anything else?"

Aldridge's annoyance about being shut down by Claire was obvious. "No. As I said, not yet. There was a complete absence of anything on the body that could have identified him. No wallet, no phone, nothing. Highly unusual these days, of course, suggesting that said items were almost certainly removed by the killer to prevent us identifying the victim."

"We already know who the victim is, doctor," Dave said. "His name's Mark Smith. He's a good friend and possibly relative of the Kerry family." He looked across the autopsy table to the sombre face of his boss. "I think I know where our next port of call is going to be."

*

"You don't think Aldridge is right, do you?" Dave finally dared to ask on the drive back to the estate where the Kerrys lived. "About a...?"

"Of course, he isn't," Claire snapped. "What we might have is someone who has a grudge against the family but even that might not hold up." She massaged her temple. A familiar headache was beginning to grow there. "Mark Smith's death was clearly murder. Clayton's death appeared to be an accident. Now, I'm not so sure."

"You're thinking autopsy, aren't you?"

Claire nodded. "We assumed Clayton had brought a wall down on himself by pratting about where he shouldn't have been. Maybe something was missed."

"I'll get on it when we're back at the station. At least they haven't had the funeral yet. Less paperwork than an exhumation."

"And lower cost. That should make Madden slightly happier, at least. Hold fire, though, just until we've spoken to the Kerrys again. Let's see what pans out before we go overreaching for connections."

"Fair enough."

Claire leafed through the preliminary SOCO report on the scene of the crime they'd brought with them. "Like we thought. Grass was way too churned up with the recent rain and all the traffic that's been through there in the last few days to provide any clear picture of who was there at the time of the murder." She closed the thin file and tossed it over her shoulder onto the back seat of the car. "Get them to go over it again."

"Madden will *not* be happy at that cost."

"Tell him to take his own magnifying glass and shovel then."

Summerskill and Lyon pulled up outside the Kerrys' house. As before, two children were playing out the front. Dave couldn't be sure if it was the same two as before given the ubiquitous Kerry features and the thick layer of dirt. The distrustful glares were the same though. *Resting Kerry Face*, as he was coming to think of it.

The door was opened again by Mrs. Kerry, still with baby in her arms. "You know the way," she said before disappearing back into the house.

"Déjà vu, all over again."

"Oh, I don't know," Dave said. "That might have been a different baby."

Had they forgotten the way to the living room, the earthy smell of weed would have been a handy guide. Inside the room, the scene was just as they had left it the last time: Kerry the father at one end of the sofas; Kerry the son on the other; a lager can in the hand of the former and a roach in the hand of the latter. The only thing different was the programme on the outsized television: something to do with antiques, incongruously enough.

"Mr. Kerry." Claire nodded at the father. "Caleb."

"How come I ain't Mr. Kerry too?" Caleb said sullenly. "I'm eighteen, y'know."

Claire ignored him. "I'm afraid I have some bad news for you. It's about Mark." She paused. "I'm sorry, I'm not sure exactly what the relationship is. He said uncle, I think the last time we were here?"

Callum Kelly's bloodshot eyes squinted, as if he was trying to focus on her or her question. "He's family." He struggled to pull himself up in his chair. He was definitely even more drunk than last time. She glanced across at Caleb. Yes, and he was more stoned. Was that all the pair of them had done since the last time she and Dave had seen them: get drunk and high? She tried to put her distaste to one side. What were men like this supposed to do? She remembered what Callum Kerry had said to her back at Foregate Street. *What else could I do?*

Caleb gave a wheezy laugh. "He gone and got himself in trouble, has he?"

Claire took a second to collect herself. There was never an easy way to deliver this kind of message. You just had to do it and get it over with. "I'm sorry to have to tell you that Mark is dead. He was killed, we believe late afternoon yesterday. I'm very sorry for your loss." She stood facing Callum Kerry, looking for his reactions, knowing that, as she had instructed him, Dave would be watching Caleb. She could practically see the news filtering into Callum's fuddled head, working its way through the swill of alcohol he was using to numb his pain. It took him several seconds to articulate any reaction.

"Where?"

Where? Not *how* or *who*. "The old Fitzmaurice brewery."

Callum frowned, the effort to think plain on his ravaged face. "Where our Clayton...?"

"Yes."

"Who did it?" Caleb called out.

"We don't know yet."

"Well, you'd better find out quick then, hadn't you?" Caleb spat. "Like Dad said, he was family."

"I was about to ask you both," Claire said with a forced, icy calmness, "if either of you had any idea who might want to kill or at least hurt Mark?"

"No one," Caleb said, affronted. "He was a good guy. No one would want to hurt Mark."

Claire turned back to Callum. He was sitting there, eyes unfocused, as if still trying to understand what he had been told. "Mr. Kerry? Can you think of anyone who might want to hurt Mark?"

The answer came slowly and with difficulty. "No. No, it's like what our Caleb just said. He was...a good guy."

"I suppose you're going to ask where we were when he was killed, aren't you?" Caleb demanded.

Claire looked down at the young man sprawled on the sofa. "No, I wasn't going to," she said. *Not yet anyway.* "But since you mention it. Where were you, yesterday afternoon, Caleb?"

"We were here, weren't we, Dad?" Caleb said immediately, as if the speed of the statement made the truth of it undeniable. "You can ask Mum or any of the kids. They'll all tell you."

And what a reliable bunch of witnesses they'd be. Claire put that thought to one side as irrelevant. Much as she'd have liked to smack the sneer off Caleb's ratty face, she and Dave hadn't come round to interview the Kerrys as suspects. For the moment at least, the Kerry family seemed once again to be the victim of tragedy, and she had no reason to see things otherwise. Yet. "Thank you. Well, Sergeant Lyon and I will be on our way. I'm sorry, but we'll probably have to talk to you again later as part of our investigation. For the moment, though, I'm sure you need some time alone. One thing before we do go. What do you think Mark was doing up at the Fitzmaurice brewery?"

Caleb gave another coughing laugh. "Knowing Mark? Probably laying flowers. For Clayton."

*

"What d'you think?"

"I think," Claire said, winding the car window down, "that if we were pulled over by Traffic now, you'd be done for driving under the influence of drugs just from the effects of passively smoking Caleb Kerry's bloody weed."

"Right. Nice tip about the vinegar by the way. Worked a treat. What I was meaning, though, was about the case? Think either of them were involved?"

Claire leaned back against the car head rest. "Why would they be? Mark kept Callum in drink and took Caleb off to Brum when he was feeling down. On brief acquaintance, he seemed the best adjusted of an admittedly maladjusted bunch. And you heard what they said. He was such..."

"...a good guy."

"Exactly."

"They were very insistent on that."

"Weren't they just? Thing is," she sighed, "maybe he was."

"He did save you from a nasty bump on the head."

"He did, didn't he?" Claire closed her eyes to think. "But there's *got* to be a link with Clayton's death, hasn't there? Family connection. Scene of crime. Within the space of a week. Too many coincidences?" She opened one eye and looked at her sergeant. "Or is that correlations? Anyway—" she closed her eye again. "What would be the motive? I mean, if either Callum or Caleb was the killer both times that would mean they'd killed either their son or brother as well. That's pretty heavy. No." Claire shook her head. "If the family isn't the link, what if it's the place? Why were both Clayton and Mark there in the first place?"

Dave considered what he knew about the former brewery's dodgy reputation. He held back from commenting. Not only did it not seem relevant in the case of Mark Smith, he also didn't want to risk Claire asking him for the source of his local knowledge. "D'you think it might have something to do with the owners, what was it, the Fitzmaurices?"

Claire snorted. "Don't be daft. I know they sound an inbred bunch of tossers, leaving the place to fall down and become dangerous while they all fight over who gets to actually inherit it, but I can't see the likes of them having any connection with the Kerry family, can you?"

They sat in silence for the rest of the journey back to Foregate Street. "It's no use," Claire said, as they got out of the car. "I need someone to have another look at Clayton Kerry. And this time I want them to look for other possible causes of death."

"Apart from part of a building collapsing on him? Okay. But I think we both know who's going to be cutting the Y section."

"Inspector Summerskill?" The desk sergeant was holding up his hand as they entered the station.

"What is it, Andy?"

"Visitor for you. Says it's urgent. Mr. Alun Blake?"

"The Kerrys didn't look like they were back from stoning teachers again," Dave said.

"No, it's not about the Kerrys this time," Andy said. "Mr. Blake says his daughter has gone missing."

*

Who do I like dealing with least? Dave wondered, as he watched his boss deal with a coldly angry Alun Blake. *Roughneck rogues like the Kellys, or tight-arse, middle-class pricks like Blake?* Reluctantly, he considered how unfair he was being to Blake. After all, the man was claiming that his daughter had possibly been kidnapped. On the other hand, as Claire was trying patiently to explain, it was far more likely she had run away. And if he'd had a father as uptight as Blake, Dave thought, he might quite possibly have run away too. Dave regarded him, sitting in front of Claire at her desk, a mirror image of their previous meetings with her sitting in front of his desk. Of course, Blake's office was a lot neater and more impressive than this one. He wondered if Claire felt the same.

*

"So you are saying, inspector, that after a verbal assault on the steps of my own school, a physical attack on myself in my office, and a near fatal attack on myself and my daughter in our car, you don't think my daughter's disappearance is anything to worry about?"

"I didn't say you shouldn't worry, Mr. Blake. Of course, you're going to worry, and I completely understand that. I'm a mother myself. But by your own admission, it's only been, what, six hours since you last saw her?"

"She has run away from *school,* inspector. She has left the premises without permission. She has *never* done that before. One of my staff had to come and tell me that my own daughter had truanted. Can you imagine the position that put me in? If you have children, inspector, can you begin to imagine how you would feel if someone told you one of your daughters had run off from school and gone God knows where?"

Claire made sure she avoided eye contact with Dave. He knew she had to be thinking of the day Tony had skipped school. "I have two sons, Mr. Blake."

"It's different with girls."

"Perhaps. However, I have to say again, a person, even a child, cannot be considered as missing until much longer than…."

"It's the Kerrys." Blake's face was pale with anger as he sat there, hands in his lap balled into fists. "You must know it was the Kerrys."

"Mr. Blake. I…"

"The attack in my office. The brick on my car. Are you honestly saying you don't know those were that man Kerry and his son?"

"Sergeant Lyon and I have just come from speaking to the Kerrys, and I can assure you…"

"About this?"

"No, Mr. Blake. About…another issue. But I can assure you, it is extremely unlikely that either Callum Kerry or Caleb Kerry have had anything to do with your daughter's disappearance." Vandalism and violence, quite possibly. But kidnapping? That just didn't fit the Kerry MO. "Has Anne ever run away from school before?"

"I told you, inspector, no."

"Has she ever run away from home before?"

For a moment, Dave thought Blake was about to surge up from his chair and pound Claire's desk with his fist. "No! That is... There have been...a couple of times over the last year or so when Anne has been late back home after school."

"A couple?"

"Perhaps as many as four times. No more. And we are only talking about a matter of an hour or so each time. Certainly, no more than two. Most parents probably wouldn't even have noticed such short absences, but I run a tight ship at home, inspector. Unlike some families."

Are you thinking about the Kerrys' family or mine?

"And do you know where she was on these occasions? With friends, perhaps? That's usually the case in these matters."

"Anne doesn't have any friends."

"I'm sorry? None? At all?"

If he felt any discomfort at Claire's obvious incredulity, Blake didn't show it in the slightest. "Anne is...a very private girl, inspector. Very self-sufficient. She doesn't make friends easily but then she doesn't really need them either. She enjoys her own company."

Or she doesn't want you to know what friends she has got.

Blake pressed on before he could be challenged. "And my being the headteacher of the school she goes to does place her in a slightly awkward position, socially."

Yes. It can't be easy being the daughter of a headmaster, let alone a headmaster as disliked by staff, pupils, and parents as you seem to be. "So, why send her to your school, Mr. Blake?"

Blake visibly bridled at the question. "I don't think that is any of your business, inspector."

"I'm sorry," Claire said, without regret. "You're right of course. No offence intended. Just curious. Is there anyone else then who Anne might be with at the moment? A relative? A friend of the family? Someone she could talk to?" She thought again of that time Tony had truanted. He'd run off without any clear thought of where he was going, just desperate to get away from a place and a situation that was making him want to explode. No thought of what to do when he did or what might happen after. Typical boy, she supposed. He'd just been lucky to bump into Dave. This time she did glance across to her sergeant, but as was typical when she was leading an interview, his head was down over his notepad as he took notes.

"No," Blake said, as if daring her to challenge him on that one.

Okay. No friends and no family. Right. If that's the way you want to play it. But at this moment, I've got more important fish to fry. "Mr. Blake. I understand your concern and I appreciate that recent circumstances have made you keen to know where your daughter is at all times. More so even than normal." She pressed on before he could rise to that one. "But I'm afraid I can assure you this kind of thing happens all the time. To every kind of family. Adolescents are pressure cookers. Sometimes they need to go somewhere else to let off steam."

"Inspector. I am the headteacher of a school of over thirteen hundred adolescents. I know what they are like."

"Quite. And I'm a police inspector, and as such I can tell you that the majority, the *vast* majority, of teenage runaways return within twenty-four hours, most well before that, certainly long before the police can or need to become officially involved. Now, ordinarily, I would advise you to go home and ring around friends and family to see if any of them have seen Anne. But," she said, raising her voice slightly to forestall the repeated objection she could see coming, "as you assure me there would be no point to that, I still say go home so that you can be there when she returns. And I *am* sure she will turn up very soon indeed. Please let us know as soon as she does. In addition, though, I will instruct the desk sergeant to circulate a note about Anne amongst duty officers and tell him I want to know immediately if a young girl in a Monastery Grove uniform is seen out and about tonight later than would be expected."

"Will you need a description?"

"I think the uniform will be enough for the moment. Now please, Mr. Blake. I'm sorry but I really must press on with other business."

Chapter Eleven

By the time she got back home that night, the threatening ache in Claire's temple had developed into a well-settled stabbing pain that no paracetamol or cold beer could touch. Once, not that long ago surely, she'd have asked Ian for some kind of massage, and he'd have been only too happy to help. Time was he would have offered before she needed to ask. Now, he didn't offer, and because he didn't offer, she felt she couldn't ask. When had that ease of communication stopped? When Sam had come along? But even before Sam, as far as Ian was concerned there had always been Tony. No, Claire didn't think it was down to the kids that the days of massages and roses had petered out. If she let herself think about it, she knew it had happened about the same time all of Ian's long meetings had begun.

Claire closed her eyes, massaged her temple, and refused to think about that. God knew she had plenty of other material crowding her brain, the sheer volume of it more than explaining her splitting headache.

Sitting at her kitchen table now with her husband and boys, she pecked at the microwaved meal that was all she'd had time to make for them. "It's fusion!" she'd told Tony as he'd wrinkled his nose at the combination of spaghetti Bolognese and chow mein. After a muttered complaint from Ian about high sugar and fat content that she'd shut down with a murderous glare, everyone had lapsed into a moody silence. Sam had been hyperactive since returning from the childminder. Claire suspected the minder's policy of no sugar or food additives was far from rigorously upheld. Now, the four-year-old was clearly on the down side of a sugar spike, and obviously struggling to stay awake as he pushed his food around his plate, more of it ending up on his table mat than in his mouth.

Claire speared a bean sprout with her fork and tried to wrap it in a strand of spaghetti. It was getting harder to deny that something was wrong with her family, broken even, and she hadn't got a clue what to do about it. Or the energy. But she knew she had to try.

It would be highly unethical to talk to her family in any detail about cases she was working on, and that wasn't something she normally ever wanted to do. Work and home should be two different worlds and Claire worked hard to keep those worlds separate. But work right now seemed determined to force itself into her private life. First, a boy from the school her son attended and where her husband taught had been killed. Now, a second young man linked to that family had been murdered, and the daughter of Ian and Tony's headmaster had gone missing. It was inevitable that she was going to have more to do with Monastery Grove. At least mentioning that possibility now might give both Tony and Ian a chance to ready themselves for seeing her on their turf as cop rather than mum. She's already witnessed Tony's meltdown when she'd had to do her police thing at school. Perhaps this would prevent him from doing it again. And Ian. She stabbed at a water chestnut distractedly. But she didn't want to do it in front of their youngest.

"All finished, Samby?" she asked the littlest with forced brightness. Sam nodded dumbly, less than half the food on his plate actually eaten. Claire took the fork from his sticky fingers and ruffled his hair. "Go on. Run along and get your jim-jams on. I'll be with you in a minute."

Too tired by now even to speak, Sam meekly did as he was told. Claire saw Ian's quizzical look. Normally one or the other of them would have taken Sam upstairs. Even coming down from sugar it was generally not wise to leave him to his own devices for too long. "He'll be all right. I just wanted to talk to you both about something." She pushed her own half eaten food away. "Look, it's going to be all over the news tomorrow, so I might as well tell you now. There's been another death at the Fitzmaurice brewery. And this time it's a murder."

"No way!" A sharp look from his mother told Tony he'd got the tone of his response wrong, and he sat back, trying to cover his obvious interest a little but more alert now than he had been all evening. "Was it Caleb Kerry?"

"What? No. Why would you think that?"

Tony shrugged. "Two deaths, one after the other, in the same place. There's got to be a link, hasn't there? And that one's the most obvious."

Claire gave a look of grudging approval. "Not bad detective work. Perhaps you take after your mam in more than just looks."

Unable to help himself, Tony grinned. "Besides," he went on, but then stopped.

"Besides what?"

"Nothing. Nothing really." Tony picked up his fork and poked at a half-eaten strand of pasta.

"I think what Tony was going to say," Ian said, "was that Caleb Kerry is as much of a git as his brother was. Sorry to speak ill of the dead. So, no one would be surprised if someone had offed him. That right, Tony?"

Tony shrugged noncommittally but didn't look up from his plate.

"Right. Y'know, I do wish you wouldn't use words like 'offed'. It makes you sound like a would-be East End gangster."

"So, who was it then if it wasn't Caleb Kerry?" Ian asked, paying no notice to Claire's rebuke.

"I...can't say," Claire admitted, aware both that she was skating on thin ethical ice discussing this with anyone outside Foregate Street, and that she had started a conversation in which she wouldn't be able to answer half the questions Ian and Tony might reasonably ask her.

"Well, can you tell us how he was killed?" Ian asked.

"He was stabbed."

"Figures," Ian said.

"Oh really?" Claire gave her husband the kind of look she might have given some wet behind the ears uniform who was a bit too full of himself. "And how exactly do you arrive at that conclusion?"

"Knife crime. It's on the rise, isn't it? That's what it says on the news anyway."

There was a lot Claire could have said about the way crime was reported by the media, particularly by certain local reporters, but she held back. Ian had, after all, been right. "Fair comment."

"At least this time," Ian went on, serenely unaware of his wife's irritation, "Blake won't be called on to deliver a eulogy." He waved his fork at Tony. "A eulogy..." he began.

"A speech about someone who's died. I know," Tony said. "We did it in First World War poetry last year. Jeez."

Claire shot Tony a warning mum look. "Yeah well, your head has got more than enough on his plate at the moment to be writing speeches about ex-pupils as well. Sorry, *students*." Husband and son both looked at her with even more interest. She began to wonder about the wisdom of this conversation. She hadn't pictured them both being quite so eager for gossip. "Okay," she said, rubbing her eyes. "Maybe, I shouldn't have said that. I'm tired. Forget it. It's nothing." When she took her hand away,

Tony and Ian were still looking at her, like dogs waiting for treats. *Well, at least we're sitting around a table talking together,* she thought. "Look, let anyone know I told you this and I'll have you both banged up for...pissing me off. Got it?" Tony and Ian nodded. "All right. Mr. Blake turned up the station today, worried because his daughter had gone missing. It'll be nothing," she added quickly in a bid to play things down. "She'll be back by tomorrow. She's probably back by now."

"Unless she's gone too far this time," Tony said.

"What do you mean by that?"

"Well, you know what she's like, don't you? You've seen her?" Tony shifted, uncomfortable at suddenly becoming the focus of his mum's interest. "She's like this real Goth chick, y'know?"

"'S true," Ian said.

Claire tried to recall Anne from the one brief moment she had seen her, sitting in the back of an ambulance. She hadn't appeared particularly Goth then, but she had been in school uniform, and at a distance. "So?"

"So," Tony said, "she's into the whole Goth vibe, isn't she? Dyed-black hair, white face. Really into doom and gloom all the time."

"Well, I don't know about the face and hair," Claire said, "but perpetual gloom doesn't sound that different from certain teenagers I know." It was meant to have been a light-hearted comment but sometimes, Claire realised, as Tony scowled at her, there was no such thing to an adolescent. They were as sensitive as exposed nerves.

"Well, at least I don't self-harm," Tony shot back.

"What?" Claire reined herself back. *More mum, less police officer.* "I mean, what do you mean?"

Tony ducked his head, looking at his mother through his fringe. He clearly knew he'd crossed a line somehow and wished he could retreat. Long experience, though, meant he knew there was little chance of that. "She cuts herself, all right? Everyone knows."

"No. Hang on," Claire said. "How could everyone know but no one be doing anything about it?" She looked to her husband. "Was anyone doing anything about it?"

"Well, yes and no," Ian said. "There's a lot of it about these days. More and more in fact. And there's not a great deal teachers can do about it. I mean what with all the reports and paperwork, and..."

"Yes, yes." Claire shut that one down before he could get going. "So, nothing is done for Anne or anyone like her? Even though, as you say, she is cutting herself?"

"There's a register," Ian said. Claire waited. "We call it a passport system. Any girl who is at risk from self-harm, and it does tend to be girls, has a passport, which means all their teachers are aware and have to look out for signs of it. Plus," he added, in a bid to beef up what, even to him, sounded pretty inadequate, "they'll get referred to CAMHS if..."

"CAMHS?"

"Community and Mental Health Services. If, as I was saying, there's a space, which increasingly there isn't, and if"—here Ian hesitated—"they have parental support."

Claire began to see where this was heading. "Alun Blake didn't give support for his daughter to be referred to CAMHS, did he?"

Now it was Ian's turn to shift uncomfortably in his seat. "Look, I shouldn't really be talking about this, y'know?" And he inclined his head in a not very subtle way in Tony's direction.

"Yeah, well, you and me both. So, Blake didn't give support?"

Ian sighed. "No. He didn't. Like Tony said, everyone knew about Anne, and everyone kept an eye out for her, but no one could officially do or say anything."

"They say she wears these really long-sleeved shirts, even in PE," Tony said, "so no one can see what she's done. But you can. Some of the girls make a thing about pulling her sleeves up so you can see the scars." He wrinkled his nose. "Some girls aren't very nice."

"Tell me about it," Claire said. "But what about, what do you call it, her form tutor? Isn't that the person who's supposed to have some kind of pastoral responsibility? Wouldn't he or she be doing something about it?"

Tony glanced at Ian and then down at his plate. Ian, too, looked unhappy about something. "Yes, she does. But like I said, it's difficult."

"Yeah. Right." Tony gave a weirdly mordant laugh. "It really is like *Romeo and Juliet*, isn't it?"

Claire frowned. "What do you mean by that?"

*

"Hello, David."

"What are you doing here?"

Sean Cullen pulled a mock-pained face. "If that's how you greet all your visitors no wonder you're such a lonely person."

Dave stood in the entrance to his flat, surprised by the MP's appearance, and painfully aware he'd been caught in his oldest T-shirt and bed shorts. As far as he could remember, he had never given Cullen his home address. "Who said I'm lonely?" he demanded, regretting the question the instant he'd asked it. Seconds into this meeting and Sean already had him feeling defensive.

"No one who isn't lonely goes to bed looking like that." Cullen indicated Dave's outfit. "I mean, please tell me you were going to bed. Alone. You don't actually walk around like that when people might see you, do you?" He smiled, enjoying, inevitably, the banter. "May I come in? Thank you."

Knowing that he shouldn't just let Sean into his home, that he should demand to know first why he was there, Dave stepped back to allow him to enter. Before he closed the front door, he took a quick look outside. No one there who might have seen Cullen. Good.

Turning back into his flat, he was struck immediately by how Sean's tall, broad-shouldered frame horribly emphasised the pokiness of his current home. The walls seemed to actually shrink around him. *Is that because of his size or his ego?* Dave wondered. But then he caught the smell of him, that rich, complex cologne, the muskiness that immediately stirred memories of their recent enthusiastic and energetic encounters. His mood lifted, at least a little, but he was still wary as to why Sean was there. Although the possibility of the obvious was not unwelcome.

Sean stood in the hall with a carefully contrived puzzled look on his face, hands held out as if he was slightly lost. "The living room's straight ahead," Dave said drily. "You literally can't miss it."

"Ah. Thank you."

In the living room, Sean looked around with the expression of polite interest he might have worn on being invited into a constituent's home to discuss bin collections or some other matter of local politics. Hotly aware of the disorder of his cramped home, and of the undeniable contrast it made with Sean's much more spacious and elegant flat, Dave gestured to the single armchair. "Please," he said, after having darted forward to snatch up the work shirt he had left there.

"Thank you." Sean went as if to sit but then turned and kissed Dave on the lips. Dave doubted he did that very often with his constituents. Surprised, he instinctively stepped forward to return the kiss properly, but Cullen had already sat down, and the moment had passed.

Sean sat there, looking up at Dave, smiling that self-satisfied smile. "Well. This is nice."

"Why have you come here?"

"Why, thank you. Yes, I will. I'll have a whisky, please."

"All right. I'm sorry. I'm a poor host. I'm just...surprised, that's all." Dave thought of the cheap bottle of supermarket whisky he had in one of his kitchen cupboards. He knew exactly what Sean would say if he offered him that. "I'm out of whisky though. Beer?"

"Imported?"

"All the way from Basement Booze round the corner."

"Then I think I'll pass. Are you going to sit down? Or is this how you interrogate suspects at your station?"

"You know how we interrogate suspects at Foregate." A cheap shot perhaps, but a small payback for Sean's condescension.

Sean nodded, understanding the reference to one of their earliest meetings. "True, though I was hardly a suspect."

"No. Just suspicious." Dave pulled over a small, wheeled chair from its position at his computer desk and went to sit down facing his unexpected guest.

Sean patted his leg. "You could always sit here."

"Like a ventriloquist's doll?"

"If that's where you'd like me to put my hand. But I was actually thinking like one man who...enjoys physical contact with another."

Dave sat down on his office chair. "And is that all this surprise visit is about? Physical contact?"

"Well, maybe that's not what it is *all* going to be about. But it would be a good start." Sean tipped his head to one side, as if scrutinising Dave. "Y'know, sometimes you're very..." He paused as if searching for just the right word.

"Spiky?"

"I was going to say stiff, but context is everything, isn't it? So, all right then, let's go with spiky."

"Perhaps I just don't like being messed around."

"And why do you think you're being messed around?"

Sean had joked about being in a police interview, but that was where Dave wished they were now. Police interviews were easy compared to conversations with Cullen. Even with the slipperiest, slimiest bad guy, he knew what he was doing, what he was trying to get out of someone. But this... "Why have you come here, Sean?" he asked again, trying to get a grip on the conversation.

"I was going to say I was in the area visiting constituents." Sean smiled. "But I wasn't. I came because I wanted to see you."

"Why?"

Sean affected surprise. "Because I enjoy having sex with you. Quite a lot. And I was hoping we could have some."

"And is that all it is? Sex?"

"Well, it will be while we're having it, yes. Have you got something else in mind? I warn you, I'm hopeless at multitasking."

"Everything's a joke with you, isn't it?"

"And I'm beginning to think that nothing is with you." Sean adopted a quizzical expression. "Can anyone make you laugh, Sergeant Lyon? Go on, name someone. That previous boyfriend of yours? What was his name? Dick?"

"Richard."

"Understandable mistake. So, did he? Make you laugh? No," he continued, before Dave could answer. "I didn't think so. And you've not mentioned any boyfriends before him. So, what about at work, down at good old Foregate Street? I can't imagine my dear friend Tom, that's Chief Superintendent Madden to you, is exactly a bundle of laughs. How about your other colleagues? Bunch of buzzkills the lot of them from what I've seen. Though there is that rather handsome one..."

"Cortez," Dave said immediately, just as quickly wishing he hadn't.

"...who had a bit of a fling with my friend Susie."

"Hardly a..."

"Although she said in the end he was as scintillating as a glass of milk."

Terry Cortez's ham-fisted attempt to gain Susan Green's confidence in a previous case had been a long way from anything remotely resembling a fling or a flirtation. But her withering description of him hadn't been far from the truth. Dave held his tongue.

"And as for your boss, well. She's hardly going to raise a smile, is she? Let alone anything else."

"DI Summerskill and I get on very well, actually." Dave stopped, annoyed at again being baited so easily, and by sounding so embarrassingly wet.

"Well," Sean said, obviously amused, "I hope you'll both be very happy together." He tilted his head to the other side, as if studying Dave from a different angle this time. When he spoke again, it was in a noticeably softer tone of voice. "I really do have your best interests at heart, you know."

You're handsome, intelligent, successful, Dave thought, looking at the man sitting across from him, as if it was he who owned the room, not Dave. *You come here just to see me, and you say things like that, and I don't know whether to believe a bloody word of it. You are unlike any man I have ever met, and I don't know if I like that or hate that or if I should like that or hate that.* "Oh, for God's sake," he said out loud, "Why is it so hard for two men to just...get on?"

"Get on? Or get on *with it*?"

Dave threw his hands up. "You see? There you go again. Joking. Laughing. Point scoring. Is this what gay relationships are all about?"

Sean leaned forward. "Don't you know? And is that what this? A relationship?"

Dave raised his hands as if surrendering. "All right. I've got to say that right at this moment, I admit to feeling..."

"Spiky?"

Despite himself, Dave laughed. "I was going to say stiff."

Cullen reached forward and laid his hand on the top of Dave's thigh. "What a happy coincidence. Can I suggest therefore we move this meeting on to somewhere more appropriate? I noticed a delightful little broom cupboard off the hallway on my way in."

"That's my bedroom, as well you know."

"Charming. Shall we?" Cullen rose from his chair and held out his hand. Dave stood up, took it, and let Sean draw him in close. They kissed again, for much longer this time. "See," Sean murmured. "I can put a smile on that handsome face of yours. Now let's go and see what I can do for the rest of your body."

*

"It's just, like...people dying and a girl missing. And a dagger. Stabbings." Tony ran his hand through his hair. Claire recognised it as something he did when he was nervous. He got it from her. "Look, why are you grilling me like I'm some kind of suspect?"

"Because you're not the kind of lad who routinely compares real life with Shakespeare. And I want to know why that Shakespeare in particular. There are loads of Shakespeare plays where people are killed with daggers, and this was a knife by the way, so why choose that one and not—" She paused, suddenly aware that knife crime in Shakespeare was not one of her strengths. "*Hamlet*." She caught her husband's eye. "Belt up!"

"Because," Tony said, with the resignation of someone finally submitting to torture, "it's about lovers, too, isn't it? Anne Blake and Clayton Kerry. Everyone knew that Anne Blake and Clayton Kerry were...together."

"What? Like, boyfriend and girlfriend?"

Tony snorted. "I was going to say shagging, but I thought—"

"Okay, okay. Don't go getting snarky with your mam."

"This other dead person, the stabbed one. Was he like their Mercutio?"

Unwilling to admit she couldn't answer because she didn't have a clue who Mercutio was, Claire turned to Ian. "Did you know this?"

"Well, it was one of those things that people knew but..."

"...but didn't do anything about. Y'know, I'm beginning to wonder if anyone actually does anything about *anything* in that ruddy school of yours. I can't imagine why you need all these bloody meetings. Why didn't anyone tell me this before?"

"You going to tell me who the stabbed guy is first?" Tony asked, thinking for a moment he might have some kind of trading advantage.

"Don't try bargaining with me, sunshine," his mother growled. "I've banged up better than you for less."

Ian and Tony exchanged wide-eyed looks of surprise. Another time, Claire might have been pleased at that brief instance of son and stepfather on the same page. But not now. "Why didn't anyone tell me about Anne and Clayton?"

"Why should we have?" Tony said.

"He's right," Ian said. "You haven't even mentioned Anne before tonight."

Frustrated by the logic of the response but determined to ignore it for the moment, Claire sat and thought through this new, unexpected information. Could it have something to do with Anne's disappearance? Could it even have something to do with Clayton's death? "All right. Say for the minute that it's true. How did people know? Was it an out in the open thing?"

"Like, yeah! They were all over each other. Breaks. Lunchtimes. Kissing in the corridors, tongues and everything. Groping each other's..."

"I get the picture."

Tony grinned, clearly pleased he'd been able to get at least some payback for this interrogation by making his mum squirm. "And the tagging of course."

"What? Graffiti?"

"Yeah. Everywhere. *I heart Clayton. Anne and Clayton for ever. A4C.* You know the kind of thing."

"Oh yes. I know the kind of thing." One of Claire's earliest jobs as a young WPC on the beat had been engaging local youths in endless cat and mouse operations aimed at stamping out their graffitiing anything and everything that didn't move, and some things that did. She could still see the brightly coloured, angular designs, all as unreadable as Arabic to her, until a young lad called Diesel, brought in for petty theft, had sat down with her in the station and taken her through the most common tags while he was waiting for his brief, explaining which gangs or individuals they referred to and how they came to look the way they did. Yes, the images of many of them were still clear in her mind. And there was something else there too. Something more recent. "Hang on a minute!"

Claire got up quickly from the table, came back with a Biro, and hastily scribbled something on one of the paper napkins she'd put ready to mop up Sam's inevitable mess. "Anything like this?" She shoved the paper over to Tony. On it she'd sketched the design from the handle of the knife that had killed Clayton.

"Yeah, that's one of them," Tony said. "*A4C.*" He pushed the napkin back to his mum. "They say one of them went and wrote it once on the door to the head's office and he went apeshit. After that it was a competition for everyone to see who could get it anywhere near where he would see it. One Friday afternoon after last lesson, I..." He stopped, just on the brink of an unfortunate confession. "I mean, someone wrote it in the dirt on the back of the head's car. Since then, he's always kept it really clean."

"Nice one," Ian murmured.

Tony needn't have worried that he'd nearly incriminated himself in an act of minor vandalism. Claire was too focused on the napkin. Of course. It was obvious, once you knew, like one of those puzzle pictures that was just a mess of lines and colours until you concentrated and suddenly it twisted and came into focus. Whoever had scratched the tag onto the knife handle had had to use straight lines instead of curves and then stylised it by superimposing the letters onto the number but once you understood that it was clear. *A4C. Anne for Clayton.*

So, Clayton and Anne had been an item. Clayton had been killed. Less than one week later a close friend, some sort of relation of the family, was killed, too, murdered by a knife that had Anne and Clayton's tag on it. Hate it though she did, she agreed with Aldridge that the knife was a girl's, so it was probably Anne's. And she had gone missing.

Anne's absence from home was suddenly a lot more significant. Claire half rose from the table. She should tell Dave. She sank back down again. What was the point? There was nothing more they could do that night. Tomorrow, though, she was going to have to rethink her approach. She became aware that Ian was saying something.

"There was the truancy too," Ian said. "It was pretty obvious that when one of them was off, so was the other. And everyone knew that Alun wouldn't have let Anne have a day off for anything less than open heart surgery."

Interesting. Blake tried to make out that Anne's truancy from school today had been a one-off thing. Was that protecting his daughter's reputation or his own? "I'm beginning to see now why Mr. Blake found it hard to say anything good about young Clayton when he died."

"That's not the half of it. Rumour is that Blake's wanting to keep his precious little girl away from Clayton was what really got the lad permanently excluded."

"Whoa, whoa, whoa." Claire held up her hands. "Slow down and rewind. You're saying that Clayton wouldn't have been kicked out of school if he hadn't been..."

"...shagging," Tony volunteered.

"...going out with the headmaster's daughter?" She thought back to her first interview with Clayton's father in the Foregate interview room, the protests that his son's exclusion had been unfair. *"There's worse up at that school."*

Ian was looking uncomfortable, realising, like Tony before him, that he might have gone just a bit too far. "It was just gossip."

Claire concentrated, forcing herself to ignore her headache as she worked to put together these new pieces of the picture. "But I thought Clayton was this real troublemaker. A bad lad. Where did I...?" She clicked her fingers. "It was you," she said to Tony. "You told me he was trouble."

"He was," Tony insisted, all outrage. "I didn't say he was the only one though. Or even the worst."

"He was a handful, love," Ian said. "I didn't teach him in his last couple of years, but I had him lower down in the school and he was hard enough to deal with then. But I'll agree with Tony. We've got kids who are as bad as Clayton was, if not worse, and yet we still seem to hold on to them, whereas we let Clayton go."

"Maaaa-aam."

Sam's plaintive wail from upstairs brought all of them quickly back to the there and then. Claire shoved the napkin to one side and rose from the table. "Well, thanks for finally telling me all that. And I'll tell you now, you'd better watch out for me tomorrow. I need to be back down that school of yours and asking a few questions."

Neither Tony nor Ian could conceal their dismay at this, both uncomfortably aware that what they'd just told Claire might quite easily be traced back to them. "Who're you going to be talking to?" Ian asked.

"If she's there, Anne Blake will be top of my list. But I've a bad feeling now she won't be. So that means I'll want anyone who knows her, kids and staff. I'm not waiting forty-eight hours before moving on this one."

"D'you think she did it then?" Tony's eyes were wide. "Do you think she killed this, whoever it is, with a knife? That really would be like *Romeo and Juliet*."

Claire regarded her eldest with disbelief. "It is *nothing* like *Romeo and Juliet*. Juliet did not kill Romeo." *That much I do know. I think.* She paused, something about that image triggering unexpected and as yet half-formed thoughts. She shook her head and headed once again for the stairs and the more immediately needy Sam. "I'll want to talk to Mr. Blake of course," she called over her shoulder, "if he's in with all this going on."

"He'll be in," Ian said dourly.

"And Anne's, what do you call her, form tutor? The one who's supposed to be pastorally responsible? What's her name?"

She stopped at the foot of the stairs. Suddenly, unexpectedly, everything had changed. For just a few minutes there, the horrible tension of recent weeks between her son and her husband had eased as they had all come together over this one topic. But now, the atmosphere had soured again, the contrast with what it had been just before making it even more horrible.

"It's Ms. Grant," Ian said quietly. "Cassie Grant."

Tony pushed his chair back roughly and hurried from the room.

*

Interesting, Dave thought.

Not the sex. That hadn't been interesting. That had been great. It was how he was feeling now, afterwards, lying in bed with Sean. Inevitably, given the hour and their exertions, they'd both fallen asleep, and Dave had woken to find Sean still asleep, turned into him, one arm across his body, his head on Dave's shoulder.

Dave didn't think of himself as a callous man, certainly not one of the "wash and go" brigade from hookup apps. But during his recent experiences with online "dating" he'd yet to find a guy he wanted to stay around for very long after they'd done what had been uppermost in their minds from the start. And now...he wasn't sure how he felt about Sean. Did he want him to stay? What for? To chat? They hardly seemed able to do that without trying to score points off each other, and that was only fun as foreplay. Should Dave ask him to stay? Would Sean want to? Sod it. Was it just gay relationships that were this much hard work? Was it his fault or Sean's? Was this even a relationship? Was it...?

"Penny for them?" Sean said without moving or opening his eyes.

"How did you know I was thinking about anything?" Even in the darkness of his bedroom Dave knew that Sean was smiling.

"I don't believe there's ever a time when you're not thinking, David." Sean leaned over and kissed him lightly on the check and then rolled back and got up. He turned on the bedside lamp and reached for his clothes. Dave noticed they were quite neatly folded in a pile on the floor while his were just thrown in a heap. How had Sean managed that? He'd thought they'd both been too eager to get naked and into bed to worry about where the clothes fell. "You can stay if you want to?" There, he'd said it. Now the balls were in Sean's court.

Sean didn't pause getting dressed. "And leave your flat in the morning wearing the same clothes as when I arrived last night? What would the neighbours think?"

"You've got a comfortable majority. What do you care?"

"My, my, sergeant. We are beginning to loosen up a little, aren't we?"

Irritated by the patronising tone, Dave went to get up from the bed and dress, too, but stopped. It was three in the morning. Where would he go? He sank back, deciding instead to go for a replay of the last time he and Sean had been together, except this time it would be him lying back being all nonchalant and sexy. So, he lay there watching Sean dress, and quickly realised that he felt neither nonchalant nor sexy, just posed and uncomfortable. "All right," Dave said, looking for something to fill the silence. "A penny for *your* thoughts."

"Oh, I never sell anything so cheaply," he said, "but, if you must know, I was thinking about young PC Jones."

"What?" There were a number of things Dave had thought Sean might have been thinking about. Joe bloody Jones had not been one of them. "Why were you thinking about him?"

Sean whipped his tie round in three decisive moves that somehow managed to create the perfect knot. "I was just wondering what it would have been like to be in bed with two policemen. At the same time, that is. You know me. Always up for new experiences."

Dave sat up, completely uninterested now in appearing cool. "Is that all this is? An experience? How many coppers can I cop off with? Why don't you just carve a notch on the bedpost on your way out?"

"Don't be silly, David," Sean tutted. "I'll carve it on *my* bedpost, not yours. I could hardly keep count if I had to keep coming over here to tot up, could I? Oh, and I like that line about copping off with coppers. Very good. Used it before?"

"You are a cold bastard, aren't you?"

Sean paused in the act of pulling on his jacket. "Yes. But not here and now. I'm just playing the game, and I'm playing by the good guys' rules. I haven't lied to you or cheated on you or made you do anything you haven't wanted to do, very enthusiastically I might add. I...like you, I really do, and I hope you like me. And that's all there is to it. Isn't it?" He stood, fully dressed now, looking down at Dave, waiting.

"Yes."

Sean looked thoughtful for a moment and then nodded. "Good. Then you'll allow me a little fantasy about improving my police-politician liaisons. That's all it is: a bit of fantasy."

"Or a bit of a challenge?"

Sean laughed. "Aren't they the same thing? I'd better be going. Good night, David." He walked back to the bed and for a moment, Dave thought he was going to lean over and kiss him. Instead, Sean just stood there, looking down at him thoughtfully. "You know, you really ought to get to know PC Jones better."

Dave was incredulous. He was getting the same advice now from the man he'd just been to bed with that he'd been getting earlier from his boss. "Why? Just because he's gay?"

Sean's smile appeared almost wistful in the shadows cast by the bedside lamp. "Don't be dense, David. Because he's very good-looking and you have a great deal in common. Believe me, it's not easy sharing your life with someone who doesn't understand the demands of your day job. And also, because I think he seems a very decent young man. *Au revoir.*" Sean left, closing the door behind him.

Dave sat in his bed, listening to the sound of Sean walking down his hallway, opening the front door, and closing it behind him. "*Decent young man,*" he said to the empty bedroom. "Like you'd fucking know!"

Chapter Twelve

"You're late."

"I thought that was my line."

"It usually is." Claire scrutinised her sergeant. As neatly groomed and well-turned out as ever. But there was...something. She couldn't quite put her finger on it. "Late night?"

"Yes."

Claire settled back in the car seat. At last. And good timing too. Something to take her mind off what lay ahead in the day. "Do tell."

"Working on these." Without taking his eyes off the road, Dave pulled a folder from the door well next to him and passed it to his boss. It was the work he had managed to get done before Sean had called, but Summerskill didn't need to know that. "Proposed schedule for today. Madden sent the go-ahead down last night after you'd left."

"Did he give us what we wanted?"

"Of course not. He's cut you back by about twenty-five percent. You me, two other officers. That's your lot."

She left the folder unopened on her lap. "It doesn't matter anyway. We've got a change of direction." She outlined what she had learned the previous night.

"Okay. This is interesting. You might even squeeze another officer out of Madden for that. Station first to rally the troops then back to school?"

"Yeah. Though I want to give Mr. Blake a call first, to see if his daughter came back last night. I've already checked in with the overnight desk and they didn't see anything of her. I've got a feeling she won't have come back. According to Ian, that won't stop Blake going to work, so a trip to Monastery will kill two birds with one stone."

They drove on for another few minutes. "You know you're driving even more slowly than usual."

"Probably the extra weight the car's carrying. Ma'am."

"Meaning what exactly?"

"Y'know. The elephant in the car."

"I don't..." Claire stopped. What was the point? "All right. Ms. Grant." She drew the *Ms.* out in a sarcastic buzz.

"That's the pachyderm."

"Stop showing off."

"Sorry. So?"

"Like I said"—Claire looked out of the passenger window as she spoke—"what Tony told you about Ian and this Ms. Grant was just gossip. There was nothing to it."

They drove on for another couple of minutes.

"And yet?" Dave said.

"What?"

Dave considered. Was he misjudging this? Three months now they'd been working together. Too soon to comment on his boss's personal life? He'd kind of got sucked in, though, hadn't he, when Tony and he had had their little coffee shop chat. And personal and professional looked like getting even further tangled today. "Look, you've obviously not really been yourself for a couple of weeks. At the same time, Tony's been getting more and more sulky. And when you mentioned Ms. Grant's name just now...you got that look."

"What look?"

"That look you have when you know you're going to have to arrest someone and you're pissed off because of all the paperwork it'll involve."

"Show me."

Dave contrived to frown, lift one eyebrow slightly, and thin his lips.

"You look like you're going for a dump."

"That's what I thought first time I saw you do it."

"I do not have a look."

"If you say so."

They drove on.

"Speaking of Tony by the way." Dave indicated the empty seat in the back of the car.

"I've given him the day off. You saw what he was like the last couple of times we were on the school premises. If he saw us in full investigation mode, I think he'd combust."

"And Ian? He going to be okay with his missus casing the joint?"

"Don't ever call me his missus. And yes, I did suggest he take the day off, too, but you know what he's like. 'More trouble than it's worth, setting work, letting kids and staff down, yada yada yada.'"

"Shame. Might have made it a bit easier if you have to bump into Ms. Grant."

"And we're back to the elephant."

"Unfair. She might actually be quite attractive. Sorry, that really wasn't very helpful, was it?"

"No. And there's no *if* about it. I *will* be bumping into Ms. Grant."

Dave chose his next words very carefully. "Is that, altogether, the best course of action? Potential conflict of interest and all that. I could interview her. You don't have to..."

"I want to see her, Dave."

Dave noted that use of his name rather than his rank and stopped. They drove on for a few more minutes in silence before he cleared his throat and spoke again. "You know I'll be there if...well, if you need anything."

"I'll need you to make notes like you always do in that notebook of yours. But, thanks," she added.

They were nearly at Foregate Street before Claire spoke again. "Oh, by the way," she said, "I'm asking for PC Jones to come along."

"Because he's good with kids?" Dave said suspiciously.

"Partly, but mainly because, as you have worked out, I am having a shit time of things right now, and I need to get my laughs where I can."

Despite himself, Dave relaxed slightly. Now that sounded more like the Inspector Summerskill he was coming to know and...like. "You do know that gay men were not put on this planet just to be a source of amusement for straight women?"

"Not true. Name any Hollywood film you like. The gay friend is always there for comic relief."

They pulled into the station. "By the way," Dave said as they got out, "you've still got that look on your face."

*

One phone call was enough to confirm both that Anne Blake had not returned home that evening and that Alun Blake had indeed gone into work at Monastery Grove as Ian had predicted. Summerskill and Lyon assembled their small team and set off for the school. On arrival, Claire and Dave left their small contingent of officers in the reception area to enjoy coffee with the excited receptionists while they went to speak to the headteacher.

Lot neater here than the last time, Dave thought on entering Blake's office. He shook hands after Claire, sat down, took out his notepad, and watched Blake as his boss began to talk. Outwardly as calm and corporate as ever. Dave doubted if he would have been so composed if his own daughter had gone missing. Not that that was ever going to be a problem. Surely, there must be some sign of anxiety, tension at the least? Maybe those lines around the eyes and mouth?

Summerskill got straight to the point. "The situation seems to have changed somewhat since the last time we spoke, Mr. Blake. We've received some new information. Why didn't you let us know that there had been a relationship between your daughter and Clayton Kerry?"

Dave saw it then, the small tic in the corner of Blake's eye, the slight flexing of the hand resting on the top of his desk.

"It was hardly a *relationship,* inspector. And why on earth would I have referred to Clayton Kerry? Who's been saying that there was anything between them?"

"In the last two weeks," Claire went on, ignoring the last part of Blake's question, "you have been attacked in your office and in your car. I'll concede now that the people responsible were almost certainly from the Kerry family, possibly because of some bad feeling connected with your having expelled, I'm sorry, *excluded,* Clayton from this school. Now your daughter has gone missing and you don't think it's relevant to mention that he and your daughter were, at the very least, close?" She paused a moment, not really expecting Blake to say anything. "Why did you exclude Clayton, Mr. Blake?"

There was no doubting Blake's surprise at that question, nor his anger. "What the hell does that have to do with my daughter's disappearance now?"

"Perhaps nothing, perhaps everything, but it is a start. We know that Clayton was far from being a model pupil..."

"Student! And yes, he was. Very far."

"But we've also heard that he was no worse than others you've managed to keep on roll. So why was Clayton kicked out when others haven't been?"

Blake was silent for a few seconds, and Dave could almost feel the effort it was costing him to keep still and his voice level. Summerskill had rattled him more than that howling mob on the steps of his school the other day. Interesting.

"The boy was a vandal, a bully, and quite possibly…involved in a range of other antisocial activities. Just exactly where are you getting this information about our exclusion record, inspector? And, as I have said, it was my understanding you were here to ask questions relating to the disappearance of my daughter, not the exclusion of a known troublemaker."

"And that is exactly what we are going to do, Mr. Blake," Claire said, once again sidestepping the potentially awkward matter of her sources.

Never grass on your snitches, Dave thought, *especially if they're your son and husband.*

"So, let's get down to it, shall we? We'd like a couple of rooms we can use as interview rooms and the names of any students Anne would consider friends."

"As I told you last time, inspector, Anne has no friends."

Not bothering to conceal her scepticism, Claire went on. "Then we'll need registers of the classes Anne is in and of her teachers."

"You're going to interview staff?"

There it is again. That tic. He'd be a terrible poker player. Or maybe, Dave thought, *I'd be a good one.*

"Yes. Is that a problem?"

"No. Of, course not. It's just… One doesn't relish one's private and public life being intertwined in this way."

"Believe me, Mr. Blake, I understand that," Claire said. "But your daughter is missing. There have been two deaths in the past week that may, and I stress may, be connected with that in some way. I think the sanctity of our private lives may well have to take second place for a while, don't you?

"Two deaths?" Blake frowned. "Do you mean to say…? That murder on the news this morning?"

"Yes, I'm afraid so."

"Is there anyone else Anne might have gone to, Mr. Blake?" Dave asked, partly to take the man's mind away for a moment from that startling piece of news Claire had dropped on him. Just occasionally, he did wonder about his boss's people skills. "You say there are no friends, and I think you ruled out immediate family too. What about more distant relatives. Grandparents? Any uncles, aunts, cousins Anne might feel close to?"

"Nobody."

"Is that nobody near or simply nobody?"

"Nobody. That is..."

"Yes, Mr. Blake?"

Summerskill and Lyon watched as Mr. Blake wrestled with some private thought. "There is her mother," he said at last.

"I'm sorry?" Claire said. "Her mother? You weren't going to tell us about Anne's *mother?* But I thought..." She stopped. She'd thought Blake was a widower but then realised she didn't know why. Was it something Ian had told her, or had she just assumed that any man bringing up a child, especially a girl, on his own must be doing so because his partner had died?

Blake's face was absolutely impassive, his tone carefully neutral. The effort it was costing him to keep them that way was almost palpable. "Anne's mother is not very maternal," he said. "They are not close. Anne hasn't seen her in nearly three years."

"I see."

Dave could tell that Claire couldn't, and knew they were both going to be very interested in finding out why. "If you'd be so kind as to give us an address, Mr. Blake," he said, "we'll make contact to see if your daughter is with her. Unless," he added, "you have been in touch already?" Blake shook his head. *Thought not.* "Right."

Blake gave them the address. They noticed he didn't need to look it up. It was for somewhere on the outskirts of Birmingham. Not one of the nicer parts, Dave noted, but not that far away if a mother and daughter wanted to see each other. Or if a daughter needed somewhere to run away to. Dave flipped his notepad closed.

"Thank you. One more thing, Mr. Blake," Claire said.

And here's the crunch, Dave thought. He and Claire had both agreed, walking in, that this was going to be the hardest part of the interview. "I'd like to send a couple of my officers to your house, with your permission of course. To have a look in Anne's bedroom."

"Police in my house!"

And there's that tic again. And the hands.

"Yes, Mr. Blake."

"What the hell for?"

"I'm afraid we won't know until we look. Letters perhaps? A diary. Something that might give us a clue as to where your daughter has gone. You may, if you wish, accompany the officers we send. I would actually prefer it."

Dave watched the head as a conflict of feelings played itself out.

"Very well, inspector," Blake said. "And yes. I would definitely like to be present when police are on my property."

"Thank you. Put a call through to Jenny, will you?" she asked Dave. "Tell her to take one of Chris's new team and meet Mr. Blake at his house. The desk sergeant has the address." She turned back to the headteacher. "All right," she said briskly. "Shall we make a start?"

*

The morning passed in a succession of interviews with Anne Blake's teachers. Again and again, Summerskill and Lyon were presented with the same description of a quiet girl who kept to herself, was no trouble in class, and who was most definitely coasting in all of her subjects.

"Yes, I taught her when she first came to the school," an English teacher told them, "and she was a quiet little thing even then, though there were signs of enthusiasm and ability, especially in her writing. But then it was like a switch had turned and suddenly she was this silent knot of hostility, sitting in the back of the class and doing the absolute minimum."

"Like a switch you say. When was that? And do you know of anything that might have caused that?" *Like trouble at home? A mother running away? Or being forced away?*

"Between Year Eight and Nine," said the teacher, a man who, Claire thought, looked hardly old enough to be out of school himself. Was this how people felt when they said young policemen made them feel old? "And no, I'm afraid I don't know of anything in particular that might have been the cause." He gave a small laugh. "I blame the summer holidays. God knows what happens to the kids then, but they leave in July normal and friendly, and come back in September hostile monsters. Hormones I suppose."

Claire assumed an expression of mixed sympathy and understanding, even while thinking of Tony's current truculence. She briefly wondered what testosterone-fuelled hell Sam might have in store for her in ten years' time.

"And did Anne have a boyfriend, d'you know?" Claire inserted this question or a variation into every interview, and the response was almost always the same. The teacher questioned looked away briefly into the middle distance, as if considering how best to answer, and then told of how Anne and Clayton, having previously given no signs of even being aware of each other's existence, had somehow come together at the start of Year Eleven and become virtually inseparable until Clayton's exclusion from the school. "But," another teacher had concluded, "I don't think they could really have been boyfriend and girlfriend, could they? I mean, they were so different, weren't they?"

The interview with Anne's form tutor, Cassie Grant, was fixed for the end of the morning. Dave noticed that Claire had rearranged his schedule to make this so. "Want me to pop out for a coffee or something?" he asked as one of the secretaries put her head around the door to announce that Ms. Grant was on her way. That would hardly have been standard practice, but then he suspected this was hardly going to be a standard interview.

"No. Shift." Claire reached for his chair. The room they'd been allocated was a curiously long, narrow space that must have been difficult to teach in. The secretary who had taken them to it had practically apologised for it, explaining it used to be a locker room until the increasing size of the school intake had necessitated its conversion into a classroom. Dave and Claire had set up their chairs close to the door, arranging them in as informal and relaxing a way as was possible under the circumstances. Now, Dave watched as Claire took the chairs and moved them all the way to the far end of the room, setting hers behind the desk there, his to one side and the other directly in front of it. Whoever came in now would have to walk the length of the room to get to them and sit like a naughty pupil in front of the teacher's desk. *Or like an accused woman up before the judge,* Dave thought. The two officers took their places and waited. Eventually the knock came. "Come in," Claire said.

Dave watched Cassie Grant as she took the long walk his boss had made for her. She was tall, dressed in a long skirt and plain blouse. Dave tried to remember what subject she taught. He was guessing English, something in the arts anyway, given her appearance, that balance of casual and business-like that female teachers in general and the "artsy" ones in particular seemed to achieve so well. She might have been a year or two younger than Claire though he was a notoriously bad judge of female age. Undoubtedly attractive, her most striking feature was her hair, a mane of fiery red that swept down well past her shoulders. Yes, on the whole a looker. Dave wondered why he'd never had such attractive female teachers when he was at school. But then again, perhaps he had. He'd only ever had eyes for the male teachers. That one Geography teacher in particular... He shook his head and dragged his erring mind back to the job in hand.

Claire held out her hand, but it was only to gesture to the chair in front of the desk. "Please sit down, Miss Grant."

Right, thought Dave. *Game on.* They'd both noticed the use of "Ms." in all the lists and registers they had been given. There had even been a slight emphasis on that title from the secretary, along with just a whiff of disapproval. Claire had pointedly ignored it.

If Claire's failure to use her chosen title annoyed her, Cassie Grant gave no sign. "Thank you, sergeant," she said.

"Inspector."

"Oh yes, of course. I'm sorry."

Fifteen all. Dave took out his pencil and held it poised over his notepad.

"I'm sorry I'm a bit late," Ms Grant continued. "I'm afraid I was caught up in a little incident in Piccadilly. That's a T-junction in the main part of the school," she explained in response to Dave's puzzled expression. "No one's really sure why it's called that. I think it's because it's always a bit of a circus when the bells go."

Nervous chatter? She does look a bit on edge. More so than any of the other teachers? Being summoned to help police with their investigations did tend to make people anxious. But if the woman in charge was the wife of someone you...knew. That might *really* make you feel tense. *Does she know?* Dave wondered. Claire used her maiden name professionally. Cassie Grant might not even be aware that Mr. Webster was Inspector Summerskill's better half. *She must do,* he decided. *But does it matter?* Claire had insisted that any talk of hanky-panky between Ian and this teacher was just gossip. But that had been before an attractive redhead had walked into the room. Dave stole a glance at Claire. *Yup. There's the look.*

"You're Anne Blake's form tutor, I believe," Claire said.

"Yes, I am."

"And have you been her tutor since she started here at Monastery Grove?"

"No, Anne's previous tutor was a Mr. Steward. A music teacher. Odd man. Went off to Brazil, I think. Or Gloucester." She attempted a smile, dropping it quickly when she saw it wasn't returned. "Anyway, I'd been a Year Eleven tutor, and when they left school, I took over Mr. Steward's form."

"Wouldn't you normally have started with another Year Seven?" Dave asked, trying to offset Claire's coldness with a touch of polite interest.

"Ordinarily," Cassie Grant said, addressing him with obvious relief at his friendlier tone. "But 10.9 had always had a bit of a reputation, you see, some of it not entirely their own fault. Mr Steward really had been a very odd man. Anyway, instead of giving it to one of the new teachers in the school as would normally have been the case, it was given to me. I don't want to blow my own trumpet, but I get on quite well with some of the more difficult kids."

"Good for you," Claire said.

"And for the school," Dave quickly added.

"And was Anne Blake a difficult kid?" Claire continued.

Reluctantly, Ms. Grant looked back to Claire. "She...had her challenges. Every child does."

"Which doesn't really answer the question."

At what point, Dave wondered, and in what way could he remind his boss that they were there to pick up useful information, not to interrogate a murder suspect?

"What precisely were Anne Blake's challenges?"

"Anne is a young woman with certain...issues."

"She's fifteen so legally very much still a child not a woman. A child who has been a self-harmer."

Ms. Grant blinked in surprise. "I believe she was, yes. How did you...?"

"You *believe* she was? Wasn't she on some kind of register or something? My understanding is that any kid with a challenge or issue like that would be on some kind of register, have some kind of care plan."

"I'm sorry, inspector." Dave noted Ms. Grant's shift into a more clipped, almost prissy tone of voice. It was the defensive tone that harried witnesses adopted in court when being subjected to hostile cross-examination. Cassie Grant had recognised that she was in for a confrontation. "One gets used to a professional reticence when talking about our students. I'm not used to speaking to the police about them. Yes, the school has a system of PSPs. Personal Support Plans. We call them passports in this school."

"I know. And Anne had one of these passports?"

Cassie Grant hesitated. "No."

"No? Why not?"

"Being given a passport, put on the PSP list, it can't be done...without the family support."

"Ah. Which in this case means the father?"

"Yes."

"The headmaster of this school?"

"We prefer headteacher, but yes."

"That must have made Anne even more challenging."

Ms. Grant said nothing.

"Did Anne have a boyfriend, Miss Grant?"

Cassie Grant didn't seem as surprised by the question as most of the other teachers had. Dave even had the feeling she'd been waiting for it. "You mean Clayton?"

"You taught him?"

"Yes. Or rather, he was in my form too. Before... Well, before he was excluded."

Claire indicated to Dave who quickly shuffled through the sheets of printouts and registers they had been supplied with. He found the register for Ms Grant's form and scanned it. "He's not on here."

"His name would have been taken off all lists, quite quickly after he was excluded. Certainly, before he...before he died."

"His exclusion must have made your form a bit less challenging."

Dave saw a flush creep up Ms Grant's neck.

"Not really. If you must know, I quite liked him. I even tried to stick up for him when it looked like he was on the way out. As much as I could." Ms Grant pulled her shoulders back a little, as if steeling herself for something. "I didn't really think that he deserved exclusion. Clayton was—well, all right, he was challenging, too, but in a very different way and for very different reasons. He came from a difficult background. His older brother had been excluded before him and his parents had not been happy with the school."

"Caleb had been excluded from school too?"

"You know him?"

"We've met."

"Yes. We held on to him until Year Eleven but had to let go of him before he could do his exams. Some kids just can't handle that pressure."

Another little fact the head didn't think he needed to tell us.

"The Kerry family seems to have a very troubled relationship with your school. Why are they staying with it? Why not just take their kids out and off to another school?"

The teacher gave Claire the look Dave recognised from his own brief relationship with his last boyfriend, Richard, a primary school teacher. It was the look that had come up many times when they had tried to talk about schools, and could be translated as *you haven't got a clue, have you?* "With all the cost of a new school uniform?" Ms Grant said. "And the hassle of getting to the next nearest school which is the other side of the river? And the kids having to leave all their friends behind?" She shook her head. "And besides, families like the Kerrys don't think like that. It's the school that has to give in to them, not vice versa. To families like theirs, school is just an annoying irrelevance until the kids can leave at sixteen and get on with their real lives. Look, I think some of us thought we could win Clayton over, help him make a success of things in the end. Okay, if he didn't like you, he could make your life hell, disrupting lessons, being rude, etc, etc. But if you could get him on your side, he was okay, really. I actually think he was trying to find his own way, be his own person, not defined by his background. That can be enormously difficult."

Dave wondered briefly if his own schooldays might have been easier if he'd had someone like Ms. Grant in his corner, telling him it was all right to be his own person. He suspected she was one of those teachers who really tried to make a difference and who was probably adored by a lot of kids in return. He wondered if Claire was sensing that too. A quick glance, however, made it clear that DI Summerskill was not feeling the love.

"Can we get back to the relationship between Clayton and Anne?" Claire said.

Ms Grant gave a sad smile. "Ah yes. That. You could hardly miss it. In fact, I had to have a word with Clayton about what was and was not suitable behaviour in public. Even had to sit them at separate desks. Don't get me wrong. They weren't doing anything outrageous. Nothing that we probably didn't get up to when we were at school." Her smile quickly faded in the face of Claire's frostiness. Dave's attempt to convey *if only I'd had the chance* in one expression was ambiguous at best.

"You had a word with him?" Claire said. "Not with her?"

Grant shrugged. "Sometimes it's easier to talk to boys about things like that. They can be simpler, more direct. No offence," she added for Dave.

"None taken," he said. *You should meet Sean.*

"Was Clayton making a nuisance of himself? Forcing his attentions?"

"No, not at all. What they had going was completely mutual. I even think it would have been good for both of them. She calmed him down. I think she was letting him see that he didn't have to be like his brother or their father."

"And what could he possibly do for her?"

"I think..." Ms. Grant said, obviously choosing her words carefully. "I think she was lonely. I mean," she added in a rush, "she has her father of course, but he..."

"Is a very busy man," Dave concluded for her. "I should think being the head of a large school like this doesn't leave a great deal of time for family activities."

"I'm amazed he has any at all. I'm just a head of department, not head of school and I can hardly find time to breathe."

"Which department?" Dave asked.

"Maths."

So much for my people reading skills.

"It must be all those meetings," Claire said. "Taking up all your time."

And now it was Cassie Grant's turn to look stony-faced. "Yes," she said.

"My husband is a teacher, you see."

"Yes. I know. I..."

"So, I know all about the meetings. How was Anne Blake after Clayton Kerry died?"

Dave watched as Cassie Grant struggled to deal with the abrupt changes in direction Claire was taking with her questions. It was classic Summerskill technique, one he'd already seen her use many times. He just hadn't expected her to use it on someone who was supposedly helping them with their enquiries.

"She..." Cassie Grant began. "Well, she... Actually, it was kind of hard to tell. She was always quiet, introvert. Except with Clayton of course. A real Goth kid. The horrible thing is, I think she's been getting some hostility from other kids after Clayton's death."

"Why?"

"It's like I said. Boys are simpler than girls. Clayton had a lot of mates, boys, and I think some of them took against her because of what her father said, or didn't say, after his death."

"Yes. We've seen some of the reactions. Was there anyone in particular who was unpleasant to Anne?"

"They're just kids, inspector. I don't think any of them would do anything..."

"A girl is missing, Miss Grant. And...there are other circumstances I'm not at liberty to comment on at this time. We need to consider all possibilities."

"We're just looking for leads at the moment," Dave said, "not suspects. Anything you know that could help us would be greatly appreciated."

The teacher nodded. "Well, that does rather bring me on to what I wanted to say earlier. There's one particular bunch of boys. They were friends with Clayton. Just the other day, in fact the last time I saw Anne, I caught them giving her a hard time outside my room."

"You mean they were bullying her? What were they saying, Miss Grant?"

"I came along too late to hear exactly but I could see she was upset and wanted to talk."

"And what did she say to you?"

Ms. Grant looked down at her hands in her lap. "She...didn't say anything in the end. The bell went before she could, and she disappeared. It can be hard trying to find time to just talk in this place sometimes."

"Can you give us the names of these boys, please?" Dave asked, pencil and notepad at the ready.

Reluctantly, Ms. Grant did. "I have to say, I think Pedro and Ryan are just hangers-on. The ones you might want to start with are Alex and Owen."

"Thank you very much for your help." Dave flipped his notebook shut.

"Not at all. I only wish I could do more. Actually, I was wanting..."

"That's all we need for the moment, thank you, Miss Grant," Claire said.

"But I..."

"Thank you," she said. Dave winced inwardly at the sharpness. "I think I have everything I need now."

Dave saw that flush again along Ms. Grant's neck. "Understood." She rose from her chair. "Nice to meet you," she said, facing Dave, nodding just once at Claire before taking the long walk back to the classroom exit.

"All right," Claire said when the door had closed behind her. "I'd like you to take one of the uniforms and go and have a word with these boys."

"You don't want to...?"

"No. Thank you. I'd just like...a little thinking time."

"Fair enough, ma'am."

Dave left Claire sitting at the teacher's desk, looking out through one of the windows but obviously not seeing anything. Her expression was unreadable.

Chapter Thirteen

Chris McNeil shook his head as he saw Dave approach. "Whatever it is, sergeant, the answer's no. Word from the station is Madden will have my head if I'm here a minute longer."

Dave waved his notebook at McNeil. "And you know Summerskill will have my, let's say head as well, if I don't get these interviews done before she's finished...what she's doing. Seems a couple of lads have been giving Anne Blake a hard time. We need to talk to them, and you know I can't do it on my own."

McNeil gave a sympathetic grimace but stood firm. "I can let you have one of my babies."

"All right. Give me Dennison. Good to have a woman when talking to kids."

"Bit of sexism there, sergeant?" McNeil said half-seriously. "Two problems with that, I'm afraid. One, I've sent her off with Jenny to check up on this Mrs. Blake who's popped up out of the woodwork. And two, well, she's a bit shit with kids to be honest. I've been watching her today, and community liaison material she ain't."

"So, who can you let me have?"

"PC Jones," Chris said.

Of course.

*

"Alex Skutt," Dave said, reading from his notepad.

"'S right."

"And Owen Thatcher."

"Yeah."

Dave looked up from his pad at the two fourteen-year-olds sitting across the desk from him. "This is just an informal chat, all right, lads. Nothing to worry about."

"You going to arrest us?" said the one called Alex.

And what part of "informal chat" was so hard to understand? "Is there any reason why I should?"

The one called Owen sat back and folded his arms across his thin chest. "I ain't saying nothing without my lawyer."

"Um, do you have a lawyer?" Dave asked, half-irritated, half-amused.

"We get one call, don't we? And mine is going to be to a lawyer."

Dave cleared his throat. "You are not under arrest. You are not anywhere near to being under arrest. Constable Jones and I would just like to talk to you about Anne Blake. You do know she's gone missing, don't you?"

Owen looked down at his trainers, but Alex met his gaze. "Course I do." His voice rose in pitch and volume. "You're not trying to pin that on us, are you?"

"No, I am not trying to 'pin' anything on anyone," Dave said with all the patience he could muster. *And stop talking like some cheap seventies American cop show.*

"That's what they do," Alex said to his mate. "My dad told me. They get you to say all kinds of things you didn't mean to say and the next thing you know you're banged up." He looked back to the police officers. "I don't know nothing, and I wasn't there when it happened."

"Weren't where?" Dave asked.

"When what happened?" Joe added.

Alex spluttered, trying to process this obvious police trick. "See? See? They're trying to stitch us up."

If Dave had been asked a couple of minutes previously, he'd have said he was okay with kids. But these two were really getting up his nose. Maybe it was the unhelpful cockiness. Or maybe it was the presence of Joe Jones. Dave was uncomfortably conscious of being on show, obliged to set a good example. Or was it that he *wanted* to set a good example?

"Guys," Joe said. "Straight up, Sergeant Lyon is not trying to trick you, or get you to say anything that you don't mean to. We just want a bit of help, is all. Nobody's looking to arrest you. And no one's going to think you've been grassing anyone up."

Alex, radiating suspicion, considered this. "All right then."

He is good with kids, Dave thought. He considered whether his junior officer's interjection should have annoyed him. Probably not, and anyway, it hadn't. Members of a team should complement each other. He tried again. "On the afternoon of the twentieth, you were seen having an altercation with Anne Blake..."

Alex was on his feet in an instant. "He's at it again, isn't he?" he said, talking to Joe and jabbing a finger at Dave. "What's that mean? Is that like a legal word? If I say yes is it going to go down on my record or something?"

"It just means a bit of an argument," Joe said. "And you were, weren't you? I mean, weird Goth girl? I know the type. They can be a handful, right?"

"Yeah, yeah. Too right," said Alex, glaring at Dave but sinking back down into his chair. "Too right."

"What was it about then? She said something to piss...to annoy you?"

The boys shared a grin at what they assumed to be the PC's near slip into inappropriate language. "Nah, not really. I mean it wasn't so much her, was it? It was Blakey, her old man."

"The head?"

"Yeah." Alex packed more contempt into the one word than Dave would have thought possible.

"Was Clayton a mate of yours?" Jones asked.

"Yeah. And her old man had been a right bastard to him." Alex paused, obviously hoping his swear word would provoke a reaction.

"But Anne Blake was Clayton's girlfriend, wasn't she?"

"Nah, that was well over, man."

"I'm sorry?"

"Yeah, he was getting ready to move on. He'd done the deed, you know? It was time to move onto new fields—if you know what I mean?" Alex leered at Owen who leered back.

If they high five, Dave thought, *I will be sick.* "How do you know that? Did Clayton tell you?"

"Nah, but it was all over the hood."

"And by hood you mean playground?"

"It's called the yard actually," Alex said, suddenly on his teenage dignity. "Only the little kids have a playground."

"If you say so. So, what? Had they argued? Shouted at each other? Had there been any physical violence?"

"I dunno. I just heard that they'd split and then Blakey chucked him out of school and the next thing he's dead under a pile of bricks and Blakey's badmouthing him on the telly."

"Wait a minute. You're saying they split *before* Blake...Mr. Blake excluded Clayton?"

"Yeah. No. I don't know. He didn't used to talk to us about stuff like that."

Owen guffawed. "Naw. That would have been well gay."

There was a moment, completely missed by the tittering boys. "What?" Dave said quietly.

"I said it would be well gay," Owen said, slowing the last two words down to give them emphasis, aware that he had finally scored a reaction, unaware of just what that reaction was.

"By which you mean wrong?"

"Course. Wrong. Bad. Not good." Owen sniggered.

Dave stood. "Okay then, constable," he said, addressing Joe, "I think we've learned all we're going to from these...fine upstanding young men. I don't think I want to hear any more from them, do you?"

"Definitely not, sir."

"Unless of course," Dave said, addressing the boys directly, "you do in fact know anything about where Anne Blake might be right now? I thought not. All right. Thank you."

Alex stood and Owen followed suit, both uncertain, both aware that the tone of the interview had shifted though not quite sure how or why. "We can go then?" Alex asked.

"Please do." Dave watched them look at each other and then move slowly to the door, suspicious no doubt of some devious entrapment. *Should I say something about that 'gay' crack?* Dave asked himself. *It's just one of those things kids say, isn't it? It doesn't mean anything, does it?* So why was it stinging? How had these two little shits managed to get so under his skin?

"Lads."

The boys stopped. Joe smiled at them, his tone friendly. "You do know what a hate crime is, don't you?"

Resentment was instantly reignited. "There you go again with the crime thing," spluttered Alex. "I told you, we didn't have anything to do with Anne."

"Or Clayton," Owen added, his alarmed imagination now really taking flight.

"Nah, not that, lads," Joe said, still smiling. "I'm talking about that little bit of homophobia there. Y'know, 'well gay'."

Anger gave way to genuine bemusement. "It's just what people say, innit?"

Joe shook his head. "No, it isn't, lads. Not any more. In fact, it's illegal, did you know that? Homophobic language is illegal."

Alex spluttered indignantly. "You can't be arrested for just saying something." Joe nodded slowly. "But it's not like I was calling someone gay. I just said 'it' was gay, you know, Clayton talking to us about his girlfriend. I mean, that's obviously not *gay* gay, is it?"

"You said it was."

"No, I meant..."

The officers watched as Alex tried to make sense of the conundrum he had created for himself. "It's not like I was saying he was gay. Or that anyone was gay. I mean it's only bad if you shout it at someone, isn't it? I mean. It's not as if I pointed at you and said, 'You're gay?' is it?" He grinned at Owen, composure recovered having stumbled across a foolproof way of winning his argument and scoring against the police at the same time. "See? I can call you gay and it's not a crime because you're not." Alex bounced on his heels, clearly pleased with his own impeccable logic.

"But I am gay, lads," Joe said, tone still friendly, face still smiling.

Alex stopped bouncing. Owen ducked his head and muttered something under his breath. It was almost certainly, "Oh shit!"

"No, you're not," Alex said finally.

Joe just nodded again.

Alex looked to Dave, as if for help.

"We are everywhere," Dave said.

*

"Sorry, sir," Joe said when Alex and Owen had closed the door behind them.

Dave regarded the young man, surprised to see that he was standing very much like a new recruit expecting a reprimand. "What for?"

"I let them get to me. The gay thing. And I shouldn't have done. Shouldn't have made it personal."

"You mean, like I did?"

"You were backing me up. And I appreciate that, sir. But I shouldn't have put you in that position. I should have just taken it for what it was—

a bit of laddish banter—and let it go. That's what Chris—Sergeant McNeil—would have said."

"Chris isn't gay."

Joe's brow furrowed. "So, we get to be treated differently because we're gay. Because *I'm* gay. I meant to say, *I'm* gay."

"Relax, constable. *We* are gay. You can say that. And no, we don't get to be treated differently. We get to be treated the same. Everyone has the right not to be insulted. We don't have to parade our gayness. But we don't have to hide it either. Sometimes it's a bit of a balancing act, that's all. And by the way, you did it without making it *look* as if they'd got to you. Good job there."

Joe looked as if he was about to say something, maybe ask a question, but in the end, he said nothing and simply nodded.

"And let's not forget the main reason we gave them that very well-deserved lesson in hate crime legislation," Dave added. "It was bloody funny!"

*

"The man's a really nasty piece of work, ma'am."

"And can you phrase that in a way I could actually include in a report?"

WPC Dennison ducked her head. When she spoke again it was in a classic copper-in-the-dock tone of voice, "Miss Clarke, formerly Mrs. Blake, reported to myself and WPC Trent that she left her husband just under three years ago because he was, quote, 'manipulative and controlling'. Every aspect of their lives, both hers and her daughter's, had to follow the guidelines he laid down."

"And if they didn't?"

From across the table came the sound of conspicuous throat-clearing. "Inspector," said Dr. Aldridge, "while I can't deny that all this *detective* work has a certain melodramatic appeal, it doesn't appear to be about the subject of the report you have called me here to deliver, and I really would appreciate it if I could pass on what I have to say and then leave to let you get on with…this." He waved his hand to take in the small meeting room that barely accommodated the six officers, himself, and a table.

"Thank you, doctor," Claire said, "but what you may not be aware of"—*because you are a pathologist not a police officer and therefore not in charge of this case or this meeting*—"is that certain facts have come to light that may indeed link the two cases. If I may, therefore, have your patience just a minute longer."

Aldridge relapsed into his chair with bad grace that he didn't trouble to hide.

"If they didn't?" she prompted WPC Dennison.

"Miss Clarke was...evasive. She said he became very angry. She wouldn't go any further than that. We, that is, WPC Trent and myself, were pretty sure, though, that he used physical violence."

"You were pretty sure? Although the woman herself didn't actually say this had been the case?"

Dennison swallowed. "She seemed very...nervous, ma'am. Really not happy to talk to us."

"Right." Claire didn't need to look at Dave to know he was thinking the same as her. They might just as well have sent PCs Poll and Harper who were built like gorillas and had the people skills of a block of concrete to interview Anne's mother for all they'd got sending Jenny and this limp lettuce. Dennison might be proving to be a liability, but didn't Jenny used to be better than this? And speaking of Jenny... "Where is WPC Trent anyway?"

"Station's down two officers, ma'am," McNeil said. "When she got back, we had to send her to Mr. Blake's house with South to take a look at Anne Blake's bedroom."

Claire glanced at her watch. "So that would have meant Mr. Blake hanging around his house for three hours waiting for us to call? Great. That'll help community relations."

Seated across from his boss, Dave gave young Dennison a smile. She might be limp, but it should have been Trent reporting back and taking the flak, not her. He suspected the lack of anything useful was the real reason it wasn't.

"Did she give any indication why Anne is with her father rather than with her?" Claire asked.

"Not as such," Dennison said hesitantly, obviously nervous about getting any further on the inspector's wrong side. "But I don't think that was ever going to happen, ma'am." She rushed on to justify this statement. "I mean, she was in rented accommodation, a very small flat, not much more than a bedsit really. And—" Dennison chose her words carefully. "I'd say she wasn't in the best of health. I'd say she'd been drinking, ma'am." She waited, obviously unhappy at the expectation that Summerskill was going to ask for the proof to back up her statement.

To her relief, Claire didn't. She got the picture. Helen Clarke was a weak woman. Alun Blake was an undoubtedly dominating man, one moreover who could afford a good lawyer. Any judge could easily have been persuaded that it was in a child's best interests to stay with the father rather than the mother. "All right. Thank you, constable."

WPC Dennison sat back and closed her eyes to collect herself. Dave wondered whether she'd be sick as soon as they left the room.

Claire continued the meeting. "Sergeant Lyon and I got precious little from the teachers and other staff we interviewed. And Dave, you say you and PC Jones got nothing from the lads you spoke to?"

"Nothing useful, ma'am, no."

"Great. And it seems, we do indeed come to you, Dr. Aldridge. May we ask what you bring to the table?"

"Thank you, inspector." Aldridge perked up in his chair, visibly delighted to be once again the centre of attention. "As was completely obvious, the cause of Mark Smith's death was the wound to the thigh. The wound to the lower abdomen, though undoubtedly unpleasant and probably fatal if left undealt with, was almost certainly made after the other. Relative blood discharge," he said in response to Claire's questioning look. "It's hard science. Trust me."

Dave glanced at Dennison, who was beginning to look even paler than she had after her grilling by Summerskill.

Aldridge continued. "Toxicology reports carried out since the preliminary examination have confirmed that this young man was no stranger to illegal substances. There were trace residues of amphetamines, MDMA, and clear indication of recent use of marijuana."

"He could have got that just from sitting in the Kerry living room for five minutes," Dave murmured.

"Perhaps more interesting, however," Aldridge went on, putting to one side the manila folder he had been referring to and opening another, "is what I have discovered about the young Clayton Kerry."

Claire frowned. "I didn't think we'd had the request for another autopsy processed yet?"

"We haven't. Those things take forever. Not that I'm too disappointed. Trying to find anything in a body as badly battered as young Clayton's can be like trying to find a pea in a pile of mashed potato."

Hold on, girl, Dave thought, glancing again at Dennison.

"No," Aldridge said. "I'm referring to Clayton's medical records." He flourished the folder. "I took the liberty of doing a bit of detective work myself and liberated these from Worcester Royal."

"Go on." Claire knew the doctor was grandstanding as usual but was intrigued despite herself.

"Clayton Kerry's left arm had been broken once," Aldridge said reading from his folder, "his right arm twice, firstly when he was ten and then again later when he was thirteen. He needed two stitches for a cut at the base of his skull when he was twelve and there was evidence of fracturing along the right side of his ribcage, though at what age that had occurred is not known."

"Fights?" Dave said. "A brawler?" Given the family that wasn't exactly unlikely.

"Only if he started from a very tender age," Aldridge said. "The earliest injury, that first broken arm, dates from when he was only four years old."

"Good work, doctor," Claire said. It was only the truth. Aldridge *was* bloody good. That, and the fact he knew it, was what made him *really* insufferable.

"Oh, there's more, inspector," the doctor said, throwing Clayton's folder onto the desk and picking up yet another with a flourish. "Caleb Kerry's medical records, also from the Royal. I, er, had to call in a favour to get this one given that the subject is not actually deceased as of this moment. Of course, if you'd rather I didn't infringe doctor/patient confidentiality?" He paused. Claire said nothing and waited. "As I thought." He read from the folder. "Another broken arm, a cracked cheekbone, and a dislocated shoulder. Oh, and an interesting little note from one of the doctors who actually saw fit to question just exactly what was going on in the Kerry household. Quote, 'Caleb is a clumsy lad. Just like his brother.'" Aldridge looked up and round the table. "That was from his mother, Mrs. Kerry. There is a recommendation from that doctor that a social worker be allocated but that seems to have been as far as that got." He snapped the folder shut and tossed it on the table with the other. "You will be relieved to hear there are no records of the youngest son, the alphabetically consistent Carl, being admitted for injuries, or either of the daughters, Calista and Connie. So far."

There was silence in the room for a moment. "Thank you again, doctor," Claire said finally. "Very useful information indeed." She caught Dave's eye and knew he was remembering the same thing she was, that first time in the Kerry living room, and Mark Smith's not so subtle hints as to Callum Kerry's bad temper.

"Well, unless there is anything else I can do for you, inspector?"

"Thank you, no, doctor. Not right at this moment. I think you've given us more than enough to be going on with."

"In that case—" Aldridge rose from his seat, pushing his small pile of folders to the centre of the table. "I will be on my way. Gentlemen. Ladies."

There was another silence after he left the room. McNeil, Dennison, and Jones looked to their senior officers. "Well," Claire said. "Dr. Aldridge has indeed given us some very interesting information to go on there. Now, all we have to do is put it all together with what we know and try to make some bloody sense out of it all."

"Cue the incident board," Dave said, standing, swapping his pencil for a whiteboard marker, and walking over to the meeting room's whiteboard.

The board had been split down the centre by a line dividing it into two halves, "Clayton Kerry" written at the top of the right side and "Mark Smith" on the left. "What have we got then?" Dave began. "Two deaths in the grounds of the Fitzmaurice brewery. Both from members of the same family, although Mark Smith's exact relationship with the Kerrys has yet to be established. Chris?"

"I've got South on it," McNeil said. "It seems to be taking a little longer than expected."

"Right." Dave respected Chris for his protective approach to his "babies". He just wished sometimes he'd use a bit more stick than carrot. "One death clearly murder," he went on, "and one an apparent accident, subject to review." He stopped. "And that's about it. Throw in a missing girlfriend, the fact that the weapon used to murder the second man belonged to the girlfriend of the first, and there you have it. Lots of jigsaw pieces, but we still can't tell what the picture on the box is."

Claire leaned back in her chair, tapping her teeth with a pencil. "Anne Blake must have known Mark Smith. She was Clayton's girlfriend. She must have been round his house. I get the impression Smith was round there a lot, if not actually living there, so she must at least have bumped into him from time to time."

Dave was doubtful. "I don't know. She may have fallen for a bit of rough, but I can't really see her sharing the love with his dad, brother, and all the other little Kerrys. And I definitely can't see them welcoming the daughter of the man running the school who'd already excluded one son and obviously didn't like the other."

"Kids and their families, eh?" Claire mused. "Like *Romeo And Juliet*." She caught Dave's surprised expression. "What? I read Shakespeare."

"Right," Dave said. "Anyway, the bottom line is, I don't think Anne Blake is the kind of girl to curl up on the sofa with Connor, Caleb, Clayton and all the other little C word Kerrys, sharing a spliff."

"And that," said a voice from the office door, "is where you are wrong."

"Hello, Jenny. Good of you to join us."

Jenny Trent took a seat at the table, looking not at all put out by Claire's clear sarcasm. In fact, she looked extremely pleased with herself. "Sorry I'm late, but I've just come from a very interesting visit to Mr. Blake's house."

"Don't do an Aldridge on us, Jen," Claire said, just a touch of irritation in her voice. "You've obviously turned something up. What?"

"Well, I didn't find any useful diaries, letters, or pictures of Anne Blake wielding a knife, but I did find this." Jenny tossed a small evidence bag onto the table.

Claire reached across and picked it up, peering at the small sachet within the larger plastic bag. "Weed."

"And that's not all of it," Trent said. "Altogether, there were another fifteen packets like this one. And a selection of pretty coloured pills too. I'm guessing E, speed, shit like that."

"More than for just her personal use?" Dave asked.

"Er, yes!" Jenny said, as if the question was obvious.

"You mean," WPC Dennison said in shocked tones, "you're saying that Anne Blake was a drug dealer?"

Sergeant McNeil bit his lip. "That's probably overstating it, constable."

"It does however put a very different slant on matters," Claire said. "How did Mr. Blake take it?"

"You could say he was surprised," Jenny said. "Or more accurately, furious, at first. Then he tried to deny it was Anne's. Bit tricky when it was stashed away in her bedside table. He was definitely not a happy bunny."

"Great. One more fun interview with him to look forward to." Claire turned to Sergeant McNeil. "I need another couple of uniforms down at that school. Anne's bound to have a locker or something, I know Tony's got one, so I presume all of the kids have. Find it and search it."

"You think she was supplying other kids?"

"Maybe. I don't... No, wait. Belay that." Claire ran her fingers through her hair. "I don't get it. Everyone was quick enough to tell us about Anne and Clayton, how they were all over each other, graffitiing their tags everywhere. Even those little toerags Dave and Joe interviewed. But there was never any mention of drugs."

"Well, there wouldn't be, would there?" said Jenny. "I mean, no one's going to be daft enough to admit to substance abuse to the local police, are they?"

"Not the kids, no," Claire snapped. "But you'd have thought the teachers would have got a whiff of something."

"Literally," Dave suggested.

"But I guess it was like that English teacher said. Anne closed up like a clam. I'm guessing at about the time her mum left home."

"Although," Dave ventured carefully. "There was one teacher she seemed ready to talk to."

"Shit!" Claire checked her watch. An hour before the school closed. "C'mon, you," she said to Dave as she rose and grabbed her coat.

"She was trying to tell us something, wasn't she?" she said to Dave as they walked briskly from the building to the carpark. "That Ms. Grant."

"She may have had more information she was willing to share."

"Stop being diplomatic. It doesn't suit you." They got into the car, Claire running through their interview with Cassie Grant in her head. Twice towards the end she had tried to add something to what she had already told them, and twice Claire had shut her down because the sight of the attractive woman her husband might or might not be having an affair with had wound her up just too tight. Her personal and professional worlds had collided again, and she'd let the one badly compromise the other. "You should have said something," she snapped at Dave.

Chapter Fourteen

Back at the school, in the absence of Mr. Blake, they were shown into the office of a personable young man who introduced himself as Tom Hall, an assistant deputy head. Assistant deputy, Claire thought, sounded even more confusing than some police ranks. Mr. Hall had to be a good ten years younger than her husband, and a lot further up the career ladder. *Just the kind of thing to tip a man over into a midlife crisis.* She shoved the thought to the back of her mind with all the other personal crap she didn't have time for right then.

A quick consultation of his computer, and Mr. Hall confirmed that Anne Blake did indeed have a locker in school. "Room G5," he said. "Ms. Grant's room. Ms. Grant is Anne's form tutor." *Of course.* Mr. Hall consulted his computer screen again. "She's not teaching at the moment so the room should be free. Would you like me to show you the way?"

"Thank you," Claire said. "We know the way."

When they arrived at G5 they found Cassie Grant at her desk, pen in hand and a pile of papers on her desk which she was in the process of marking. At first surprise and then definite apprehension flickered across her face at the sight of Claire, though this was tempered by a faint suggestion of relief at the sight of Dave.

Claire didn't waste time on pleasantries. "We believe Anne Blake has a locker in here."

"Yes, she does. All of the kids in my form do." She stood and indicated the ranks of metal lockers at the back and to one side of her room.

"Could you show us which one is hers, please?"

"Of course. Let me just... Here it is." She pulled out a sheet of paper from her desk drawer, and quickly scanned it. "Number twenty-six." She led the officers to the back of the room. Most of the lockers were covered in stickers, pictures cut from magazines, or graffiti scratched, drawn, or painted on the metal. Anne's stood out for having none of those things. It also stood out for having a neat hole punched into the panel where the lock should have been. Claire bent down to peer at it. The lockers were flimsy, cheap affairs. It wouldn't take much in the way of either skill or specialised equipment to break into any of them. "Did you know about this?"

"No, I certainly didn't." Cassie Grant's annoyance was evident. "But I can tell you it must have been done in the last twenty-four hours."

"How do you know that?"

"I like to work in a neat environment, inspector. You take your eye off the ball for a minute and the next thing you know, your desks are covered in doodles and your displays have been torn from the walls. I have a quick look round my room at the end of each day to check everything's in order. I would have noticed this if it been done by then."

"If you say so." Claire hooked a finger in the hole and pulled the locker door open. The small space within was empty.

While she did that, Dave scanned the room looking for the modern policeman's best friend. He quickly spotted it. "CCTV," he said, pointing to a camera in the corner of one room.

"One of Mr. Blake's less popular innovations," Ms. Grant said. "But I suppose in this instance we can be grateful."

"So, if you're sure the locker was fine at—what, four o'clock yesterday?"

"I left at six actually."

"Okay. And I'm guessing the school was locked up pretty securely not long after that. Say half six? Seven at the latest. Open again at eight in the morning?"

"Seven thirty. I was in by about quarter past eight."

"And then you would have been in here most of the day?"

"Apart from break, lunchtime, and one free lesson."

"Then it shouldn't be too difficult to work out the times we need to review on the CCTV recordings, should it?"

"I'll get onto our IT support now," Ms. Grant said, and left the room.

Dave turned back to his boss and the wall of lockers. Claire was kneeling now, head well into the locker. Her voice came from within, strangely hollow. "You can bloody smell the stuff in here."

Dave's eyes drifted along the bank of lockers. Some of the "artwork" on them was quite impressive. And then one of the metal doors caught his eye. "Ma'am?"

Claire pulled her head out of the locker. "What? Another one broken into?"

"No. Quite secure but interesting." Dave was pointing at a locker door devoid of all decoration except for one large graffiti tag: the stylised symbol they both knew from the handle of the knife that had killed Mark Smith. *A4C.*

"Systems are on it," Cassie Grant said, re-entering the room.

"Whose locker is this?" Claire said, indicating the one Dave had spotted.

Ms. Grant consulted her list again. "Oh," she said. "It's Clayton's. I mean, it *was* Clayton's. I suppose it should have been cleared out by now if there is anything in it. I'll admit, it slipped my mind."

"Do you have a key for it?"

"Master keys are kept in Reception. I'll go and get it."

As they waited, Dave and Claire looked around the room. The walls were covered with brightly coloured posters about mathematics, frenetic in their efforts to make the subject look cool and interesting. "I hated school," Claire said. "Couldn't wait to get away. You?"

"I quite liked it. Took my mind off things."

"You any good at maths?"

Dave made an ambiguous sound.

"Course you were. I'll bet you were a real swot and teacher's pet."

"I was definitely trying to please. To fit in."

"When did that stop?"

"Approximately the same day I came out. Saves a lot of time and energy."

Cassie Grant returned within a couple of minutes with the key which she handed to Claire. "Pay dirt," Claire declared on unfastening the lock and swinging open the locker door.

"Is that...?" Ms. Grant asked, trying to see over Claire's shoulder.

"Yes, Miss Grant. Weed. Marijuana. Are you surprised?"

"Truthfully? Not really. At least, I'm not surprised that Clayton used it. You could smell it on his clothes most of the time, though how much of that was down to him or the rest of his family it wasn't for me to say. Maybe I'm surprised he brought it into school. Then again..."

"You know it is illegal for minors to use this shit?"

Hardly the official police description of a Class B drug, Dave thought, but was Claire reacting as a police officer or the mother of a boy who went to this school?

"I'm saying," Cassie Grant replied coldly, "that like it or not, inspector, they do. Of course, we'd rather that children didn't use drugs, even stuff like weed..."

"*Even* stuff like weed?"

"But," Ms Grant continued, ignoring Claire's interjection, "I don't suppose either of us is naive enough to think that they don't experiment."

Don't say, "Didn't we?" Dave thought. *Don't say, "Didn't we!"*

"I mean, didn't we?"

Dave tried not to wince as Claire's already cold demeanour dropped at least another ten degrees. "Ms. Grant," she began.

"Got the fuckers!"

A very happy Abbi Sharpe, the school's CCTV specialist who had helped them before, bounded into the classroom, triumphantly waving a printout.

"Hello, Abbi," Dave said.

"Hiya." With a beaming smile of satisfaction, Abbi held out her paper for either of the police officers to take. "Five minutes, that was all it took. Personal best. The little shits got in at eight oh one, just one minute after the school opened up and about ten before you got in, Cassie."

Dave and Claire examined the printout of the picture Abbi had brought them. It was as grainy as these things generally were, but the two figures it showed crouched over Anne Blake's locker, hammer and punch in hand, were by now very familiar to Dave at least. "Alex Skutt and Owen Thatcher, ma'am. The ones I told you about. Can you tell me, Ms. Grant, where these two should be right now, please?"

Ms. Grant walked over to her computer.

*

"We didn't do it."

"We weren't even there."

"You did and you were," Claire growled. She stabbed a finger at the screen capture from the CCTV. "And there's the proof. So, stop wasting my time."

"All right. All right," Alex cried. Owen jumped like a startled rabbit and shot his mate a nervous look, obviously worried that Alex was about to drop them both in it from a very great height. "What?" Alex demanded when he saw his friend's expression. "They've got us bang to rights, haven't they?"

Again with the seventies cop show speak, Dave thought wearily.

"But it's all gone," Alex said, turning back to Dave and Claire. "All of it. None left."

Claire pointed to the number of packets that were clear even in the blurred picture they had. "If you'd smoked that much weed in just under six hours, you'd be flying around the rafters not standing here lying through your teeth to me. Now, a bit later on, we'll be getting around to exactly where you two thieving magpies have stashed your little haul, but right at this moment, what I'm more interested in is how you knew it was in Anne Blake's locker in the first place."

Alex looked confused by the question, but then as Dave knew from earlier experience, it wasn't hard to confuse him. "I dunno. Bound to be, weren't it?"

Claire reached for a patience she was far from feeling. "Why was it bound to be?"

"Alex. Owen. It's all right. You know that…"

"Miss Grant! Please!" Claire's tone was only marginally less hostile than the one she was using on the boys. "If you would kindly let us carry on with our investigation."

There was that flush of red along Cassie Grant's neck Dave had noticed in their last interview, and for a second, he was worried she was going to snap back. In the end, though, she simply nodded and held her tongue.

Claire turned back to the boys. "As I was saying. Why was it bound to be?"

The two boys stood, wide-eyed, all attempts to bluster and appear older and more streetwise than they were abandoned. Dave thought he knew why. They might play up and cheek Cassie Grant every chance they were given, but she was still a teacher, on her turf. And now a scary Welsh policewoman had come in and put her in her place. That made Claire Summerskill one badass mother in their eyes. *Lads,* Dave thought. *You have no idea. So, spill the beans.*

"We always got our gear from Clayton," Alex began. At his side, Owen nodded dumbly, eager now to show he was helping the police with their inquiries just as much as his mate.

"By gear you mean weed?" Alex nodded. "Anything else? Speed? Ecstasy?"

"Just weed," Alex said.

Yeah. Right.

"Clayton had always got it, and she, Anne, was always with him. So, we reckoned she might have some in her locker. And we were right." Alex brightened before realising this wasn't the best moment to be showing pride in his guesswork.

"If Clayton was your usual dealer," Claire said (she had been about to say supplier but reckoned dealer sounded just that bit scarier), "why did you go to Anne's locker not his?"

"He was a mate," Owen said.

"That'd be stealing!" Alex said. Both of them were clearly shocked at the suggestion.

"*Iesu Grist*," Claire swore, under her breath. Dave's phone rang. He stepped to one side to answer it while she tried to fathom the mindset of these two morons. Something, quite apart from the ridiculous honour code they were spouting, wasn't adding up. "Clayton's been out of this school what, a week, ten days? Why wait until now to break open Anne's locker? Had she been supplying you until she went missing?"

Owen snorted. "That skank! No way! We had..." He stopped and glanced at Alex. They both had the look of boys realising they had just run to the edge of a very tall cliff, with a sheer drop in front of them, and a very scary female police officer behind.

"What? What did you have?"

"We had another...supplier," Alex admitted. "Actually, it was the one who used to fix up Clayton. When Clayton got kicked out, he stepped back in again. Said he'd got someone lined up to fill in again but till then he'd keep us happy. I thought he might have been going to ask me, y'know? Recruited me, like." Owen dug him in the ribs with his elbow. "Not that I'd have done it, like. No way."

"Me neither!" chimed in Owen.

"He'd meet us on the Ash Path after school or sometimes at lunchtime, and we'd, y'know, do our deals, and that was that. But he's not been around for a couple of days, and we were running low, so we thought, like, why not try Annie's locker? That was what he called her: Annie."

"What was his name?"

Alex shrugged. "Never heard his last name. Don't think he wanted us to know. But his first name was Mark."

Mark Smith. Claire saw again that fuggy Kerry front room, thick with weed fumes. The bling on Clayton's wrist. That bloody plasma screen. Even the pearl-handled knife. The one that had been used to kill Mark Smith. Maybe now she could see where the money for it all had come from. *Back up a minute. There's something else here. Something one of these braindead idiots just let slip.* "You said this Mark called Anne Blake 'Annie'?"

Owen sniggered. "Yeah. Used to really get on her tit...nerves. On her nerves." He blushed deeply and fixed his eyes on his feet.

"He knew her?"

Alex snorted. "I think he fancied her. Stuck up for her, he did, after Caleb had gone."

"Did she like him? I mean, would she have...gone out with him after Caleb?" She tried not think how Tony would have put it.

"How would I know? Might have done. Miss High and Mighty didn't have any time for..." He stopped.

"Kids?" Claire suggested. "Like you?"

"Ma'am." Dave had walked back over to her, pocketing his phone. "We've got a situation."

"Did you just call her 'mum'?" Owen snickered. A glare from both Summersill and Lyon silenced him instantly.

"And I think I've got an idea where Anne Blake may be. What's the situation?"

"Station says they've had reports of a disturbance at the Kerry house. They've dispatched a couple of uniforms but thought we might want a look too."

"There's a coincidence," Claire said grimly. "That's just where I want to go next. What kind of situation?"

Dave glanced at Alex and Owen and then took a step closer to his boss and lowered his voice. "Seems like Mr. Blake is there demanding the Kerrys release his daughter."

"Blakey?" Alex exclaimed.

"You! Butt out!" Claire turned back to Dave. "And we've got a connection. Mark Smith knew Anne Blake and was selling weed to this pair of idiots."

"Hey. You can't..." Another glare shut Alex down again.

"Right. Back to the Kerry house?"

"Bloody quick. But before we do." Claire turned to address Alex and Owen one last time. "You two are bloody morons, right? If I hear anything, and I mean *anything* about either of you again, even if it's riding a bike without a helmet, I will have you banged up in a reform school where you'll be passed round like a bag of jelly babies. Do you understand me?"

"Yes, miss," Alex and Owen chorused immediately.

"And you—" Claire looked to Cassie Grant, open-mouthed, perhaps in reaction to what she had just heard about her headteacher, perhaps because of the highly unorthodox threat delivered to two of her pupils. For a moment, Claire just stood there, looking at the other woman. *The other woman?* "Thank you very much, Miss Grant," she said.

It sounded more of a threat than her promise to the boys.

*

"We've been thinking too small," Claire said as they drove at speed to the Kerrys' house. "Too focused on individuals and not seeing the bigger picture."

"County Lines?"

Claire nodded. "I should have seen it. Worcester's a prime hunting ground for the big city gangs wanting kids to ferry their shit around. Large number of rural kids with bugger all to do and not many prospects, but Birmingham close enough to reach out and scoop them up. Rich pickings for the headhunters looking for the disaffected, the truants..."

"The excluded."

"Exactly. You can be knee deep in them at the malls, arcades, underage watering holes."

"Or hanging around abandoned breweries?"

"Sweet-talk them. Buy them a coffee, a beer, give them a spliff. Say you understand what it must be like living with domineering fathers and how you're too cool for school and wouldn't you like to be earning some money and having a good time instead. Damn it!" Claire thumped the car fascia hard. "He was telling us, wasn't he? Mark Smith. He was bloody laughing at us with all that talk of taking Caleb to Brum."

"Could be," Dave conceded.

"Mark bloody Smith. If that's even his real name. Charming, kind and helpful. *A good guy.* Shit!" She hit the fascia again. "He was cuckooing."

Dave eyed the dashboard. He didn't want to be the one to explain to the car pool why their car had cracks in the panelling. "What's cuckooing? Sounds like a dodgy sexual practice."

"Keep up with the jargon, sergeant, if you want to get ahead. We had a County Lines specialist come down to the station last year. God, she was boring. But she did tell us about cuckooing. It's when one of these groomers actually moves into a household and effectively takes it over."

Dave pictured the Kerry house: a father kept drunk on expensive booze; a brother, maybe two seduced by bling and weed. "So, Mark Smith is the cuckoo in the Kerry nest? Okay, I can see that. Except, he's dead. Are we saying the Kerrys turned on him? Or are we talking about some kind of rival gang action? Other gangs from Brum taking out the opposition?"

"Maybe." Claire's tone was doubtful, her face a mask of fierce concentration as she tried to work the information through. "God knows the guys who do this are hard. I mean real scum. They'll use kids for…for everything and then throw them to one side like they were nothing. But I'm not seeing it somehow. We've heard nothing about that kind of turf war going on. I'm certain we'd have heard something. And Anne Blake's disappearance just doesn't fit into that kind of scenario. No. I think our answers have got to be much closer to home."

"An angry dad?"

"Oh God, I hope not. Am I stupid for finding it impossible to believe a man could kill his own son?"

"No," said Dave. "I don't think so." He pulled into the road the Kerry house was on. "Well, that leaves us with the other angry dad." He pulled up outside the Kerry house, behind the police car already parked there. "Which brings us here."

Claire undid her seat belt buckle and threw it to one side. "C'mon."

*

The front door was open. Down the hallway, they could see a cowering Mrs. Kerry, grizzling baby in her arms, a small girl clinging to her legs. Wordlessly, she pointed to the living room door. The sounds of violent argument coming from it this time were not from a television. "It'll be all right, Mrs. Kerry," Claire said, as she and Dave entered the house. "Everything will be fine. Just take the kids into the kitchen. Or next door, maybe, eh? Let us handle it." The woman just stood there, wordlessly miserable, unwilling or perhaps unable to tear herself away. Claire shook her head in resignation. "C'mon," she said to Dave.

The air in the living room was as stifling and as bad as they remembered it: thick and heavy with the earthy reek of weed, and the sour afternote of stale lager. If anything, the room was even more oppressive, given how many people were packed into it this time. Callum and Caleb, as ever, were in their places at either ends of the sofas, both, as far as Claire could tell, wearing the same clothes as the last time they had seen them. Callum's face looked even more haggard than last time, though, skin grey and sagging, eyes deeply sunk in his skull. Caleb leered at them with familiar contempt, pulling on a spliff, enjoying the hit as much as he was enjoying the conflict playing out in front of him.

In the centre of the room, PC Joe Jones and Sergeant Chris McNeil were doing their best to deal with an incandescent Alun Blake. Claire took note that Joe had positioned himself near Caleb: a good move. He'd be close if the boy tried anything, although at the moment, given Caleb's skunk happy high, that didn't seem likely. Chris had put himself between Blake and Callum Kerry, hands raised in a placatory gesture that was wasted on the raging headteacher, having constantly to shift position as Blake tried to lunge past him to get at Callum.

"She's here! I know she's here!" Blake was yelling. "Just let her go, you fucking degenerates. Let her go!"

"Language!" Caleb jeered.

"Mr Blake. Mr. Blake!" Claire yelled.

Sergeant McNeil gave a small but heartfelt smile of gratitude at the sight of Summerskill and Lyon, and relaxed, just a fraction, while maintaining his position as a shield to Callum Kerry.

"Mr. Blake," Claire said. "Why are you here? Please, just tell me. As calmly as you can."

Blake took a deep, shaky breath. "I am here," he said, enunciating each word with icy clarity, "to collect my daughter."

From his place on the settee, Callum slurred something that none of them could understand. Claire ignored him for the moment, focusing on the distraught father. "Mr. Blake. I understand how you must be feeling at the moment..."

For a second, Dave thought Blake might actually go for Claire. He made a movement towards her. Both McNeil and Jones did the same in response. But Blake stopped, closed his eyes, and took another deep breath, both hands curled into fists so tightly his knuckles were white. Claire gave an almost imperceptible nod to her officers. *Stand down.* She hadn't, Dave noticed, so much as flinched. "You have no idea how I feel right now," Blake said slowly through gritted teeth.

"Yeah. And we don't fucking care, mate." Caleb sniggered.

"Please, Caleb, that doesn't help," Claire said, as Blake whipped round to turn a murderous look on the lad.

"Eh, eh, I'm fucking *Mister* Kerry to you, all right?" Caleb said, waving his spliff up into the faces of the police officers. "'S my house, yeah? Just as much as that drunken old fart's over there, so you come in here and you show some fucking respect, right?"

"I think," Claire said, "that the best thing we can do right now is for you, Mr Blake, to come with us back to the station where we can talk this through and I can fill you in on...one or two matters that have come to light." She looked at Caleb. She'd like to have seen him back at the station, too, specifically in one of its cells. But that would just have to wait, for the moment. She had no doubt the time would come.

"I am not leaving this stinking hole until these bastards give me back my daughter."

"What makes you think that Mr. Kerry and his son have your daughter, Mr. Blake?" Dave asked.

"Yeah. Why would we have that stuck-up cow here?" Caleb jeered.

"These people," Blake said, sweeping his hand from father to son, "have attacked me outside my school, inside my school, and even in my car. They have abused me on social media." His volume rose as his fury threatened to overwhelm him once more. "And you're standing there telling me that now my daughter is missing, you honestly don't think they have something to do with it? And you're the *police,* for Christ's sake?"

"You've got no proof any of that were us," Caleb sneered. "'Cept the social media stuff, and everyone does that." He giggled as if he had said something profound yet deeply amusing.

"Mr. Blake..."

"He groomed her, that's what it was," Blake went on. "They might have been the same age, but he groomed my daughter. He did it *because* she was my daughter."

"He? You mean Clayton?"

"Of course, I mean Clayton!"

There was more uncontrollable giggling from Caleb. "Bollocks. She was all over him. Right from the start. Couldn't get enough of him. She liked her bit of rough, she did."

"You...!" Blake lunged at the seated boy who lay back on the settee, arms spread wide in mocking invitation, and laughed as Jones and McNeil leaped forward and pulled Blake back.

"Yeah. She *really* liked it rough."

Blake screamed with fury as he struggled against the two policemen. Caleb laughed again. And Callum Kerry shouted.

"Mr. Blake, please," Claire said. "This isn't helping. It's only making things worse. And you." She glared down at Caleb. "Give it a rest." She looked to Callum Kerry, not thinking he'd have anything of worth to contribute to this mess but hoping that maybe drawing attention to him would shut the others up. "I'm sorry, Mr. Kerry. What was that you said?"

Callum Kerry sat, fuddled, on his sofa, so apparently out of it, Claire wasn't even sure he was fully aware of what was going on around him. She saw him gathering himself, as if to do something immensely difficult, and then he spoke again, the words slow and slurred but, this time, just about intelligible. "She killed him," he said.

Blake stopped struggling against Jones and McNeil who cautiously released him. Caleb's leer vanished.

"What was that, Mr. Kerry?" Claire said.

Callum stared up at her blearily, as if the effort of stringing together three articulate words had burnt him out.

"She killed him?" Claire insisted. "Who? Anne killed Mark? Anne Blake killed Mark Smith?"

"Are you insane!" Blake screamed.

Callum coughed, once, twice, and then, incredibly, his coughing turned to wheezing laughter.

"That's enough." Caleb lurched to his feet. "Shut the fuck up, old man! Just shut the fuck up! And you. All of you." He swung his arm round savagely to take in everyone in the room. "Get the fuck out of my house." He reached out and shoved Blake in the chest.

Blake stumbled, but before Jones and McNeil could go to help him, he recovered, surged forward, and threw himself onto Caleb. Dazed by weed, Caleb crashed backwards onto the settee behind him. Blake fell on him and began beating him repeatedly with his fists.

"Get him off! Get him off me!" Caleb shrieked, trying to protect himself with raised arms.

McNeil and Jones seized Blake and, aided by Dave who had rushed forward, dragged him back off the lad. "Stop it, man! C'mon, stop it!" Dave shouted, but provoked past his limits by Caleb's taunting, Alun Blake was in a frenzy and beyond listening.

Claire watched as the three officers struggled to contain Blake. *He'd kill him,* she thought. *If we weren't here to stop him, he would kill Caleb Kerry.* "Mr. Blake! Calm down!" she yelled out loud.

"Fuck you!" Ignored by everyone for a moment, Caleb surged back up on his feet. For one crazy second, Claire thought he'd picked up his spliff again and was lunging forward to stub it out on Blake. Too late, she realised just what it was Caleb had pulled out from the pocket of his jeans. "No!"

Stupefied, Blake looked down at his stomach, at the red stain soaking through his shirt. All the fight left him in a single instant. He went limp in the arms of the police officers, his head lolling forward as his legs buckled under him.

The shocked silence was broken by a scream. "Dad!"

Standing in the living room doorway, hands over her mouth, horrified eyes fixed on her father, was Anne Blake. "Dad?" She pushed her way past Claire to throw herself on her knees at her father's side.

Before anyone had a chance to react, Caleb reached down, grabbed a handful of Anne's hair, and pulled her back up to her feet and close into him, his knife, still wet with her father's blood, pressed against her throat.

Shit! Claire tried to take stock of the nightmarish scenario that had exploded in their faces. Sergeant McNeil was on his knees, Blake's head cradled in his lap, frantically pulling out a handkerchief to ball up and press into the wound in Blake's stomach. There was already a lot of blood. Lyon and Jones were standing in front of Caleb, poised to jump him but unable to do anything while he held on to his hostage. Callum lay sprawled on his settee, apparently incapable of taking in what was happening any more.

Right. Priorities. Blake. Slowly, deliberately, Claire reached into her coat pocket. "It's all right, Caleb," she said quickly, as Caleb reacted to the movement. "I'm only getting my phone. I'm going to call for ambulance."

"Leave it!" Caleb spat. Anne whimpered as his knife pressed into her skin.

"Mr. Blake is badly wounded. He needs help. If he dies..."

"D'you think I'm fucking stupid, or what? Leave it. You're not calling any more of your mates."

"If he dies, Caleb," Dave said.

"Like I give a fuck."

"Caleb," Claire said, pitching her words in as calm and reasonable a tone as she could manage. "This has got bad. But we can still..."

"Shut it!"

Claire looked at him closely. He'd reacted without thinking and now hadn't got a clue what to do. If she could just keep things calm... "Caleb. Caleb," she said softly, repeating his name to form as much of a connection as she could. She held her hands up to show that she didn't have the phone. "What do you want us to do, Caleb? Where do you see this going?"

Caleb's eyes darted wildly around the room. There was only the one door leading out. The only thing between him and it was Claire. She saw him realise that at the same time as she did.

"I'm getting out of here. And you're not going to stop me." He shoved Anne forwards. She gasped, stumbled, and Jones and Lyon instinctively took a step towards her. "Stay where you are!" Caleb screamed even as Claire quickly signalled for them to stop. Caleb pushed Anne forward another step, then another, closer to the door, and closer to Summerskill. "Out of my way."

Claire shook her head slowly and stood her ground. "No, Caleb. I'm sorry, I can't do that."

"Please!" Anne begged. "Please!"

"I'm not going to let him hurt you, Anne," Claire said. "But I can't let him go." Now behind Caleb she could see Dave and Joe silently edging towards him. Claire made herself keep eye contact with Caleb, watching her men without making it obvious, holding his attention so that he wouldn't look round. "Your mum's out there, Caleb," she said, "with your sister and the little baby. You don't want them to see you like this, do you?"

Caleb made a sound like a laugh smothered by a sob. "I don't give a fuck about them. I've got friends. Lots of friends. In Birmingham. Mark's mates. They'll sort me out. They'll put me somewhere you won't find me."

He laughed hysterically. "Me and her. That was the plan anyway. To get her away. That's why she came here, wasn't it, Annie?"

Anne shook her head, straining to catch sight of her bleeding father. "I don't want to any more. Not now."

"Shut up! Shut up!" To his one side, Joe took a step forward. Caleb heard the movement and dragged Anne round to face him.

"It's not going to happen, Caleb," Claire said.

The boy looked at her, panicky, then back to the two men, then back to her.

In her head, Claire counted to three and stepped forward. Bizarrely, she realised she was thinking of Sam. "Just put the knife down," she said. "Let me call an ambulance for Mr. Blake and we can sort all this mess out before it gets any worse." Struggling to control her breathing and her voice, she held out her hand. "Give me the knife, Caleb."

With a roar, Caleb released Anne and shoved her forward and into Claire, sending both of them sprawling backwards and onto Callum Kerry. Caleb made a dash for the door even as Dave and Joe threw themselves on him from behind. Joe went low, to rugby tackle the lad to the ground. Dave went high, locking off Caleb's arm and twisting it in an attempt to make him drop the knife. Caleb kicked back, catching Joe in the head, sending the young officer flying backwards, blood spraying from his nose. With his free arm he punched Dave in the stomach and tried to knee him in the crotch. Dave clung on to the arm he had locked but stepped on a discarded beer bottle in their struggle. Unbalanced, he fell, hitting his head against the wooden arm rest of the settee as he went down. Knife hand free, Caleb stood over the dazed sergeant. "Fuck you!" he spat and raised the knife high.

From behind, Joe leaped on Caleb's back, grabbing the wrist of the hand wielding the knife. Caleb whirled round in an effort to dislodge him, but Joe clung on. With an inarticulate roar, Caleb threw himself backwards and crashed back down onto the settee on top of Joe. Completely winded, Joe let go of Caleb's wrist. Caleb staggered to his feet again and spun round to face Joe. "Fuck you all!" He raised the knife again.

This time, it was both Summerskill and Lyon on his back, Dave twisting the arm with the knife, Claire throwing one of her arms round Caleb's neck and pulling back hard on his hair with the other hand, as all three of them crashed down on top of Joe.

"Let! Go!" Dave yelled, pulling Caleb's arm up tight in a back hammer, ignoring the screams of pain until Caleb released the knife and it fell to the sticky carpet. "Okay, ma'am, let go!" Dave yanked Caleb up and off Jones, hauled him round, kicked the back of his knees to bring him down, and forced him facedown onto the floor. He held him there while Summerskill pulled out the cuffs and jammed them onto his wrists. When he was sure the boy was secure, he looked up and round for Jones, even as he pinned Caleb where he was with a knee in his back. "You okay?"

Face smeared in blood from his injured nose and looking like he couldn't quite believe he was still alive, Joe replied. "Yeah," he said. "I guess so."

"I'm okay too," Claire said as she reached once again for her phone. "Thanks for asking."

Dave grinned. "You're always okay, ma'am."

As Claire called for an ambulance and backup, Anne Blake pushed past her and ran to sink down at her father's side. "Dad." Blake lay silent. Chris McNeil, still applying pressure on the blood-soaked handkerchief, looked up bleakly at Claire.

"Get him up," Claire ordered. Dave and Joe dragged Caleb up to his feet and held him facing their boss.

"Caleb Kerry. I am arresting you on suspicion of the murder of Clayton Kerry and Mark Smith, and for aggravated assault with a deadly weapon against..."

"It wasn't me, you stupid bitch," Clayton spat. "It wasn't me. It was him." He jerked his body in the direction of his slumped father but was pulled up sharp by Lyon and Jones. He laughed. "And her."

Down on the grubby carpet, Anne Blake, tears streaming down her face, hugged her dying father.

Chapter Fifteen

"I've had enough, Mark. I want out. No more weed. No more pills." Clayton Kerry took out the mobile phone he'd brought in his pocket and held it out, waiting for Mark to take it.

Mark Smith smiled at Clayton—that familiar, open, friendly smile—and didn't accept it.

"Suit yourself." Clayton tossed the phone onto the grass.

"What's brought this on, buddy?"

"I want to make a new start." Even as he strove for defiant confidence, Clayton eyed Mark nervously. He'd known him for nearly eighteen months now. He knew he was as dangerous when he was smiling as when not. Maybe more so. Mark enjoyed making other people do what he wanted them to. Clayton had seen him do it often enough now. Flattery. Bribery. Threats. Mark had many different methods. The growing realisation that he was just another puppet, not a friend of the puppet master, had brought Clayton to this point.

Across what was once some kind of courtyard in the old Fitzmaurice brewery, Anne Blake sheltered from the light rain against one of the building's crumbling walls. Clayton searched her face for some reaction to what he'd just said but could see none. That, even more than Mark's shark smile, shook his confidence, but he held fast to his decision. His feelings for her were giving him the strength he needed.

Mark laughed and shook his head slowly. "Clayton, Clayton, Clayton. You've just been chucked out of school, m'man. Bit late to be turning over new leaves, isn't it? What are you going to do, eh? Get a new job? Oh, wait. No qualifications, no references." He adopted an affected posh accent, peering at a pretend piece of paper. "Oh. I see here it says you were permanently excluded for being a right like knob end." He dropped his mimicry. "Get real, boy. Who's gonna take you on?"

"I'll get something. Something'll come along."

Mark snorted. "Get real! Look around." He held up his arms to take in the ruined brewery around them. "This city's as had it as this place.

This whole country is going down the drain. You need mates like me, Clayton, me and my friends. We'll look after you. Stick with us. We'll see you right."

"Yeah? And how many of your friends have been put away since we've known you? No thanks, Mark. It's just a matter of time. We're getting out now before it's too late."

Mark Smith shrugged. "You're talking occupational hazards, mate. Okay, so you do a couple of months here and there. You're looked after while you're away. And then you're out again, and everything's rosy. Hey, I've taken care of you this past year, haven't I?" He smiled across at Anne. Her face remained unreadable. "Both of you." He looked to Clayton. "You. Your family. Kept your old man and your brother off your back. That hasn't come cheap, y'know?" And now Mark's tone changed, took on a harder edge. "You owe me, Clayton."

Clayton swallowed nervously, recognising the change of tack, but stood his ground. "I don't think I do, Mark. You got us stuff, yeah. Cheers. But I worked for it. Did the lines, did the deals. It was good. It was a laugh. But that's it. I'm done with it now." He glanced across again at Anne. "We're done with it. Maybe getting thrown out of school was the best thing that could have happened. Shook me up a bit. Made me think. 'S like Ms. Grant says, it's never too late."

"It's never too late," Mark mimicked in a high-pitched voice. "Listen to yourself, mate. Are you a boy or a man?" Clayton flushed but said nothing. "Is that what happens when you shag a headmaster's daughter? You're a real teacher's pet now, are you? Whoa, whoa, whoa." He backed off, laughing, as Clayton raised his fists, but just one pace. "I wouldn't do that if I were you, bud," he said. He was still smiling, but the laughter in his eyes had gone. They were cold. He jerked his thumb in Anne's direction. "And what about her, eh? How about it, Annie?" he called across to her. "You going to be okay not hanging out with the cool kids any more? Thought you liked playing with the bad boys."

"Leave her, Mark."

"He talk for you now, Annie, does he? Thought you didn't like that. Thought you had enough of that at home with Daddy." As he spoke, Mark strolled over to Anne, paying no notice at all to Clayton who was anxiously watching him. When he got to her, he reached out and gently cupped Anne's cheek in one hand.

Clayton sprang forward. "Hey!"

"Back off," Mark snapped, without removing his hand. He waited. Clayton was pale, breathing hard, but he stayed where he was. "Good boy." He turned his attention back to Anne. "You don't want to go back to being the weird kid in school again, do you, Annie? All on your own. No pretty toys from your boyfriend. No." He stroked the side of her face with his thumb.

Anne turned her face away but stood where she was. "I don't need toys, Mark."

"Of course, you don't," Mark said softly. "You're not a schoolkid, are you, Annie?" He leaned in so his lips were close to her ear. "You're a beautiful young woman."

Abruptly, he dropped his hand and turned round again to face Clayton, his tone once more cheery and upbeat as if there had been no disagreement at all. "Okay. Let me put this another way. I'm trying really hard here to be nice about this, okay? We're mates, yeah? Pals. Shit, I'm practically one of the family now, right?" Just as quickly the smile and tone of voice dropped. "So, I like you. But this is business we're talking about, my business, and in business it doesn't matter whether you like someone or not. Get my drift? You're signed up, Clayton boy. And you don't get out unless we say so. Am I making myself clear?"

"Yeah. You're clear, Mark. More clear than you've ever been. But I'm not a kid any more either." Clayton gave a bitter laugh. "I've left school." He stood, braced, arms at his sides, hands still curled into fists. "And I can look after myself."

Mark stared at him, inexpressive. Then he burst into laughter. "Course you can, buddy. Course you can." Without looking, his hand shot out and he had hold of Anne's face again. Involuntarily she gasped. His touch was not so gentle this time. "But it's not just about you, is it?"

"You keep away from her!"

Mark pantomimed dismay. "Or what?"

"Clayton! Don't." Very slowly, Anne reached up and put her hand on Mark's wrist. "Please. Just give us some time to think about this, to talk it through."

"Oh Annie," Mark crooned. "Didn't lover boy tell you what he was planning before he dragged you all the way here?" He wagged a finger at Clayton. "That's not the way to treat the ladies, m'man. It's not all about treat 'em mean to keep 'em keen any more these days. They like

to have a say. They like to be treated as if they're special." He brought his face close to Anne's again. "Because you are special, you know that, don't you, Annie?" And he went to kiss her. Anne twisted and pulled away. Laughing again, Mark let her. They both knew he could have prevented her if he'd wanted to.

Hardly taking his eyes off Mark, Clayton moved quickly over to Anne. "You all right?" She gave a tight nod but didn't meet his eye, her arms wrapped tightly around herself. "We don't need to be frightened of him, Anne. Why'd you say we needed time to think about it? I thought this would be what you wanted. It is what you want, isn't it?"

"Yes. No," Anne said miserably. "I...I don't know. You didn't tell me what you were going to say. Why didn't you say?"

"Did I need to?"

"Yes. Of course, you did!"

"I don't get it. We can be together again. I mean, really together. I thought you were breaking up with me because of all this. We can be better without it. Without him."

"Better!" Her tone was bitter. "It won't be better. It'll be just like it was before. Kids dumping on me at school. Dad watching my every move. A mum who doesn't give a shit. And now you won't be there, and God knows what you're going to do."

Clayton reached out. "I'll be there."

Anne flinched away. "As what? A trolley boy? One of those guys who cleans cars at traffic lights? That's the future is it, Clayton? I don't want that. I want... I want a life."

"Course you do, Annie," Mark jeered from one side. "That's what you deserve, and if you stick with me that is what you will get. I tell you what, Clayton, she's got more balls than you. Maybe we should just forget about old Clayton here, altogether, eh, Annie? Make it so it's just you and me. What d'you say? Fancy that?"

"You keep away from her."

"Why not let the lady answer for herself?"

"All right. Go on, Anne. Tell him. Tell him where he can shove his pills and his weed, and then let's get out of here. Anne? Anne?"

Anne stood, her face wretched. "I'm sorry," she said, so quietly they almost didn't hear her.

Mark waited a second, two, then... "So?" he said brightly. "We back on track again? Best buddies once more?"

With a wordless roar, Clayton hurled himself across the space between them. He knocked Mark to the floor and landed on top of him, raining punches down.

Anne screamed.

Clayton had had the element of surprise, but with that gone, the older, stronger Mark easily flipped him over, pinned his arms with his knees, and sat on his chest, grinning down at him. "Bad move, buddy," he said softly before drawing his fist back and swinging it hard into Clayton's face. There was the crack of breaking cartilage, and Clayton's nose fountained blood.

Clayton bucked and twisted under Mark's weight, but it was no use. "Fuck. You."

"From down there? I don't think so." Mark leaned down, bringing his own face close to Clayton's so that only Clayton could hear his words. "But maybe I'll fuck her. Would you like that? I think she would. You heard her. She's really too good for a shelf stacker or road sweeper. Grow up, Clayton. True love doesn't come cheap. Trust me. I learned that a long time ago." He drew his hand back again, laughing as Clayton struggled helplessly, flinched, and grimaced, before bringing it down, this time as a hard slap. "Wake up."

"Please," Anne pleaded. "Please stop."

"Okay, princess." Mark got back up off Clayton and moved over to one side, wiping the blood off his hand on his jeans, and watching to see what Clayton's next move would be.

Anne reached down to help Clayton to his feet, but he ignored her, clambering up to stand again on his own.

"So, what's it going to be, Clayton?" Mark called across. "You with me, or...?" He let the question hang.

Clayton faced Anne. "I'm leaving," he said. "Are you coming with me?"

Anne hesitated.

"Well, I think that answers that, doesn't it?" Mark began to saunter over to Anne. "C'mon, Annie. Why don't you and me head off to Brum for the evening? I can take you to a party that's going on tonight. You like parties, don't you?"

"Get away from..." Clayton snarled, readying himself to leap on Mark again.

"Clayton! Don't!" Anne thrust herself between the two young men. Without thinking, Clayton shoved her to one side. With a small scream she fell to the ground.

"Anne!" Clayton stopped in his tracks, face stricken as he realised what he had done. "Anne. I'm sorry. I didn't mean..." He reached down to help her up. She slapped his hand away. "Anne, please!" He reached again.

"Get off me!" she shouted as she scrabbled to her feet. "Get off! Get off!"

Behind them Mark laughed as Clayton tried desperately to apologise, pleading, reaching out for her as she backed further and further away. "Anne. Please!" he begged. He took her by the shoulders, but she yelled and squirmed out of his grip. He grabbed her again, harder this time, his face twisted in misery. "Anne, please. I just..."

"Let go! Just leave me alone!" Anne pushed him away.

Clayton stumbled backwards, caught his foot on the cracked, uneven paving of the disused courtyard, lost his balance and fell, crashing back into the rotten wall of an old outhouse.

The wall fell.

After a century and a half, a ton of crumbling brick and corroded metal collapsed in seconds onto Clayton Kerry. He didn't even have time to call out.

"Annie!" Mark ran forward and yanked her to one side and away from the collapsing wall. Anne screamed, fought against him, but Mark was too strong. And then, it was all over.

For what seemed like an hour, the two of them stood there, Mark's arms around her, holding her tightly, one hand on the back of her head, her face pressed into his chest until she pulled away to stare dumb and frozen at the pile of stone burying Clayton. "Stay here," Mark said at last. He stepped gingerly over to the mound of rubble. He knelt and carefully moved some of the heavy stones. After less than a minute, he looked up. He shook his head.

"I..."

Mark walked back over to her and took her in his arms again, pulling her in close and stroking her hair. "Shhh," he said, soothingly. "It's going to be all right. I'll look after you."

"I... I killed him," Anne gasped.

Mark continued to stroke her hair, looking past her head to the pile of rubble burying the broken body of Clayton Kerry. "I know," he said, "but it was an accident. I'll look after you. Don't worry."

*

"This is DI Summerskill concluding this part of the interview at eighteen fifty-five hours."

Claire reached over and switched off the recorder, and for a moment there was silence. "It *was* an accident, Anne," Claire said. "Smith was using the situation. It was his way of keeping you under control."

Anne hung her head in misery. "No."

"That building was old. It should have been knocked down years ago. There's even talk of prosecuting the owners for not having done that, or at the least for not having done enough to keep people out of the place."

"You don't understand," Anne persisted. "It wasn't that. It was what I did to him *before* the wall fell. I... I didn't go with him when he wanted me to. I held back." She threw herself forward, arms over her head, head on the desk, and sobbed uncontrollably. The three adults in the room, Claire, Dave, and the legal rep the station had fixed Anne up with, exchanged awkward looks and waited. "If...if I'd gone with him when he asked me to, we wouldn't have fought. I wouldn't have pushed him, and..." She collapsed into wordless sobs again.

"It happened, Anne," Claire said. "There's no blame and no point in torturing yourself."

"But I didn't know," Anne cried out. "Just for a minute, I didn't know."

"Didn't know what? "

"If Mark was right or not. Whether I could love Clayton. If he walked away from what we were doing. What sort of person does that make me? I should have said yes!"

"I think that is enough for tonight, don't you, inspector?" the legal brief said.

Claire agreed. "Get Jenny would you, please?" she asked Dave.

Jenny Trent came back with Dave and stood beside Anne. "Do I have to stay here. In a cell?" Anne whispered, eyes wide.

"No, no. Definitely not. We've been in touch with your mother. She's outside waiting for you. You'll be staying with her tonight."

Dave tried to gauge Anne's reactions to that news, but it was impossible to read her face now. She got awkwardly to her feet, helped by Jenny, and girl, officer, and solicitor left the room.

"Romeo and Juliet had it easy." Claire sat for a moment, taking a brief respite from the draining emotion of the interview just gone and to prepare for the challenge of the ones still to come. And to think. After all that had happened in the last few hours, one thing still didn't sit easily with her.

"Penny for them?"

"Nothing." Dave sat and waited with a sceptical expression. Claire sighed. "Something I haven't got time to be thinking about at the moment, but I just can't help myself."

"What?"

"Ms. Bloody Grant. She was right, wasn't she? About Clayton. I'd got him written off as just another bad kid from a bad family, but he wasn't, was he? He was trying to go straight, get out of the County Lines operation. Maybe I would have seen things more clearly sooner if I'd given him that benefit of the doubt. If I'd listened to her. And if I'd given her more time to talk that first time instead of using the interview as an opportunity to score points."

"I listened to her, and I didn't hear it either."

Claire grunted. "They don't pay you as much as me. You get to screw up. Now and then."

"Thanks. I'll remember that." Dave inserted the next memory stick into the recorder. "Ready for suspect number two?" He thumbed the intercom switch. "Sergeant McNeil. Could you and PC Jones bring in Caleb Kerry, please?"

"Oh God, I need a drink," Claire said.

*

"Why here?" Caleb Kerry spat on the ground.

"Does it bother you?" Mark Smith asked.

Caleb looked around himself at the ruined brewery buildings, at the pile of flowers lain to mark the site of his brother's death. *"Nah. Not really."*

"Thought not." Mark took a cigarette out of his jacket pocket and lit it while talking. He did not offer one to Caleb. *"We're here because in about ten minutes I've got another meeting also taking place here, so*

I'm killing two birds with one stone." He glanced at the floral tributes. "Metaphorically speaking."

Caleb's forehead furrowed, not just because he didn't know what a metaphor was. "Who?"

Mark took a drag of his cigarette and let out a long plume of smoke. "Not that it's any of your business, but it's Annie Blake. She wants to have a little chat."

"What about?"

"Guilt. Confession. Fresh starts." Mark shrugged. "Who cares? It doesn't matter. Let's just say she just needs reining in a bit, and I thought this would be a good spot to do it. Somewhere to jog the memory a little. Romantic associations and all that." He laughed, clapped his hands, and rubbed them vigorously together. "But, in the meantime, you said you wanted to talk to me about business, and since it's practically impossible to find a room in your house that doesn't have a whingeing child, miserable mother, or drunken father in it, I thought this would be as good a place as any. So, go ahead, shoot. Again, speaking metaphorically."

Scowling, knowing he was being mocked though not sure exactly how, Caleb gathered himself and then came out with what he had to say, the rehearsed words spilling out in a rush. "I want to take over from Clayton."

Mark waited for the rest. When it became clear that Caleb had said everything he had to say, he nodded, as if considering. "Okay. Direct and straight to the point. I like that." He took a pull on his cigarette. "And how exactly do you want to take over from Clayton? I mean, do you want to take over as Daddy's main bitch? Do you fancy yourself as Annie's next boyfriend? Or do you just see yourself under one of those walls?" He waved his cigarette at the flowers.

"I want to do what Clayton did for you. Help run the lines from Brum. Do the deals."

"I see. You do realise you're a bit old now for working the school?"

"Yeah. Course. But I know all of Clayton's mates, the ones he was selling to. I can still see them outside the gates, at the Youthie, the park. Here. And Clayton wasn't going to be doing that forever, was he? You'd got him lined up for other things, hadn't you? I can do those."

"Can you now?" Mark took a final draw on his cigarette and flicked it away in the direction of Caleb's flowers. "But when all was said and

done, Clayton was a bright boy. He had something about him." He stepped up to Caleb and prodded him in the chest. "He stood up to your dad."

"I stand up to him too," Caleb protested.

Mark laughed. "Now you do, now that the old fart can hardly put one foot in front of the other."

From behind them came the sound of feet on stones. "I didn't... You didn't say he..." Anne Blake began, seeing Caleb.

Mark walked over to her, put his hand on her shoulder, and kissed her on the cheek. "It's all right, Annie. He's not staying. We'll be finished in a minute."

"I can look after her for you," Caleb said in a rush.

Mark frowned, slowly walked over to the boy, and stood so close to him that when he spoke only Caleb could hear him. "And what do you mean: look after?"

Caleb licked his lips uncertainly. "Whatever you want," he said.

"Good." Mark leaned in even more closely. "Then, listen very carefully. If I ask you to look after Annie here, that means I do not want a single hair on her head hurt. Do you understand me, you dumb fuck?"

Caleb nodded furiously. "Yeah. Yeah. I get it."

Mark's face brightened. He stepped back, punching Caleb on the shoulder as he did. A playful gesture but with enough force to make Caleb wince. "Good. Good man. You know, buddy, I think we probably will be able to find a place for you in our operations." Caleb's face relaxed into a huge smile. "Now. Fuck off."

Caleb's smile wavered. "Okay, Mark. Whatever you say." As he passed Anne, he spoke to her, in a voice intended to carry to Mark. "You know where to come, yeah?" he said. "If you're in any trouble like?" He snuck a look back at Mark to see if this offer had been noted and appreciated.

"Bysie bye, Caleb," Mark said, waggling his fingers in a mock wave of farewell.

*

"Just trying to follow in the family business then, Caleb?"

The boy across the interview desk from her glared balefully at Claire and said nothing.

"Except," she continued, "people usually follow their parents rather than their younger brothers."

Caleb grunted. Several hours in a holding cell with no weed had left him a grey and unresponsive shadow of his previous self.

The door to the interview room opened and the desk sergeant put his head round. "Ma'am?"

"For the record," Claire said into the recorder, "the interview was paused at nineteen thirty-five while Inspector Summerskill left the room." Thumbing the off key, Claire went out to speak to the sergeant.

While they waited, Dave studied Caleb and the duty solicitor sitting next to him. *Got to hand it to these guys,* he thought. *There he is, sitting next to a real scumbag, knowing that he's a real scumbag, and he's not letting any of his feelings show. Just doing his job.* He felt the stirrings of admiration, until he reminded himself that's what he was doing, and they were both being paid for it.

Claire re-entered after barely a minute and started the recorder up again immediately. "Interview recommenced at nineteen thirty-seven. You're a lucky boy, Caleb," she said. "Mr. Blake is hanging on there. For the moment. You might not be a murderer after all. Well, not of him anyway."

"I didn't kill anyone." Caleb's voice sounded like his mouth was full of glue.

"Like I said, not yet. Though there is, of course, still the matter of Mark Smith." She paused. "What is his real name, anyway? I'm not buying Smith." Caleb said nothing. "Doesn't matter. We'll have it sooner or later." She leaned forward. "C'mon, Caleb. You and Mark. He'd told you to sling your hook. But you didn't, did you? So, what happened?"

Caleb twisted unhappily in his seat and then went to speak, but his words were choked off by a spasm of coughs racking his thin body.

"Could we have some water, please?" his brief asked.

Claire signalled for Dave to fetch something, but he stopped when Caleb spluttered. "Don't want water. Feel sick."

Summerskill and Lyon exchanged glances. That was not an end to the day that either of them relished. Claire reached for the recorder. "Interview with Caleb Kerry concluded at nineteen thirty-nine." She switched it off. "Get Andy to take Mr Kerry here to a cell where he can sleep it off," she said to Dave. "We'll get back to him in the morning."

Chapter Sixteen

"Want to call it a night?" Dave asked as the two of them sat in the interview room after Caleb and his brief had been escorted to their respective destinations.

Claire rubbed her eyes. "You're joking, aren't you?"

"Yeah." They both knew one last interview had to be done before either of them could head home and collapse.

"Okay. But we need a break first to clear our heads." Claire checked the large interview room clock. "Say back here in half an hour?"

"Great."

"You're going to get something to eat, aren't you?"

"I assuredly am."

"God, I wish I could put it away like you do."

"All down to nervous energy, ma'am." Dave left the room and headed for the station canteen. There was the hope of a quick snack before the last interview. But there was something else he hoped he could do as well.

*

As he had expected, there were very few people in the Foregate station canteen at that time of evening, partly due to the hour, partly to the quality of the cuisine. As he had hoped, however, there was the person he wanted to see. "Constable," he said approaching PC Jones's table, adding, as he realised how formal that had sounded, "Joe."

"Sergeant Lyon." Joe went to get up, but Dave waved him back.

"It's nothing official. I don't want to interrupt your sandwich."

"It's okay, sir. Just finished really." Joe pushed the third of the sandwich to one side of his plate.

"I think you'd better finish that off. Eileen'll never forgive you if you leave any of her famed bacon sandwiches uneaten. Look, I'll just go and get a coffee. Want one?"

"Er, yes, please. Thank you."

While Dave went to fetch a couple of mugs of Foregate Street's finest, Joe wolfed down the last of his sandwich. "Thanks," he said when Dave came back, accepting one of the mugs.

"May I?" Dave indicated the free chair.

"Of course."

"Thanks." Dave sat down. "How's the nose?"

"Sore but okay. It's not broken." Joe smiled. "No damage to my looks."

"That's good. I mean... You know what I mean."

Joe laughed. "Yeah."

They each took a sip of their coffee. It was, of course, revolting.

"I just wanted to say thank you," Dave said.

"What for?"

"Caleb Kerry was about to stick a knife in me, remember? You stopped him."

"Oh that." Joe grinned. "Well, then he went to do the same to me, didn't he, and you stopped him, so I guess that makes us even."

"Ah, but I had help."

Joe guffawed. "I'll say. She's fierce for a little gal, isn't she?"

Dave wondered fleetingly whether he should reprimand such a flippant comment about a senior officer. What the hell? It was true. "She's Welsh." Joe guffawed again. "And I guess that's what they call teamwork. It's always good to know you've got someone you can rely on, in a job like this."

"I certainly get that," Joe said, raising his mug to Dave.

Dave raised his mug. "Let me buy you a proper drink sometime," he said. It was automatic, the offer sparked by Joe's gesture, and he instantly wished he could take it back. He couldn't go asking a junior officer out for a drink. Could he? But that was what guys did, wasn't it? That was what *colleagues* did. Just because they were both gay didn't mean they shouldn't. Even if, Dave thought, one of them was really good looking when he smiled. Even with a bruised nose.

"Okay," Joe said, but Dave could hear the uncertainty in his voice. *He's thinking the same as me.* But then Joe spoke again, with more conviction. And that great smile. "I mean, yes. Yes, I'd like that. Thanks."

"Good. Right." There was a beat. "I can't make tonight..."

"No. Me neither."

"But would tomorrow be any good? After about eight?"

"That'd be fine. Thank you."

"Good. Good."

There was another pause. "Where?" Joe asked.

"Oh right. Where?" Dave thought quickly. Somewhere they wouldn't bump into gossiping colleagues. Somewhere they wouldn't bump into anyone they'd had professional dealings with. Somewhere he wouldn't bump into a previous internet pickup. *Mars?*

"The Farriers?" Joe suggested.

Colleagues. "No."

"Halfway House?"

Pickups. "No."

"Gallery 48?"

Sean! Edward the barman! That bloody palm tree! "God no!"

"I can see why Jenny and DI Summerskill met at her place when they last had a night out," Joe said.

"Right," Dave said. There it was. The obvious solution.

"I mean, I'm sharing a flat with Baz at the moment, so…"

"You could come round to my place if you…"

They stopped.

"After you," they both said at the same time.

"Rank has its privileges," Joe said. "You first, sir."

"Thank you, constable. Why don't you come round to my place? I'll make us something to eat, and I can thank you properly." He winced. *For God's sake! Why can't gay men have a conversation without its sounding loaded with innuendo?* He saw the corners of Joe's mouth twitch and knew he was having the same thought. Dave relaxed. It really was a very attractive mouth.

"That would be great, sir. Thank you."

Dave reached into his jacket. "Hang on. I've had some cards made up with my address on." He stopped, scanned the canteen. Not many people about, but still. He didn't want to give rise to—what had Claire called it? *Scuttlebutt?* "Actually, I think I've left them in my jacket. I'll give you one later." *Oh. dear God!*

"That would be…great," Joe said, struggling not to laugh. "I will look forward to it. To the meal. I will look forward to the meal. Tomorrow at eight. It's a date. I mean…"

Dave wondered if Joe was blushing. It was hard to tell. "I'd better head off back to my interviews," he said quickly. *Before either of us says anything else that sounds like a come-on.* "Have a good rest of the evening, constable."

"You too, sir."

I won't, Dave thought, contemplating the final interview to come. Still, tomorrow night was a better prospect now. His mood considerably improved by that thought, Dave made his way back to Interview Room One.

*

"Revisiting the scene of the crime, eh, Annie?" Mark affected a sad expression. "I'm sorry, love. That wasn't very nice, was it? You know me. Sometimes I let my sense of humour get the better of me."

If his words had hurt her, Anne gave no sign. She was gazing at the bedraggled remnants of the flowers left for Clayton. "Two-day wonder, wasn't it? No more flowers now. No more police and reporters. Just the druggies. Just us."

"Hey, don't knock the revenue stream. C'mon then. What did you mean? Your text. I thought we'd talked about this."

"Wait, and it will all go away? Learn to live with it and move on?"

"Pretty much, yes."

Anne shook her head. "I can't."

"Okay." Mark paused. "So, what's the alternative?" He laughed. "Turn back time?"

Anne reached into her pocket and took out the knife Clayton had bought her. She flicked it open.

"Whoa whoa whoa." Mark stepped back, holding out his hands.

A faint smile touched Anne's lips. "Not for you. For me."

"Ah, yeah, right. I was forgetting the whole gloom girl, Goth thing you've got going on." Mark reached into his own jacket and took out a packet of cigarettes. He shook one out and lit it as he talked. "Go on then. Do it. Make for another great news story." He waved his hand along an imaginary headline. "Tragic Girl Kills Herself at Site of Boyfriend's Death? Or should that be, Killer Girlfriend Takes Own Life at Site of Murder? I don't know. Probably neither. They'll just think you're another snowflake emo jumping on someone else's bandwagon." His voice changed, taking on a harder edge, "'Cause that's all you'll be, Annie. Unless you cut this crap and pull yourself together."

Anne stood, the knife held out in front of her, staring at its blade. With a sobbing cry she let it fall to the ground. "What...what can I do?" she wailed, sinking to her knees.

Mark sighed, threw the barely touched cigarette to one side, hunkered down by her side, and placed both his hands on either side of her face. He turned it so she had no choice but to look directly into his eyes. "Well, for starters, you can go back to school. Very important to get an education, you know." He dropped his smile. "And to stop drawing attention to yourself, at least for the foreseeable. And while you're there, you can make sure all my happy little Monastery customers stay happy. Then..." He stroked her face with one of his thumbs. Anne, too numb to react, didn't pull away. "Well, you're not going to be in school forever, are you? Be time to be leaving soon, I reckon. Join the adults. Come up to Birmingham full time, with me. We had some fun in Brum, didn't we? You, me, and poor old Clayton. Well, now it'll just be you and me. And some friends of mine. You made a good impression last time we were up there. There's a couple of guys in particular who are just dying to meet you properly. And that would be really good for me, if you know what I mean. You want to keep me happy, don't you, Annie? You need to keep me happy. And if I'm happy, then I'll look after you. No one needs to know what you did here. Ever."

"Leave her alone."

"Wha...?" Mark shot up to his feet. To his obvious annoyance, Caleb was back. But he wasn't alone. Mark's face relaxed into its default grin when he realised who it was. "Who the fuck let you out, old man? And what are you doing here? If you're after another six-pack, you'll have to wait. I'll throw another one in your cage later."

Caleb Kerry shuffled from one foot to the other, clearly unhappy with the situation. "Sorry, Mark. He must have followed me. I told him to go back but he wouldn't listen."

"Didn't follow." Callum Kerry spoke with the careful deliberation of the very drunk and he swayed as he stumbled towards them. "Came to see this." He waved his hand at the piles of wilted flowers.

Mark laughed scornfully. "Really? Bit late, aren't you? In every possible way. Lord spare us from sentimental drunks, eh, Annie? Almost as bad as melodramatic Goths."

Callum shuffled closer. "He was my son."

"I'm your son," Caleb shouted. "Didn't stop you knocking me about when you'd had a few, did it? Me and Clayton."

Callum staggered over to Anne and Mark and sank heavily down on his knees next to Anne.

"Oh for…" Mark stepped back, distaste written across his face.

"I didn't mean to," Callum said to Anne, his voice thick, close to sobbing. "It's hard, being a dad. No one knows. Hard. With boys." He reached out with a shaky hand and touched her hair. "I heard what he was saying to you. I heard it."

"Hey, hey," Mark said, stepping close again. "Hands off the merchandise, old man."

Callum Kerry mumbled something.

"What was that?" Mark scowled and leaned down, hand cupped to one ear. "For fuck's sake, old man. You are so wasted these days you can't even speak properly. What did you say?"

Callum Kerry looked up. In his hand was the knife that Anne had dropped to the ground. His face was wet with grimy tears. "I said no." He swung the knife in a wide arc, months of humiliation and grief and self-loathing fuelling one terrible, scything sweep of the blade. Mark screamed. Callum reared up, still on his knees, and thrust the knife upwards, in deep. Mark crumpled wordlessly to the ground.

"No!" The howl of outrage was from Caleb. "No! No! No! No! No! You stupid old fuck! What the fuck have you done? You've ruined everything!"

Callum Kerry sank back onto his haunches as his son ranted around him, kicking at walls and swearing to the heavens.

Anne Blake gazed in horrified fascination at the body of Mark Smith as his blood pooled on the cobbles and weeds of the old brewery's courtyard.

*

"Had you gone there meaning to kill Mark Smith, Mr Kerry?"

Callum sat hunched over the desk and shook his head.

"For the record, Mr. Kerry just shook his head," Claire said into the machine. "So, why did you do it? How long had Smith been in your house? A month? Two? You must have known what he was up to. You must have seen what he was doing to your boys. Or didn't you care, so long as he kept you in booze and fancy goods?"

At Kerry's side, the duty solicitor shifted as if about to protest. Claire silenced him with a look.

"Was easy," Callum said, still not looking up, "at first. Just sat there, let him in, took his beer and his fags. Thought I was the one taking him for a ride. Clayton and Caleb, they was old enough to look after themselves. They knew what they were getting themselves into." He paused to take a sip from the water they had provided him. His hand shook as he held the cup. "But after a while, it was like *he* was the head of the house. Bossed us about, he did. Told us what we could do, when we could do it. It was like I was"—he cast around for the right words—"a dog, just some old dog to be kept happy by chucking scraps to it. In my own house. Clayton didn't like it either. Tried to talk to me about it but I didn't listen. Not gonna be told what to do by my own boy. And then, when he died." He looked up at Summerskill and Lyon. "At first, all I could think about was that bastard Blake. If he hadn't chucked him out of school, maybe that wouldn't have happened. And then he couldn't even say something decent about him on the telly. And Mark was there, wasn't he, giving me the beer, telling me I was right, and I should do something about Blake until pretty soon, I just couldn't think of anything else any more. Until that afternoon, when I just had to go there, had to see where my boy had...where he had..." He took another sip of water. "And then I heard him. I heard what he said to her."

"To Anne Blake? For the record, Mr Kerry just nodded."

Callum gave a snuffling half laugh. "I never liked her. Stuck-up cow. Always looking down her nose at me whenever she came round. But Clayton had liked her. And now Mark was going to... He wanted to..." Callum stopped. "I couldn't let him." His bleary eyes moved from Claire to Dave as he addressed them both. "Have you got kids? Daughters?"

"I've got two sons," Claire said.

Callum shook his head. "It's different with girls."

Chapter Seventeen

"It's called County Lines," Claire said as she reached across the dinner table for some salt.

"I know, Mam," Tony said. "I read the papers."

"That's like when organised gangs use kids to carry drugs from city to city, that kind of thing?" Ian said.

"That's right." Claire ignored her eldest's comment. She'd been a mother for long enough to know that what teenagers claimed to know and what they actually did know didn't always match up. She noted, too, how Tony was listening closely to what she was saying even as he pretended to be absorbed in his pork chop. And maybe this was something he needed to know about. She sighed. It really had been easier for Romeo and Juliet.

"And this Mark Smith was like middle management then?"

Claire smiled at Ian's comparison. "I suppose you could say that. We've seen his type before. Superficially charming but underneath it all a pretty nasty piece of work. Not called Smith at all of course. When we finally got the ident we found the usual: a list of petty theft and assault as long as your arm, all building up over time. If he hadn't been killed, he'd have worked his way up the ladder."

"All the way to SLT," Ian said, a little wistfully. "Senior Leadership Team."

"What's going to happen to them, Mam? I mean, Anne especially."

"Dunno, love. Out of my remit. My job's done." She pushed her dinner plate forward. "And yours is just beginning, my lovely. Load the dishwasher for us, will you?"

With unusual compliance, Tony did as he was told while Claire wiped round Sam's mouth and face with a paper towel and Ian skimmed the local newspaper. "I'll take Sam up, Mam," Tony said when he'd finished.

"Thanks, love." Claire was touched. A small thing but appreciated, especially tonight.

This last case had briefly brought her professional and her private world close together, and she hadn't liked it one bit. She was glad it was over. Almost. She waited until her boys were out of the room and all the way up the stairs. "You got much work to do tonight?" she asked Ian.

"Some marking. Bit of lesson preparation. Not a great deal."

"No meetings?"

"No. Not tonight."

"Good." She watched him, saying nothing. Waiting. Finally, he sensed her eyes on him, and looked up from his paper. "You know I met Cassie Grant a couple of times during this business."

Ian put his paper down. "Yes. She told me."

"Right." Claire braced herself. "Ian, we need to talk."

*

"I didn't know what to bring. I hope this is okay." Dave took the bottle of wine Joe was holding out and smiled. "What? Is it a bad choice? I don't know anything about wine," Joe said anxiously. "I mean, are you supposed to bring red or white when your sergeant asks you round for a meal?"

"No, no, it's absolutely fine. It's just...this is the same wine I took to Claire's—to DI Summerskill's—when she first invited me round to her place. And as for red or white, it doesn't matter a bit. As long as it's not pink. C'mon in." As Joe squeezed past him into the hall, Dave automatically peeked outside to see if anyone had noticed. No. Good. He checked himself. *But who cares?* He closed the door.

"Nice place," Joe said when he got to the living room.

"Thanks." *Well, that was a kinder response than Sean's.* "It's not really a home as such, just somewhere to live for the moment."

"You planning on moving on then?"

"Eventually, I suppose," Dave said. "I guess I'm still feeling my way around this new situation."

"That's right. You've not been at Foregate that long yourself, have you? I keep thinking everyone's been there forever apart from me, South, and Dennison."

"Funny. I think I still feel like the new kid on the block. Maybe Foregate's like those old villages where you can live for fifty years and still be treated as a newcomer."

Joe laughed. "Where were you before Foregate then? And where are you thinking of moving on to next?" He stopped and held his hands up. "Sorry. Too many questions. Mum says I don't know when to stop with the questions."

"It's all right," Dave said, "I don't mind." And rather to his surprise he found that he didn't. "You take hold of that corkscrew on the table there and open up the wine. I'll go and get the glasses and make sure the food's okay. It's only spag bog. That okay?"

"Very much so. Thank you."

"You're not vegetarian or vegan or anything like that, are you? Sorry, I should have asked."

"Definitely not."

"Right." Dave hit his forehead with his hand. "Bacon sandwich in the canteen. Course you're not."

"Can see why you're the sergeant."

*

When he happened to catch sight of the time, Dave found that he and Joe had been eating, drinking, and talking for over three hours. It had hardly felt like ten minutes.

All through the day, Dave had been worrying that this invitation had been a mistake. He was older. *(Only by about seven years.)* He was senior. *(It's not like I'm an inspector yet.)* He was the older, senior officer. And they were both gay. *(Well, that means we've got at least one thing in common.)* Now, at well past eleven at night, he realised he had had no reason to worry.

He'd found out about Joe's family background (mother, father, one brother, one sister); hobbies and interests (Joe played guitar and football, had already joined a local six-a-side team and wanted to start up a team at Foregate—Dave immediately excused himself), and that he'd wanted to be a policeman from the age of five when he'd seen his first cop show on telly. Dave couldn't help comparing this with Sean. He and the MP had met over half a dozen times now. Each of those times, when they'd been alone, they'd had sex. But Dave didn't know half as much about Sean the person as he knew now about Joe. Mind you, he had an uncomfortable feeling that he hadn't told Joe that much about himself. Well, he wasn't that interesting, was he? Joe, though, he found, was very interesting. He also found that he really wanted to kiss him.

"You okay there? You kind of zoned out for a minute?"

Dave blinked. He'd been thinking about Joe's lips. How they might feel on his. "Hm. Oh yeah. Sorry." He rose from the table. "Let me go and get the coffee. You'd like coffee? I promise you it'll be better than the station's muck."

"Couldn't be worse."

In the kitchen, Dave considered his discovery. How had that happened? Well, that was bloody obvious, wasn't it? Joe was a good-looking lad. He'd noticed that from the first meeting, how could he not have? But he hadn't fancied him, as such, then. Had he? Joe's junior rank had been like an invisible shield blocking off any such thoughts and feelings. He certainly hadn't been thinking that way when he'd invited Joe round for a meal. Had he?

"Thought I'd bring these through." Joe stood in the narrow kitchen doorway holding the dessert dishes. "Where shall I put them?"

"Oh thanks. Er, just over there will be fine."

Claire had visited Dave's flat twice when she'd come to pick him up on those rare occasions when she was doing the driving for the day. She'd suggested, only half-jokingly, that Dave knocked out one of the kitchen walls, either through into the living room or into the bedroom as a talking point. That way, she'd said, he'd have room to actually breathe in the tiny room while he was microwaving his meals. Now, as Joe squeezed past him, Dave was forced to admit how microscopic his kitchen was. And how much he was enjoying having Joe pressed this close to him.

"Warm in here," Joe said.

"Yeah. No window. No fan."

The two men stood, barely an inch between them. "I want to kiss you," Dave said.

"I want to kiss you," Joe said. He waited. "Now?" Dave laughed. The two men put their arms around each other and kissed.

"I hadn't planned that," Dave said later, as they sat once again at the dinner table, nursing their coffees.

"Me neither," Joe said, "though..."

"What?"

"I kinda hoped we might get at least a bit of a snog in."

"Really?"

"You're a good-looking guy. Sir."

Dave gave an embarrassed laugh. "*Sir*. That's the problem, isn't it? I'm a sergeant. And you're..."

"...not a sergeant yet." Joe grinned. "So what?"

"People could say I've taken advantage of you. I mean, they could if anything, you know, came of it."

"Like who? Far as I can tell, everybody in the damn station has been expecting us to get off with each other from day one."

"You've noticed that too?"

"Hell yes. Becky and Baz think it's hilarious. People like Jenny and...and others seem to think we should have been at it from the word go. Just 'cause we're both gay."

Dave knew Joe had been about to name Claire as one of those others. It was to his credit that he'd held back. "Yeah, but now, if we do, y'know, take things a bit further," he said, "I mean, just for as long or as far as we want to, then we'll just be proving them right, won't we? Which is bloody annoying."

"You mean, you're worried people will disapprove, but you'll be annoyed if they do approve." Joe cocked an eyebrow. "You kind of overthink things, don't you? Sir."

Dave sighed. "I kind of think I do. Why can't things be easy?"

Joe leaned across in his chair. "Sometimes they can." Dave leaned in to meet the kiss.

From across the room, Dave's phone pinged the arrival of a message. "Ignore it," Dave said.

"It's cool," Joe said. "Better check it. Might be a bank robbery in progress needing two handsome cops to come save the day. Or it could be DI Summerskill wanting to know how your date went."

Dave laughed but, of the two possibilities, the second would have been more likely. If he'd told Claire about this meal.

Free? My place now?

The message was from Sean.

"So. Bank or boss?" Joe asked.

Dave weighed the phone in his hand for moment and then turned it to silent and put it back down without answering the text. "Neither," he said, "and nothing important." He walked back to the table. "Y'know, what I really wish I had right now is a good-sized settee."

Joe laughed. "Yeah. Cuddling up on a sofa'd be nice."

The unspoken alternative to a sofa hung in the air between them. *Not tonight,* Dave thought. *Let this one grow. Let it breathe.*

"Thanks for telling me all that stuff about how you felt 'cause of our ranks and everything," Joe said. "I've gotta say, I'm kind of relieved."

"Relieved?"

"Yeah. You seemed pretty cold and distant at first. I'd thought two gay officers, we'd probably kind of bond or something over that, be friends at least, but it was looking like the opposite."

"I am sorry Joe, I..."

"No, no, it's okay. It's cool. I mean, it is now. But then, well, I couldn't help wondering if maybe, y'know, there might have been a bit of prejudice going on there."

"Prejudice?" Dave frowned, totally puzzled. "Because you're gay?"

Joe chuckled. "Are you blind as well as overthoughtful? Not because I'm gay. Because I'm black."

Dave regarded Joe, stunned. "I never... You thought that I might... Joe, I..."

Laughing out loud, Joe rose from the table, pulled Dave into him, and kissed him, long and deep. "You really do need to lighten up, Sergeant Lyon."

About the Author

Steve Burford lives close to Worcester but rarely risks walking its streets. He has loaded conveyor belts in a factory, disassembled aeroplane seats, picked fruit on farms, and taught drama to teenagers but now spends his time writing in a variety of genres under a variety of names. He finds poverty an effective muse, and since his last book has once again been in trouble with the police. (He would like to thank the inventor of the speed camera.)

E-mail

Summerskilllyon@gmail.com

Other books by this author

Summerskill and Lyon Series

It's A Sin

Bodies Beautiful

Also Available from NineStar Press

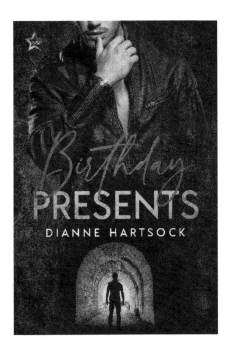

Connect with NineStar Press

Website: NineStarPress.com

Facebook: NineStarPress

Facebook Reader Group: NineStarNiche

Twitter: @ninestarpress

Tumblr: NineStarPress

Printed in Great Britain
by Amazon

87813967R00119